Also by Deborah Carr

The Mrs Boots Series

Mrs Boots

Mrs Boots of Pelham Street

Standalones

The Poppy Field

An Island at War

MRS BOOTS GOES TO WAR

DEBORAH CARR

One More Chapter
a division of HarperCollins*Publishers*
1 London Bridge Street
London SE1 9GF
www.harpercollins.co.uk
HarperCollins*Publishers*
1st Floor, Watermarque Building, Ringsend Road
Dublin 4, Ireland

This paperback edition 2021
1
First published in Great Britain in ebook format
by HarperCollins*Publishers* 2021

A catalogue record of this book is available from the British Library

ISBN: 978-0-00-843633-9

Printed and bound in Great Britain by
CPI Group (UK) Ltd, Croydon CR0 4YY

To my brilliant publisher, Charlotte Ledger. Thank you for everything. x

Chapter One

21 September 1913

Florence Boot reread the letter she had dictated to her secretary earlier that morning. Her staff were waiting patiently for her to come and speak to them, but she was nervous. It wasn't like her at all. Then again, Florence mused, she had learned the hard way never to act without considering the consequences first.

She glanced at the *Punch* cartoon depicting her declaration that she would take on fifty college girls as shop assistants in Boots stores. It had been published a week before and her husband Jesse had brought it to her the previous evening stating that her intention was likely to lead to a superior type of shop woman. Florence still felt sick at the sight of it and the reaction she feared it would cause among her girls. The last thing she wanted to do was frighten any of them into thinking that they might be in danger of losing their positions within the company to those college girls. She needed to reassure them without delay that their jobs were perfectly safe.

In fact, she thought, rather than them losing their jobs, she needed to confirm to them that the reason she had set up the series of evening classes to run in partnership with Nottingham's Education Committee was to help all her girls, not just newly employed ones.

'My intention had been to encourage my female employees to take these classes as a way of helping themselves,' she explained to Miss Tweed. 'It's taken a huge amount of work and I'm horrified to think that the magazine has pre-empted my announcement to my girls. Don't they realise that by doing this they've probably caused panic among my shop assistants?'

Miss Tweed shook her head. 'I don't think they care one way or another.'

'You're probably right.' Florence sighed heavily and unscrewed the top of her favourite fountain pen. 'I just want to ensure that this silly cartoon doesn't instil fear into my Dear Girls. I need to reassure them of my belief in the importance of their roles at Boots.' She pushed the magazine aside. 'Especially the girls who left school at fourteen and came directly to work here as shop assistants. I valued the work I did as a shop assistant very highly then and do so now. I won't allow some faceless cartoonist to take that away from either me or my loyal staff.'

Florence's thoughts returned to the letter on her desk. 'I want my staff to know exactly how much I value them and I hope this letter gets that message across.' She signed the letter before picking up her blotter and rolling it over her signature, then handed it to Miss Tweed. 'Thank you.'

Florence needed to keep her mind off her worries and looked at her notes from her most recent trip to New York on the RMS *Caronia*. She had had so little available time since returning to Nottingham that she still hadn't managed to put her notes in order for Miss Tweed to type up and file.

It had been a busy trip, as always, but, this time, she had taken her children Margery and John with her. John had been very entertaining during the voyage, as she had known he would be, but had continued his journey, travelling to Boston to carry out business on behalf of her and Jesse, while she and Margery had remained in New York City to visit suppliers.

Florence recalled fondly those blissful six days during the transatlantic crossing when she could spend time with her youngest daughter and son. She had missed Jesse and worried about him being in Nottingham without her, especially now that he was becoming more disabled each month, but his male nurse George was staying at the house and would take good care of him.

Margery was a smart twenty-one-year-old woman now and Florence thoroughly enjoyed her company. She had been concerned that Margery and her sister, Dorothy, might wish to join the suffrage movement, as Florence herself had been tempted to do, but had been somewhat disconcerted when suffragettes burned down the Nottingham Boat Club building on the Trent Embankment, because it was a men-only organisation. She did sympathise with them, but that really was a step too far.

The previous evening, before Jesse's return home, Florence had spent a few hours chatting with her two daughters, listening to their opinions, determined to let them know that what they had to say about current situations was valued by her. Once again, Margery had brought up the subject of the brutal death of the suffragette Emily Wilding Davison. Florence had now also seen the footage at the picture house of the poor woman being hit by the King's horse, Anmer, during the Epsom Derby three months before and understood Margery's horror. She was glad her daughters took an interest in the women's suffrage movement and how they could help themselves as well as other women.

'I was speaking to Father about the Cat and Mouse Act,' Margery had told them. 'I think it's disgusting that they've been allowed to force feed the women suffragists, but he explained that the act made the hunger strikes legal.'

'That's right,' Florence said, still horrified to think that the legal system could allow something so cruel to be passed. 'I hadn't realised it was the case until recently. Apparently, they brought in the act so that they can release the women from prison temporarily when their health deteriorates. Then, once their health improves again, they can re-arrest them and take them back to jail to complete their sentences.'

'Why would they do that? It all sounds so cruel.' Margery said, scowling.

Florence agreed. Personally, she didn't believe the women should be treated so harshly in any way. 'I gather they believe that if the women are weak from their hunger strikes then they'll be too unwell to commit further unlawful acts.'

'Well, I think the way they treat them is disgusting,' Margery said. 'I don't think there's any reason to inflict such torture on these poor women; they're only fighting for something we would all like to have. I'm not surprised they feel compelled to go to these lengths.'

'I read somewhere,' Dorothy said, thoughtfully, 'that there's an advertisement saying something to the effect of, "women bring the voters into the world, so should be entitled to vote themselves".'

Margery gasped. 'That's true. We can give birth to these men but not be equal to them.' She shook her head. 'How long do we have to wait for this unfairness to be wiped out?'

'I've no idea,' Florence admitted. 'It's wrong that we're not seen as equal and I completely understand your fury. However, don't think I'd be happy for either of you to take part in anything illegal.'

Dorothy laughed. 'We have no intention of doing anything silly,' she said looking at her younger sister. 'Do we, Margery?'

Margery pretended to consider her sister's words then pulled an innocent face. 'Of course we don't, Mother.'

Florence could tell that Margery was teasing her and believed her daughters had more sense than to do anything they'd later regret, which was a relief.

'Anyway,' Florence said, 'I believe I can do far more for women in leading by example. And I think that the two of you must find ways to do the same.'

She watched Margery stare back at her in awe as if Florence had just shared some incredible secret. 'Mother, that's exactly what we should do.' Margery frowned. 'But what can I possibly do to inspire others? I haven't achieved anything yet.'

'You work hard at Boots, like many other women. I'm sure you will think of something, in time. Right now, though, the most important thing you can do is live your life in a way that helps others.'

'Yes, but how do I do that?'

Florence gave her daughter's question a little thought. She didn't want to put her off from trying to help others, but also doubted she was ready to make big changes to her life. She certainly didn't want Margery racing off to join the suffrage movement and become carried away and end up in some kind of trouble. 'The most important way we can all change other's days is simply by being kind. If you see someone needing help, then step up and do what you can. You're already hard working and get along very well with your colleagues at the factory and that's a good start.'

Margery didn't seem impressed. 'But it's not very likely

that I'll make a big difference to many people by doing that.'

Florence put her arm around Margery's shoulders. She loved that her daughter was so determined to find a role for herself. 'Your time will come, I promise you.'

'I hope so.' She stared at Florence silently for a few seconds. 'When you were a shop assistant at grandfather's stationer's did you know that you wanted to achieve all that you have done since?'

Florence laughed and shook her head. 'Not at all. I do recall that I didn't want to marry and give up my independence. I thought – mistakenly, as it turned out – that if I became someone's wife then it would mean I would spend my days running a house and bringing up children while my husband achieved things outside the home.'

Dorothy leant forward in her chair, grinning. 'But you did run a house and bring up children,' she said, giggling. 'You just managed to do it while also going out to work all day with Father.'

'Dorothy's right. I've no idea how you fitted everything into your day. I still don't know how you do what you do.'

'Mother has more energy than most of us.' Dorothy laughed, raising an eyebrow at her younger sister.

Florence loved times like these, when she and her daughters could have fun together. 'I don't, I just plan my days well.'

Florence grinned as both her daughters fell back in their chairs, laughing and holding their stomachs. She hadn't expected them to find what she said quite that amusing but loved that they did so. 'It wasn't that funny, surely?'

Tears ran down Dorothy's cheeks. She wiped them away with the tips of her fingers and nudged her sister. 'It was, Mother. You are funny, but you're also someone who we look up to.'

'And love, very much,' Margery said as they both stood to move closer to her and give her a hug.

Chapter Two

Later that evening, when the girls had retired to their rooms, Florence sat quietly on her bed. She had intended reading but, although she was enjoying the novel she had brought up with her from their small library, she couldn't take her mind off what she and the girls had been discussing.

After some consideration about the suffrage movement, Florence reasoned that she had been right to suggest the girls could do more for women by example. Just like her. Hadn't she worked next to her husband since their marriage and shown that she had the brain to compete with any man, and the strength of character and determination needed to get ahead in business and make her ideas come to fruition?

It had also dawned on her that she was able to help many women already, both with her new project of free evening classes for her staff and also with her continued planned outings and help with their welfare, giving advice to those who needed it.

Her family was growing up and seemed to be settling down now. Florence loved that John had been working with the company for a couple of years and knew that Dorothy was ready for a new direction in her life. Florence had been aware of her twenty-three-year-old daughter's wish to do more with her days, but she had still been surprised when Dorothy met and fell in love with Captain Wilfred Montagu Bruce.

Florence was used to Jesse being known by people she met and all of them knew exactly who the captain was, having read about his heroic exploits in the newspapers. She was in awe of the captain's bravery in taking part in the two southern voyages with his brother-in-law Captain Robert Scott on the *Terra Nova* between 1910 and 1913. She could not deny that her daughter's beau was a real-life hero and understood why a young woman would have her head turned by someone who had achieved so much already in his life.

She was a little concerned though that he might have too much life experience for her daughter, who had enjoyed a very sheltered upbringing with her and Jesse. She had been pleased for her daughter when Dorothy and the captain had become friends before his final voyage, but hadn't anticipated anything more might come of their friendship. She looked back now thinking about the evenings Dorothy had been dressed up, excited to be accompanying the captain when he collected her to take her to friends' parties.

They always seemed to enjoy each other's company and Florence prayed that the hopes she instinctively knew Dorothy held for a future with the captain were not dashed at any point.

Now, though, Dorothy had confided in her that since the captain's return to England on the 14 June, they had become much closer and he was ready to propose to her.

Florence was determined not to stand in the way of her children's happiness – as her own mother had temporarily done with her, believing she was protecting her. She had to trust that her and Jesse's upbringing of their three children had given them the confidence and awareness to make informed decisions about their own futures.

'He's here, Mother,' Dorothy called as she stared out of a window to the side of the front door. She spun to face Florence and rushed over to her. 'Do you think Father will be gentle with him when he speaks to him?'

Florence thought back to her conversation with Jesse only an hour before, and nodded. 'Yes, I'm sure he will.' She straightened the small gold brooch on Dorothy's dress, wondering if it was a gift from her captain. 'Try not to fret. This will soon be over and, if the captain walks into this house and sees you in a state, well, it's not going to give him much confidence, is it?'

Dorothy frowned. 'No, you're right.' She straightened her shoulders and stood next to Florence, waiting for the doorbell to ring.

Seconds later, Meadows marched through the hallway, glancing only briefly towards the two women before opening the front door. Florence took her daughter's nearest hand in her own and gave it a gentle squeeze before letting it go. She recalled only too well the excitement and nerves she had felt when Jesse had come to her parents' flat above her father's stationery shop in Queen Street to ask his permission to marry her.

'I've an appointment to speak with Sir Jesse,' she heard the captain say.

Florence had already tipped Meadows off about the expected visit and waited while he welcomed the captain into the house.

The captain immediately spotted Florence and Dorothy and came up to them. 'Good afternoon, Lady Boot.' His eyes moved from hers and locked on Dorothy's. 'It's wonderful to see you again, Dorothy.'

Florence could feel the chemistry between her daughter and the man she wanted so much to marry.

'Good afternoon, Captain,' Florence replied, then, aware that they probably needed a moment to themselves, added, 'I'll go and see if my husband is ready to meet you. I won't be long.'

As she walked along the Parquet flooring to Jesse's study near the back of the house, Florence could hear the young couple whispering, their anxiety palpable. She hoped Jesse wouldn't keep him too long so that the four of them could then relax and have a celebratory drink of tea.

Florence entered Jesse's office and found him seated at his desk. Jesse looked up at her. 'Is he here?'

'He is.' She rested her hands on his desk and leant

forward, keeping her voice low so as not to be overheard. 'Now, remember what we agreed?'

Jesse gave her a stony glare. 'Yes. No lengthy diatribes and to give him my blessing to marry my eldest daughter.'

Florence laughed. 'You make it sound as if you're being forced to do this. We both like the captain, don't we?'

Jesse nodded. 'We do.'

'Then why the hesitation?' she asked, worried in case he might change his mind.

'I suppose I'm finding it a little strange to think that my daughter will be getting married. Selfish of me, I know.'

Florence stood up straight and walked around his desk to give him a kiss. 'There's nothing selfish about you, dear Jesse. I find it difficult to think that my children are all grown and making their own ways in the world now, too. But this is what Dorothy wants and she's an intelligent, sensible woman who is more than capable of making up her own mind. Now, let's not waste any more time. The poor things are going to wonder what we're chatting about in here.'

'I suppose so.' Jesse straightened the paperwork on his desk. 'Ask him to come in then. Let's get this over with.'

Ten minutes later, Florence watched as Dorothy paced back and forth in the hallway outside the library door. 'Come away now,' she said, hoping to soothe her daughter's nerves.

'He's come to ask Father for my hand,' she whispered, looking terrified. 'What if he refuses? What will I do then?'

'Firstly, I'm sure you have nothing to worry about,'

Florence said, aware that Jesse was capable of changing his mind at the last minute and not doing as she had expected him to. 'And I'm sure that you fretting out here is not going to do any good either. You don't want them to hear your footsteps, do you?' Dorothy's eyes widened in horror at the suggestion. 'Fine. Then we may as well make the most of this sunny weather and enjoy the fresh air.'

Dorothy hesitated. 'What if Wilfred comes out and wishes to speak to me and I'm not here. How will he find me?'

Florence linked arms with her daughter and began to lead her away from her father's study door. 'I'm sure your father or one of the servants will be able to find us for him, if he's unable to do so himself,' Florence teased. 'Although, I'm sure that with the captain's experience of expeditions he should find tracing you to our garden rather simple, don't you?'

Dorothy nudged her mother, amused. 'You think you're so funny, don't you?' she said, then giggled.

'I do have the occasional moment of comic genius. Now, let's leave them to it and go outside.'

Florence squinted as they stepped out into the afternoon sun. Two swifts swooped in the sky overhead and Florence heard the cooing of a dove from next door's dovecot. She knew that she would remember this day forever as the day her daughter's future was decided upon. She wished Dorothy wasn't so worried though. Florence felt sure that Jesse would give the captain his permission to marry Dorothy. The man had proved to have mettle and

Jesse liked that in a person, and it was obvious to them both that their daughter was very much in love with this man.

'I hadn't realised you and Captain Bruce were quite so close,' she said, trying not to sound too alarmed by the seemingly sudden turn of events. 'Are you certain that you are ready to be married?'

Dorothy looked as if she was about to cry. 'I know it sounds a bit sudden, but it isn't really and I'm positive that he is the man I wish to marry.' She brushed away a stray tear. 'You do think that Father will give his permission, don't you? I'd be mortified if he refused it. He is a special man in so many ways, Mother, he truly is.'

'I believe you,' Florence said, hurriedly trying to soothe her daughter's rising panic. 'I only want to be certain that you are as sure of him as you seem to be.'

'I am. We're very much in love and, after all he's seen and done these past few years, he's ready to settle down and be married as much as I am. I know we're going to be very happy together.'

Florence pulled her daughter into a hug. 'Then I'm very happy for you both, my darling. Knowing your father, he'll want to speak to me before giving his permission, just to be certain he's doing the right thing. I'll reassure him and tell him what you've said. I'm sure he'll give his blessing without any hesitation after that. We both only want what's best for you and to see you happy and settled.'

'I know you do. Thank you, Mother.'

Moments later, Florence saw Meadows hurry outside to

join her and Dorothy. 'Your presence has been requested in Sir Jesse's study, Lady Boot.'

Florence leant towards Dorothy and whispered, 'I won't be long. Stay calm and take a few deep breaths. I'll be back here before you know it.'

She walked to the study. The captain gave her a tight, nervous smile, which seemed to her more like a grimace, before making his way to the door.

'I'm going to wait in the hallway while you speak to Sir Jesse.'

Florence closed the door after he'd left and shook her head as she walked over to where Jesse was sitting.

'Meadows said you wanted to speak to me,' she said, her eyes locking with Jesse's. 'Whatever's the matter? Has something happened to change your mind?'

Jesse said nothing but stared at his twisted hands. 'It's rather strange, all this, don't you think?'

'It reminds me of the day when you asked my father if we could be married,' she replied, unsure what Jesse was leading towards.

He took her right hand between both of his misshapen ones. 'Only this time, we are not going to shatter their hopes and expect them to do as we wish, are we?' She shook her head.

'Florence?' Jesse's voice sounded unsure, which was very unlike him.

She looked down at her hand in between both of his. 'What is it, my love? What is troubling you?'

He gazed at her thoughtfully for a moment. 'Was I selfish to marry you?'

Florence's breath caught in her throat. 'No, off course you weren't. Why would you even ask such a thing?'

Jesse took gave her a wistful smile. 'You were so young and lovely.' He blew her a kiss. 'You're still very lovely. But I was thirteen years older than you and so different to you.'

'But—'

Jesse raised his hand to stop her saying anything further. 'No, it's true. The thing that troubles me is that by marrying me, you've been attached to someone who isn't able-bodied, someone who can't dance with you, as you wish, or go for long walks.'

She pushed away the anger that his words fired up in her and crouched down so her face was level with his. Taking his face in her hands she kissed him to stop him from saying another word. 'Jesse, I can honestly say that you might have enraged me at times with your stubbornness, but I have never regretted –' she raised a finger – 'not for a single moment, that I married you.' Her heart melted as she gazed at him. She truly was the luckiest woman in the world to have married such an incredible man. 'You've not only given me three strong, wonderful children, you've allowed me…' She hesitated. 'No, you've encouraged me to be the woman even I never imagined I could be.'

'But—'

'No. You're going to listen to me. I've achieved things no other woman I know has had the opportunity to do. But I wouldn't have been able to do any of the things I've done and enjoyed the life I have if I'd been married to any other man. So, don't you ever, for one second, think that I regret marrying you, because I don't. I wouldn't change my life with you even if I could. And,' she added, standing back up, 'don't you let me hear you say such negative things about yourself ever again, do you hear me?'

Jesse's mouth drew back into a smile. 'All right. You are a very bossy woman, do you know that, Lady Boot?'

Florence laughed. 'Yes, I learned from the best. Now, shall I go and fetch the poor captain, who must be beside himself by now out there in the hallway?'

'Yes, please. Then, I'll send him out to find you, so that he can propose to Dorothy.'

Florence clasped her hands together excitedly. 'This is such a momentous day, Jesse. Our first child is to be married.' She took a calming breath. 'The captain will find Dorothy and me in the rose garden.' She blew him a kiss. 'I'll return to speak with you as soon as he comes to find Dorothy. Good luck.'

Florence opened the study door, unable to hide her sympathy for the ashen-faced captain. 'You may go back in now,' she said gently. 'Dorothy and I will be outside when you want to come and find her.'

It was less than five minutes later when Florence left her daughter with the man she wanted to marry. She went to go back to Jesse's study, but saw that he had asked George to push his chair into the library.

'I thought we could watch the captain proposing from a safe distance here,' Jesse said, waving for her to join him.

Florence stood silently next to Jesse by the French windows, her hand resting on his left shoulder. Outside, the captain went down on one knee, taking Dorothy's left hand in his, and although they couldn't hear what he was saying, they could imagine his words.

Florence's hand flew to her chest when Dorothy's joyful cry rang out as she accepted his proposal. The captain, still on one knee, retrieved a red box from his trouser pocket and opened it to show Dorothy the ring inside, making Florence gasp with delight to see the two young people so clearly besotted with each other.

Florence slipped her arm around Jesse's shoulders and swallowed the lump in her throat. Her daughter looked blissfully happy. It was a joy to see such a magical event. The captain took the ring from the box and, holding Dorothy's left hand in his, slipped the ring on her finger. He stood and took her in his arms and Florence took the handkerchief from her sleeve to wipe the tears from her eyes.

'I'm so happy for her, Jesse.'

'I am, too, for both of them. I think they'll be very happy together.'

'I do hope so.'

Now it seemed that they had a wedding to look forward to. Florence would have preferred a summer wedding, but the captain had other commitments and neither wished to wait until the following year to become husband and wife.

Florence recalled only too well how desperate she had been to be married to Jesse when she was Dorothy's age, and how heart-breaking it was when her mother had insisted that they wait a year before allowing her father to give his permission. She didn't want her daughter to suffer as she had and decided that if Dorothy wanted to be married in November, then who was she to argue?

'We only want a quiet wedding,' Dorothy explained a few days later. 'With everything that happened this year, losing his brother-in-law, and his sister Kathleen still grieving for her husband, it seemed wrong to have anything too elaborate.'

Florence understood completely. The poor captain had been through so much. He might have survived the expedition, but Captain Scott and several of his friends had died tragically. 'What do you think of these wedding invitations?' Florence held one out to Dorothy as they sat in her office.

'They've done a good job in the printing department,' Dorothy said, nodding. 'We'll need to send them out in the next few days.'

'We will. The wedding is only –' Florence studied her diary and counted the weeks until she reached the twenty-fifth of November, the date she had circled in ink as soon as Dorothy and the captain had decided upon it – 'six weeks away, so it's just as well that you don't want anything elaborate.'

The Boots printing department had worked quickly to produce the plain white card with black lettering and Florence couldn't help wishing that she was helping to arrange a large wedding for Dorothy. She hadn't been able to or, if she was honest, felt the need to have a large wedding herself. Maybe things might be different for Margery, she mused, reminding herself that as long as her children were happy in their choice of husbands or wife, then that was all that truly mattered to her.

Chapter Three

December 1913

Dorothy's wedding had been a joyful affair and after heavy rain earlier that week and then the first frost of the winter striking two days before the date, everything had been perfect for the happy couple. The happy couple had returned from their honeymoon two days before to stay with Kathleen, his sister, for a few days.

Florence and Jesse had had a lot on their hands, overseeing the build-up to Christmas. Jesse was in a lot of pain, had been since the weather turned colder, and Florence had tried to persuade him to take some time off, but he still insisted on visiting the factories and stores as usual with his driver. She wondered if he would ever take a step back from the business and hoped that his insistence on working so hard wouldn't be detrimental to his health.

Now, though, it was Christmas Day and Florence stared out of the library window, her arms folded, hoping that Dorothy and Wilfred would arrive soon, so that they could all spend time together for the first time since their wedding. Florence understood their wish for a little privacy. She remembered only too well how exciting it had been spending her first Christmas with Jesse in their small home and how long ago that now seemed.

It was colder today. The thick frost on the ground gave the front garden and surrounding hedging and trees a white, magical quality. John and Margery were in the living room with Jesse. The family had eaten a little earlier and now it was the servants' turn to enjoy their Christmas lunch, while Florence's family played a few parlour games. She could hear John's jolly laugh.

She was about to turn away from the window when she heard the distinctive sound of Wilfred's car pulling into the driveway.

Happiness coursed through Florence. She watched as the young newlyweds stepped out of the car. Dorothy's husband, Wilfred – or the captain, as most people referred to him – lifted a large bag from the back and, together, they hurried into the house out of the cold.

Florence was waiting for them in the hallway as they entered the house.

Dorothy's face was pinched with cold. 'You look frozen,' Florence said, reaching up and resting her right palm gently against her daughter's icy cheek. 'Quickly, remove those outer things and come with me into the living room. It's lovely and warm in there. Hurry now.'

'It took us forever to finally get here,' Dorothy said, draping her coat, scarf and hat over the leather chair in the hallway.

'Everyone's been dying to see you again and hear all your news.' Florence turned to Wilfred. 'Your sister, how is she?'

His smile vanished. 'She's finding things very difficult without Robert, naturally, but she's doing her best to cope. She was delighted to have us staying with her for a while and, of course, we'll be returning to spend some time with her in the New Year.'

'Good. She needs her family around her at a time like this. I wish she had agreed to come with you today.'

'Thank you, it was very kind of you both to invite her here for Christmas. However, she preferred to stay at home.' He noticed the Christmas tree taking pride of place in the huge hallway. 'That's a magnificent tree. I don't think I've seen another bigger inside anyone's house.'

Dorothy took his hand. 'It's a tradition of ours to have the biggest tree my parents can find each year. Mother likes to decorate it as best she can.'

Florence laughed at her daughter's teasing. 'Dorothy knows that I love to make the most of this special time of year. I do decorate the lower half of the tree and then usually Meadows hangs up the tree ornaments on the higher branches.'

'With you pointing from below where you want them.' Dorothy giggled.

Florence noticed her shiver. 'Let's get you both into the warm now.' She led the way into the living room, laughter and giggles greeting them as she opened the door and waited for the young couple to enter. 'Look who's arrived, everyone.'

Jesse was seated in an armchair nearest to the fireplace. He waved them over to join him. Florence knew he was in worse pain than he had been recently and hoped it would ease soon, but she knew that he would be distracted from his discomfort by having his children around him for the day.

He took Dorothy's hand in his and pulled her gently down to him so he could give her a kiss on her cheek. 'You are freezing,' he said, darting a look at Wilfred. 'You two need to wrap up better if you're driving that car about this winter.'

'We know that now, Father.' Dorothy laughed, taking her hand from his and rubbing her hands together in front of the flames. 'How is everyone?'

Margery immediately began speaking, telling her sister all her latest news.

Florence stood back and surveyed the scene in front of her. She was so lucky to be spending Christmas Day with her family.

She looked from her oldest daughter to her son. John was laughing at something Margery had said. He was now working for the company and doing even better than she had hoped. Working for Boots suited him well. And as for Margery, her independent, bright youngest child, Florence hoped that she would find a passion that she could focus on in the coming months.

She clasped her hands together. This was all she had ever wanted. For her family to be happy, safe and fulfilled. They all had so much already and everything to look forward to. The coming year – 1914 – held so much promise.

Suddenly, she realised everyone was staring at her with wide grins on their faces.

Florence laughed. 'What are you looking at?'

'You seemed so far away,' Jesse said. 'Care to share your thoughts?

Florence shrugged. 'I was thinking how lucky we all are to have so much and to be able to spend today here in this lovely house. We have achieved so much, Jesse. I know it's taken years of struggle, but we've made it.'

Florence had heard a lot about the impressive Selfridges, but neither she or Jesse were worried about any competition from Harry Selfridge, despite being asked by journalists since the opening of the other store. She and Jesse had seven factories now and employed around five thousand people. It was a huge number that never failed to stagger her. She had been discussing with her lady's maid Harriet how she had read that Mr Selfridge was reported as saying that he saw his store as some sort of theatre. Florence thought then, as she did now, that a bit of healthy competition is a good thing where business was concerned.

'It keeps us all on our toes and striving to be better,' she murmured to herself.

'What was that, my dear?' Jesse cupped his right ear trying to hear her.

Florence rested her hand lightly on his. 'I was just saying how happy I am.'

Chapter Four

September 1914

Florence stared at her son John in horror. She loved him so much and the thought of him choosing to put his life in danger terrified her. 'What do you mean, you've enlisted?'

Her pulse raced, the shock of his announcement making her knees buckle, causing her to land heavily on the chair behind her. She took a moment to gather her composure. *Why would he do such a thing?* 'I don't understand.'

He frowned. 'What? That I want to fight with my fellow man? I feel it's my duty to do this, Mother.'

Florence tried to calm herself. Then, standing, she marched over to her George III mahogany circular table displaying her pristine silver picture frames of her family and selected the one of John and his new wife Margaret on their wedding day only a few short months before. She picked it up, holding it in front of his face. 'You're a married man, John. Have you forgotten?'

'No, Mother, I not forgotten.' Florence couldn't miss his determination to keep a rein on his temper. He must have known she would be upset when he broke this unexpected news to her. 'Naturally, I discussed my intentions with Margaret before I accepted my commission in the Sherwood Foresters. She understands my need to do something to help my country. We're at war, Mother, and, instead of scolding me, you should be thinking of ways that you and Father can do your bit, too.'

Florence tensed, irritated that her son was telling her how to go about her business. She stared at the photo of Margaret in her beautiful lace wedding dress gazing deep into John's eyes at St George's Church in Hanover Square in London. It had been such a joyful event and even Jesse had enjoyed the day despite the pain he was now suffering on a daily basis. Florence did her best to remain calm as she placed the photo back on her polished table.

'I'm painfully aware of that, John.' She sighed heavily. 'Please don't think for one moment that we haven't been making our own plans but, surely, your time would be better spent working at Boots? We're doing all we can right now to find ways to help the gallant soldiers. I might be too old and a woman, but I intend going to war for my country, too, albeit in my own way.'

Florence couldn't miss how his muscles near his jaw worked as he clenched his teeth together. She knew she should hold her tongue and that now was not the time to reprimand him. It was obviously far too late for that and she had no intention of falling out with her beloved son just before he left to go to war.

How could their world have changed so much in four short weeks? One minute, they had all been enjoying long, lazy summer days in the garden and the next the country was at war. It was surreal. Florence wondered if everyone else felt as stunned as she did by the sudden difference in their circumstances since Great Britain had declared war with Germany on 4 August. She suspected they did.

'John, it won't be the same as what you're used to in the Territorial Army.'

'I'm well aware of that, Mother.' John frowned and she realised she had gone too far.

'I'm sorry, dear boy. You've just taken me off guard with this news, that's all. I never expected you to join up, not when you didn't have to. I wish with all my heart that you hadn't.' She knew she wasn't seeing things from his point of view. 'I know I'm being selfish but the thought of something happening to you is too dreadful for me to contemplate,' she added quickly, her voice breaking with emotion. 'I simply couldn't bear to lose you.'

With that, John's face relaxed. He stepped forward, taking her gently by the shoulders. 'Mother,' he said, his voice gentle, 'I do understand how you must feel.'

'I don't think that's possible,' she said quietly, 'and it won't be until you have a child of your own.' She barely managed to contain her emotions.

He gazed down at her for a moment, his expression

softening further. 'Maybe not, but I can try to empathise. Anyway, it's done now, and I have to go.' He gazed out of the window as if his squadron was waiting for him. 'I want to go. Is that terribly selfish of me?'

'Oh, John,' Florence sighed heavily. 'How am I going to break this news to your father?'

John's hands dropped to his sides. 'Would you like me to go and speak to him now?'

'I wish you could but he's in a meeting with a new research chemist and the man's assistant he's recently recruited to come and work for the company. He won't be back until later. If you're free to wait for a while, you can tell him when he returns home.' She looked at the white marble and gilt mantel clock to check the time. 'He shouldn't be too much longer now, hopefully.'

Florence would have rather told Jesse herself, but this was something John needed to tell his father. Her son was twenty-five and a married man, able to make his own decisions. He was no longer a boy and someone she could protect like she used to or easily persuade to change his mind. She had to accept that this was what he wanted and support him in any way she possibly could.

'I'll write to you often,' he promised, as if sensing she was watching him.

'I know you will.'

at that moment, they heard Jesse's car and John turned and walked over to his mother, giving her a gentle kiss on the cheek. 'I want you to be proud of me, Mother. You mustn't worry too much; I'll keep my head down and won't take any unnecessary chances when I'm in France.'

Florence nodded, unable to reply. If her son going to war wasn't such a frightening prospect, then she *would* be exceedingly proud of him right now for being so brave. She would just have to pray harder that he be kept safe. Watching her son leave the room to go and speak to his father, she sat down on the sofa and stared at the flames dancing in the fireplace. She could do nothing to stop him going to war, but at least she had her work to focus her attention on and keep her mind from racing. She covered her mouth with her hand to stifle a cry. She wasn't ready for her son to go abroad and put his life at risk. She never would be. If it wasn't for this war, she knew John would be focusing on his job and his wife, living safely in Nottingham. However, he had made up his mind and there was nothing she could do about it. Who knows, she thought, trying her best to be positive, maybe one of those ideas she and Jesse had been working on might be the thing that saves their own son's life when he goes to fight?

Florence shuddered. She couldn't think of such things, it was far too terrifying. She forced her mind to focus on the reports she had read earlier that day before John's arrival. The falling sales in the fancy-goods and other high-end toiletries were only to be expected. She understood why there had been a dip since the war had begun. The last thing on her own mind right now would be to treat herself to pretty trinkets or perfumes. All she and no doubt the other mothers, wives and daughters could focus on was the safety of their loved ones and trying to find ways to give their own time to the war effort.

How did these women cope, left at home with little to distract them from their fears? At least her work at Boots meant she still needed to put in long hours each day to find ways to keep the business going as well as ensuring their staff had enough work. Florence knew that if she was worried about the situation then Jesse would already be working on ideas to produce items to help the men at the Front.

The idea of being able to do something to make her son's life easier in France calmed her slightly. She thought about the tinned heat Jesse had spoken to her about the previous day. She loved the idea of a little pocket stove and thought the price of sevenpence-ha'penny was very reasonable. She could send one to John in a care package, she decided, along with one of the new pocket air pillows to help make his nights more comfortable. Yes, she thought, she might be helpless when it came to keeping her son from going to France, but there was nothing stopping her from furnishing him with products that might make his time away a little more bearable. The notion soothed her, but only slightly.

Why were her children so obstinate and determined to do the things that they wanted even if it might be dangerous? What a stupid thing to ask herself, she then reasoned as she pulled the curtains closed against the cold evening sky. Didn't she already know the answer to that question? All she had to do was look at their parents she and Jesse were the two most determined people she knew, and it wasn't really a surprise that their children had inherited these traits of theirs.

Florence wished she could hold on to her children for just a little while longer, though, before they all found ways to go off and fight this war. She thought of the assurances she had heard staff and customers giving to each other that the war would be over by Christmastime. She hoped desperately that they were right. Maybe, this nightmare would end before John had even trained as a soldier, let alone been sent overseas. Yes, she thought, feeling a bit better, that's what she would cling to. She couldn't bear to think of her son in any danger and certainly didn't need Jesse becoming upset at the thought of John going away to fight. He was already playing with what little good health he had left by pushing himself to find ways to produce necessary medicines for the British Forces.

Yes, this dreadful war might be over even before there was reason for her to panic. She certainly hoped that would be the case, because the alternative was too terrifying for her to entertain. Yet, even if the war *were* over by Christmas, men would still die before it ended, and the thought that her son could be one of them terrified her. Even more so if he was going to war to prove to his father that he was his own man and not someone who could be told how to live his life. She wasn't sure she understood why Britain had been drawn into this war, and she had no idea what dangers John would be facing on the Continent. Her inability to protect him in any way gnawed at her insides.

Chapter Five

'But you can't truly be telling me that you're leaving, Eleanor? Not when we need you at Boots so badly.'

Florence could not imagine Boots now without Eleanor at the helm of their Staff Welfare programme. She thought back to the previous year at the Olympia trade exhibition in London when their model sickroom had been built on the site and their achievements at having four out of the sixty professional industrial-welfare workers in Britain working for them at Boots were being lauded in the press. Now, Eleanor Kelly and her three assistants were to leave, just when Boots needed their services most.

'We're grateful to you for all that you've done for the company and staff,' Florence said. 'I'm finding it difficult, however, to hide the fact that this news has rather shocked and, I'll admit, saddened me. And you say that your assistants, Miss Harrison, Miss Kerr and Miss Holme, feel the need to leave, also? But why? Is there something we've done wrong that we can try to rectify?'

Florence knew Jesse's reaction to war being announced had been to fret and hoped that his recent reactions to what was happening hadn't upset his staff. She wouldn't criticise him though. He was sixty-four now and in constant pain, crippled by his arthritis, which didn't help his moods. Florence felt certain she would also find coping with difficulties hard especially when there was so much to fear with all the uncertainty in the world, let alone if she had to cope with severe pain.

She watched the incredible woman standing in front of her who had, over the previous three years since Jesse had employed her, brought huge changes to their canteen and created a sickroom attended by nurses and a doctor brought in to see their staff several times each week.

'Your work here has been invaluable. I don't know what we'll do without you and your assistants.'

Eleanor Kelly smiled, and Florence felt slightly reassured. 'I'm very grateful to have been given the opportunity to do all that I've done for Boots and the staff here,' Eleanor said. 'Your consistent support, Lady Boot, and Sir Jesse's has been incredible and I'll always be grateful for the trust you put in my efforts. However, I feel that my work at Boots is well established now and, as we are at war, I believe my experiences will be more useful elsewhere.'

Florence could see there was nothing she could do to change the woman's mind. 'As do Miss Harrison, Miss

Kerr and Miss Holme, I assume?' Florence asked miserably.

'Yes, that is correct. We believe our individual areas of expertise should be put to good use, especially now that the country is calling for qualified medical staff to step forward and offer their services.'

Florence knew it would be selfish to expect the four talented women to stay working for the company when so many others needed their skills. 'You're right. I understand your need to do your part and, although I'm very sorry to see you all leave, I know that you will all make a big difference in your own ways.'

After further polite small talk, Florence bid Eleanor farewell and watched the woman leave her office. She stared at the closed door in stunned silence. So much had changed for them all in the past few months. She grieved for the peaceful years they were all used to living in where her biggest worry each day was whether her children were eating properly, or the books were balanced at work. What did this war mean for them all now? she wondered fearfully.

Despite trying to persuade the factory staff who had already left to work in the new munitions factories that were being set up, and the men who were enlisting in their droves, to change their minds, Florence didn't seem able to. What was going to happen to all these young people in the coming months? What was John going to have to confront? she thought, feeling sick to think of her son facing danger. At least Dorothy was now married and running her home and with Margery working at Boots she didn't have to worry about their safety. The thought comforted her slightly.

Unable to stop fretting about John, Florence decided to pay a visit to the Island Street factory to see for herself how the girls were getting along. She had only been there a few minutes and spoken to a couple of the women in the packing department when she came across a girl who, unlike the other women, didn't look up to greet her. Florence sensed there was something wrong. She watched her for a few seconds and noticed she was trying to hide the fact that she had been crying.

She walked over to her. 'Brenda, isn't it?' Florence asked, keeping her voice low.

The dark-haired girl, whom Florence knew to be only twenty, looked up, her red-rimmed eyes puffy and filled with sorrow. 'Good morning, Lady Boot.'

'Whatever's the matter?' she asked, hating to see one of her girls so upset. 'Is there something I can do to help?'

Brenda let out a cry and burst into noisy sobs. 'I'm so … sorry, L-Lady Boot.'

Florence walked around the large table to her. 'Here,' she said, pulling over the girl's chair. 'Take a seat and try to tell me what's upset you so badly.'

She sobbed into her handkerchief for a few seconds. 'It's my Frankie…' she sniffed. 'He's enlisted and I'm so very frightened I'll never see him again.' She broke into fresh tears.

Florence knew exactly how she felt. Since John's

announcement that he had enlisted ten days before, she had barely been able to think about anything other than her fear for him. Only that morning, Jesse had asked if she was unwell and she knew it was because she was so pale after barely being able to sleep since that day.

'I'm so sorry, Brenda. I understand how you feel.' Brenda looked up with a doubtful expression on her face. 'I do. My own son has recently enlisted, and I can't stop worrying about him.'

'I'm not surprised. It's horrible being left behind not knowing where they are or what they're doing.' She sniffed and blew her nose. 'I wish there was something we could do, but there isn't. Instead we're expected to sit and wait, dreading each time a telegram boy comes to the house.'

Florence sighed heavily. 'I was thinking the same thing.' She rested a hand on Brenda's shoulder. 'You take your time to gather yourself. I'd better return to my office. Who knows, maybe there might be something that we can do for our boys at the Front.'

'Do you really think so?' Brenda asked, a glimmer of hope in her reddened eyes.

'There will be, if I have anything to do with it,' she reassured Brenda, feeling a bond with the young woman who was suffering as much as her.

Florence left the factory and returned to her office anxious to make a difference for herself and the other women fearing for the lives of the men they loved, and determined to do all she could to help. She rested her elbows on her desk and cupped her chin in her palms. She might not know what the outcome of this war was going to be, but she did know that she was not going to sit by and do nothing. This battle was one that needed to be fought from home ground as well as on foreign soil. She didn't know exactly how she and Jesse could help at that moment but was certain that with their skilled staff and her and Jesse's innovative ideas, there would be ways that they could help the war effort. She stood and went through to Jesse's office.

'I've been thinking, Jesse,' she said, walking around her husband's desk to kiss him on his forehead.

'Should I be concerned?' he teased without looking up from the paperwork in front of him.

'I don't think so. I've just been speaking to one of my girls. She is distressed because her husband has enlisted. I think it's time we focused our attention on some of those ideas we've been discussing recently. We might not be able to physically leave for war but there's nothing stopping us joining the war effort from here.'

Jesse looked up at her. He held out a twisted hand for her to take. 'I agree. We can and will do all we can to keep our boy and other people's sons safe. Take a seat and let's work on a few of our thoughts. We must decide exactly what our next move will be and what's needed. Then we'll plan how best to produce it.'

'Yes,' she said determined to do her bit to ensure John and men like him were given every support possible from Boots while they were fighting so far from home.

Jesse winced. She hated to see him in pain and knew better than to ask him about it when he was working. She waited for him to speak. 'I think the first thing we should do is contact the British Forces and find out what they need most.'

'Good idea.' She tried to picture where these extra departments would fit in their current factories. 'We'll need to employ more staff to do this added work too, won't we?'

Jesse nodded thoughtfully. 'We will.'

Florence realised now was as good a time as any to mention some of the losses of staff they had already suffered. 'We've also had several women give notice to work in munitions factories.'

Jesse frowned. 'Why would they do that? Those places will be incredibly dangerous.'

She thought so too, but apart from trying to persuade the women to stay at Boots or advise them about the downsides of working in munitions, Florence couldn't see what else she could do to stop them. Thankfully, she thought, there had only been a few so far.

'I agree,' Florence replied. 'I think though that right now our real difficulty is going to be finding new men to take over in the areas where their strength is needed.'

'Also working out what new products we can begin producing for our own war effort and putting the departments and staff into place that we'll need to carry out the work.'

She looked at her husband who, despite everything he had to contend with each day, still maintained his control over the company. 'You mentioned yesterday that we're almost at the end of our supplies of aspirin and saccharin.'

'We are,' he groaned. Florence could see how concerned he was at the thought of not being able to supply things that they usually did from the factories. 'I knew our supply of chemicals we import from Germany would be cut as soon as we went to war. Now, though, we urgently need to come up with other ways of obtaining these products. I've been working on an idea of how to resolve this.'

'Don't look so worried,' she said trying to reassure him. 'You always find a solution to the problems we face. You're a clever and very resourceful man, Jesse Boot. Do you know that?'

He laughed. 'I try my best.'

'Any thoughts on what we're going to do?'

'A few.' He frowned. 'It looks like we're going to need to work on new manufacturing processes in order to develop the supplies ourselves. It'll be better for us in the long run if we do it this way despite the initial outlay in funds to cover the work. But at least then we'll no longer be beholden to other countries for those products.'

Florence heard a quiet but distinct knock on Jesse's office door.

'Come in,' Jesse called.

Miss Tweed opened the door and looked from Jesse to Florence. She seemed concerned about something and, Florence thought, whatever it was must be urgent, otherwise her secretary would never have interrupted her when she was in Jesse's office with the door closed.

'Yes, Miss Tweed?' Florence said. 'Were you wanting me for something?'

'Yes, Lady Boot. I'm sorry to interrupt your conversation but there are a few members of staff who've come up to speak to you.' She stepped into the room and closed the door quietly behind her. 'I have a feeling they're going to be giving notice.'

Florence felt a familiar anxiety coursing through her. She closed her eyes briefly to compose herself.

'Why are they all leaving when we need them most?' Jesse asked.

Florence knew he was well aware of the answer. War work sounded much more exciting than coming to work in a factory or store each day. She didn't blame the younger people for wanting to be in the thick of things and travel but wondered how long they would be kept in paid employment should the war end by Christmas, or soon after. She stood and thanked her secretary. 'Please tell them I'll be along directly.'

'We seem to be losing staff most days now,' Jesse grumbled. 'We need more of them to come and work for us not fewer, if we're to do all that we intend for this war effort.'

'I understand that, Jesse. There's nothing we can do though if staff want to leave.' She walked around his desk and kissed his forehead. 'I'd better go and speak to them now.'

Florence welcomed in the fifth member of staff who had come up to her office to speak to her. She checked the notes that Miss Tweed had given to her earlier and saw that this girl's name was Doris Traynor.

'Good morning, Doris,' she said smiling and indicating one of the chairs opposite her desk. 'Please, take a seat.' The girl, whose hands Florence noticed were shaking slightly, did as she was asked. Florence tried to put her at her ease. It can't be easy coming up here to speak to me, she thought. As much as she tried her best to encourage her staff to relax in her presence, she was aware that despite their respectful and appreciative behaviour, her position in the company, as well as her imposing height and now having the title Lady Boot, gave her a rather larger-than-life presence.

'Thank you, Lady Boot.' Doris's voice trembled as she spoke.

'I presume you've come to give me your notice?'

Doris's eyes widened briefly. Surely, she wasn't surprised by her comment, Florence thought. 'You're not the first, even today, I'm sorry to say.'

Doris gave Florence a guilty look. 'I have, Lady Boot. Sorry.'

'No, that's fine. May I ask why you've decided to leave Boots?' She kept her voice gentle, not wishing to intimidate the girl any more than she already seemed to be doing.

'I want to join the First Aid Nursing Yeomanry.' She looked down at her hands. 'That is to say,' she added as her cheeks reddened, 'I signed up with them yesterday.'

Florence's mouth fell open, surprised that the girl had already taken steps to move on from her position at Boots. She immediately closed it. 'Is this who they refer to as the FANYs?'

'That's right.'

Florence was intrigued. She had heard these women mentioned but, unlike VADs, who helped nursing staff, she had little idea what these women did. 'Do you know what you'll be expected to do?' Doris nodded. 'And if you'll be staying here in England?'

'I'll be doing whatever is expected of me. We help where we're most needed and do things like change bandages, drive ambulances. Although I've yet to learn to drive,' she added as a seeming afterthought.

Florence admired Doris's bravery in leaving all that was familiar and signing up to do something when she didn't know what exactly it could be or where she would be stationed. She could see the passion in the girl's face and hear it in her voice. The shy girl who had momentarily before entered her office was gone.

'I'm hoping to go to France,' Doris continued. 'With a few friends who have also joined the FANYs.'

Florence knew it was far too late for her to try to persuade Doris to stay working at Boots. Nor did she feel she had the right. She wouldn't have listened if anyone had tried to stop her leaving Jersey when she was younger to follow her dreams with Jesse. This girl had made up her mind and was obviously excited to go. Florence couldn't help feeling a thrill of excitement for her.

'Then I wish you well, Doris. Just please do try to stay out of any danger, if possible. And, when the war is over, if you wish to, do come back and see if there's an opening for you here.'

'Thank you very much, Lady Boot,' she said, standing. 'I

really appreciate you saying that. My mum will be grateful when I tell her what you've said, too. She's upset that I'm leaving such a good job and worried about what will become of me after all this is over.'

'Please then tell her there's no need to be concerned. You do all that you must and come back to me when you're ready. Good luck, Doris.'

Doris thanked her employer as Florence saw the girl out. She hated the sense of loss she felt at losing yet another competent girl but, before she had any time to dwell, invited the next member of staff into her office.

By the end of the morning, she had accepted the resignation of seven members of staff. Florence sat back in her chair and stared at a picture on her wall of the most recent opening of one of their stores. Boots had been going from strength to strength over the past twenty years but now it looked like they were going to have a problem keeping their enthusiastic staff. It wasn't surprising, she supposed, not when there seemed to be so much excitement out there for young people to become involved in. She didn't blame them for a moment, but struggled to imagine how they would manage to create new departments and find the staff to work in them if so many of their present staff kept leaving.

She hadn't noticed Miss Tweed enter but smiled to see her placing a cup of tea and a digestive biscuit on the desk in front of her. 'Thank you, Miss Tweed.'

'It's such a difficult time, isn't it, Lady Boot?'

Florence sighed miserably. 'It is. For all of us.' She

clasped her hands together. 'I understand them wanting to go but Jesse and I saw a few of the first wounded men being brought back to Nottingham only yesterday.' She shivered at the recollection. 'Some of their injuries are horrendous. I worry what might happen to our staff when they do get to the Front, or wherever it is that they end up.' Florence pushed away the thought of John being badly injured. She must not allow herself to even consider such a thing, she thought anxiously as she rubbed her tired eyes. 'I've lost several girls to munitions factories. Those are the jobs that frighten me the most. All those explosives under one roof with those women working long hours to fill the shells. It can't be safe, surely?'

Her secretary gave her a solemn nod. 'It's true. I worry that some of these young people are so entranced by the thought of more excitement in their life that they don't understand the risks they might be taking.'

Miss Tweed was right, Florence knew that. Then again, she thought, none of them knew how this new type of war would develop. She couldn't help thinking that there would be many shocks coming to them all before this war was over and could not manage to shake her fear that the worst was still to come. 'Do any of us know the risks, really?'

'I suppose not.'

Florence smiled at the loyal woman standing in front of her. 'As long as you don't decide to leave Boots, Miss Tweed, then I'm sure I'll be able to cope with whatever is thrown our way.'

Miss Tweed's cheeks reddened. 'There's no fear of that,

Lady Boot. I love working here for you and have no wish to go elsewhere, war or no war.'

Florence rested her palms on her leather desktop. 'That's the best news I've heard all day. Thank you for your continued support. I truly don't know what I would do without you here.'

Florence was aware that Miss Tweed knew how valued she was at Boots, but she wanted to reiterate how she felt. It was true. Her secretary ran everything so smoothly for her that it gave Florence the time to work through twice as many of the appointments in her calendar as she otherwise would have done. Miss Tweed was professional and more efficient than she suspected most secretaries could be. Her typing skills were second to none and no matter when Florence entered the woman's office it was always ordered and neat.

So much had changed since war had been declared in August. Everyone's lives were different in one way or another, Florence mused. And, like everyone else, she would simply have to find a way to achieve all that she and Jesse had been planning to support the war effort. After all, hadn't she spent her adulthood finding solutions to supposedly insurmountable problems? Yes, she thought, taking a bite from her biscuit. She was a fighter, as was Jesse. They had never let much defeat them before and having her own son fighting for his country made her all the more determined to succeed.

The world might have changed but her resolve to make things work had increased since the war began. She and

Jesse would have to ensure that Boots adapted to fit the needs of their staff, as well as their customers. And despite many people still hanging on to the idea that the war would be over by Christmas, Florence's instinct told her not to be so certain that this would happen. She might not have any military experience but she knew enough about life to understand that a war of this magnitude could surely not be ended within mere months. She needed to start thinking, and planning.

Chapter Six

October 1914

'Mother? Mother, where are you?'

Florence heard her youngest daughter's voice calling for her. 'We're in the conservatory,' she replied, wondering why Margery always had to bellow from the hallway rather than come and look in the obvious places where Florence would usually sit. 'Good afternoon, Mother, Father,' her daughter said as she appeared in the doorway. Florence smiled then said, 'Ask for another cup to be brought in, then come and join us.'

Florence watched her daughter leave to go and do as she had asked. She reached out and rested her hand on Jesse's. 'I wonder what exciting news our daughter might have to share with us today.'

She gazed at the envelope in her hand with John's

familiar writing and opened it, unable to resist discovering her son's latest news now that he was in France. She withdrew the single sheet of paper and smiled relieved he was doing as he had promised and keeping in touch with them. She unfolded the letter and began to read.

France
18 October 1914

Sir Jesse and Lady Boot,
St Heliers House
The Park
Nottingham
England

Dearest Mother and Father,

I don't have much time to write but wanted to let you know that my battalion is now in France and I've been appointed Transport Officer. I've yet to discover how good I am in this role as my duties come to fruition once we are given orders that we are to move forward and take over from another battalion. I'm expecting this to happen soon and look forward to going to the headquarters of the division we'll be relieving where I'll observe their protocols and be able to plan how to supply rations and ammunition to our men.

I believe that I have been given this appointment due to the work I've done at Boots. I probably have more experience than most of the men in organising large groups of people, so not only understand why the powers that be would think of me for this role but am grateful for it and look forward to showing what I can do.

It's fairly daunting being here so close to the front lines and I have to admit that any thoughts of glory I might have once had have now dissipated. I've heard and seen enough already to know that my thoughts of being at war were, to say the very least, naïve. Please don't worry about me, though: unlike most of the men, I won't be going 'over the top' and, although I am on the Front, I will be kept too busy arranging the transport of supplies to the men in the trenches to get into any trouble.

My fondest love, as always,
John

Florence finished reading the letter and pushed it back into the envelope. 'As much as I worry about him being so close to danger, I'm relieved to know that he will be looking after supplies and not running into battle.' She sensed that John was trying to be as honest as possible without causing them too much concern.

Jesse reached out and took her hand in his. 'He'll be fine. John is a sensible man and he's not going to put himself in any danger if he can possibly help it.' He smiled at her. 'Do you feel a little more at ease now he's told you what he's doing?'

'I do,' she admitted. She didn't add that she would rather he be miles back from the front line rather than working so close to it, but didn't want to give Jesse any reason to worry more than he already was doing.

She now heard Margery's voice again, in the distance. She loved her daughter's enthusiasm for life. It was a huge relief to her that she still had one child at home and that both her daughters were out of harm's way. How like her siblings Margery was though, Florence thought. She was determined to find a way to make her mark during this dreadful war. Florence had overheard two of the maids whispering about Margery having a big idea but she had yet to hear about it directly from her daughter. Florence had heard of other friends' daughters organising knitting circles to make scarves, balaclavas, gloves and socks for men at the Front and others setting up small charities or events to raise funds. She looked forward to hearing what her lively younger daughter had in mind.

She heard rapid footsteps and wished Margery wouldn't run on the polished Parquet flooring in the hallway.

Appearing once more in the doorway, Margery grinned at them both as she walked over to kiss first Florence on her cheek and then bent to kiss her father. Florence felt almost overwhelmed by her love for her youngest child. She noticed Margery's flushed cheeks and suspected now might be the time her daughter had intended sharing her news.

Margery sat and rested her hands together neatly in her lap, which, Florence noted, she tended to do when bracing herself to announce something momentous. 'How are you both today?'

Florence gazed lovingly at her daughter, hoping to put her at her ease. 'I can sense you have something you wish to speak to us about. Why not tell us what it is before one of the servants arrives with your teacup?'

Margery glanced from her to Jesse and winced. 'Right, then, I will: I'm planning to set up a canteen. Well, it's more of a kitchen with a café.'

A canteen? Florence struggled to picture her daughter doing such a thing. Maybe she meant to do the same as other women had by setting up small stalls at railway stations and ports to welcome returning soldiers with cups of tea, cigarettes and buns. She wondered when Margery could have visited or been taken by the idea to do it herself. Would she even know how to run such a thing? Maybe she had joined another group of women?

'Do you have an idea where you'll do this?' Florence asked, unsure where this was leading.

'Northern France.'

Florence opened her mouth to speak but her shock was so huge that she was unable to find the right words. '*Northern France!* But, surely…?' Her mind raced. She couldn't possibly allow her to go and have two of her children in harm's way. Why was Margery wanting to leave the safety of Nottingham to go to France? The second the thought entered her head she thought of Doris's enthusiasm in her office a few weeks earlier and that of the other girls who had since given notice that they were replacing their work at Boots with jobs connected to the war effort. Why should her caring daughter be any different to them?

Florence saw Margery swallow as she waited for her and Jesse to absorb her news. Margery was obviously expecting this reaction from her. Then Florence realised Jesse hadn't spoken. It wasn't like him not to have expressed an opinion by now. She suspected he must be as horrified at her at the thought of their daughter leaving to go and work in France.

'Where *exactly* in Northern France?'

'Not you as well?' Jesse said before Margery had a chance to answer Florence's question. 'Why do you young people feel this need to put yourselves in danger? Surely, there's something safer you can do for the war effort here in Nottingham? Or even elsewhere in England, if you'd rather go further afield?'

Florence didn't want Jesse to lose his temper or, worse, panic at the thought of Margery going away but could see by the reddening of his face that he was getting upset. When the war had begun she had been horrified to discover that John had enlisted but it never occurred to her that one of her daughters would also find a way to go to France whilst the war was raging.

Florence decided to try to calm herself. She needed to take charge of the situation before tempers flared. 'Why don't you start from the beginning, Margery?'

'Good idea,' Jesse agreed glancing at Florence, his

expression giving nothing away. She suspected he was also trying hard not to upset Margery. Like her though, Jesse would no doubt be concerned that if he insisted their daughter forget the idea of leaving she might storm off and leave without being fully prepared. Florence had heard of other young people hurriedly leaving their family because of arguments despite being forbidden to go, and had no intention of her daughter doing such a thing.

How many parents must be feeling frightened for their families like she and Jesse were right now? Florence thought back to only a few months previously when her children's futures had been ones she was looking forward to witnessing. Peaceful, calm futures filled with excitement and the prospect of creating their own families with everything to look forward to. How suddenly everything had changed and not just for their family but for every family touched by this war.

Was it her fault, for striving to bring her children up to be independent? Florence wondered. She had always thought her determination to help her children become adults with minds of their own an advantage; was this intention now coming back to bite her? Florence knew she would never forgive herself if either John or Margery were hurt or, worse, killed, due to their decision to become involved in the war.

Margery sat up straighter, her chin raised slightly. 'It's simply that I've heard how dreadful it can be for men travelling home by train who've been injured, especially the more severely injured of them.' She stared out to the garden, a wistful look on her young face. 'The rattling around in carriages, hour after hour, can be agony for many of them. I met a couple of nurses two weeks ago and we started talking. They wanted to find a way to help ease the dreadful journeys of those wounded soldiers and we decided that we should do something ourselves. I've met up with two other friends of mine who wish to help and together we believe we can make a huge difference to what is otherwise a horrible experience.'

Florence pictured her youngest daughter trying to cope with such a situation. 'Go on…' she encouraged, doing her best to remain calm.

'It occurred to me how nice it would be for us to offer them a kindly word, a cup of tea and some nourishing food, the offer of a cigarette or two, that sort of thing. I believe that doing something so simple can really help turn a painful experience into a more positive one.' She turned to look at Florence and Jesse. 'Surely, something like this could really help many wounded soldiers? It would also help those nurses and doctors travelling with them, if their charges have a break and are refreshed with these things. What do you think?'

Florence glanced at Jesse. He looked at her, a troubled look in his eyes. Then he turned to Margery, smiling proudly at her. 'I think it's a splendid idea, darling. How very clever of you to come up with something that could potentially make an enormous difference to many soldiers.' His gaze returned to Florence. 'But you can't cook, and you don't know anything about setting up a canteen.'

'I can learn to cook from one of the others,' Margery responded immediately, 'and, as far as organising everything, I'll simply have to ask people and figure everything out. As I said, it won't only be me doing it, there are a small group of us.'

Jesse shrugged. 'It seems, Florence that our youngest daughter is set on finding her own way in the world.'

Florence wished she could sound as cheerful as Jesse at the prospect of her daughter taking up this challenge. She wanted desperately to refuse to let her go but how could she react in such a way? She never would have stopped John leaving, regardless of how much she didn't want him to go. After all that she had said about women being equal to men, she couldn't now treat her daughter differently from John. She reached forward to take her daughter's hand in hers briefly and gave it a gentle squeeze before letting go and sitting back in her chair. Margery had always been a hard worker, first at her studies and then working for the company and as much as Florence admired her daughter's intentions it worried her that she might not have realistic expectations about what to expect in France.

'Mother? You're very quiet,' Margery said, frowning. 'I'd love to know what you think about this idea.'

Florence's head pounded and she could feel a headache coming on. The thought of her daughter going to France without a family member there to protect her terrified her. What if something untoward happened to her when she was so far away from home? Neither she nor Jesse could be at her side within hours, only days. Her mind raced. Would Margery be in danger? How would she cope if anything happened to her daughter? Florence knew she would want to die if either of her children were killed. She gave an involuntary shiver at the thought.

'Mother?'

Margery's concerned voice pierced Florence's troubled thoughts. She was determined not to upset her daughter but her plan to leave for France made her sick with fear. 'I think it's a marvellous idea, too.' It was, she reasoned, she wasn't lying, but she hesitated for a moment, aware that she needed to broach her concerns with as much tact as she could muster. 'There will be a lot of planning for you all to do before you'll be ready to leave though, I should imagine?' Before Margery could reply, she added, 'Have you thought about where you'll set up this canteen and how you'll manage the long hours it will take to run it?'

'Yes, I think so.' Margery gave them a confident smile. 'If I've learned one thing from the pair of you it's how to be organised. I'm going to need several assistants, including someone trained in nursing for helping change bandages and that sort of thing. That's where my two nursing friends have come in. I'll have to raise some money to buy equipment and provisions, of course. Then, as soon as I have everything in place we'll be leaving for France.'

'But where exactly in France?' Jesse asked.

'I'm not entirely certain at the moment, but wherever we're needed most. I intend setting up at one of the railway stations through which the wounded pass on their way to the nearest seaport. I want their journey home to be as pleasant as possible, so it makes sense to start there.'

'It does,' Jesse agreed. 'My only concern is that you are a woman and a young one at that.' Florence heard Margery groan in unsuppressed irritation. 'What worldly experiences have you ever had to help you cope with any ungentlemanly behaviour?'

'*Father!*'

'Well, it's something I believe you should consider. As distasteful as it sounds, it is something you need to be prepared to deal with.'

'I— That is… Well, I'm not sure.'

Jesse didn't wait for Margery to finish her reaction to his questions before continuing. 'Don't you think it'll be dangerous in Northern France? We've seen ourselves –' he looked at Florence for back-up– 'haven't we, dear, the shocking state those poor wounded soldiers have begun returning in.'

Margery's smile vanished. Florence wondered if her daughter had thought about having to deal with badly injured men and how she had no experience of that sort of thing either. She watched as Margery gave Jesse's questions some thought.

'The soldiers will be accompanied, Father. I don't think you need worry about that. And most will be wounded, as you said, so probably not in a position to do anyone much harm.'

Jesse scowled at her. 'I wouldn't be too sure of that, my

darling. Men can be beastly when they put their mind to it.' He looked at Florence for reassurance. 'Don't you agree, my dear?'

Relieved at Jesse's sensible comments and glad not to be the only one voicing concerns, Florence nodded. 'Your father is right, darling. Not all men are well behaved and if you and your friends are running this venture alone, who will be around to come to your aid if the necessity arises?'

Margery sighed heavily. Florence could see her daughter had been expecting this sort of opposition to her plans. 'I do wish the pair of you wouldn't worry so much. As I said, we'll set up our canteen at a railway station. There are guards there, aren't there?' She waited for Florence and Jesse to nod their agreement. 'Well, my assistants and I will be sensible enough to make friends with them, so that they will come to help us should we need them to.'

Despite Florence's fears for her daughter's safety, she could not help feeling somewhat reassured that Margery appeared to have considered various situations.

Jesse mumbled something under his breath. 'Surely you can find other ways of helping the war effort and still remain in the relative safety of Nottingham?'

Florence could see by the determined expression on Margery's face that she and Jesse were wasting their breath. She thought back to when she had been twenty-two. She had not yet met Jesse, but she had been as determined as her daughter was now to make something of herself. Florence didn't doubt that Margery was going to find a way to go to France whether she and Jesse liked the idea or not.

'Your father and I have both made choices in our lives that our parents might not have wished for us when we were younger… haven't we, Jesse?' Florence admitted. She spoke gently, not wanting to antagonise him further unnecessarily. 'We can't accept John's decision to enlist and not allow Margery to do as she chooses.'

'John is a married man,' Jesse argued.

Margery gasped. 'What has that got to do with anything?'

Florence spoke quickly before Jesse could react. 'I think it's more that your father worries less about your brother because he is older than you.'

'By three years, that's all.' Margery unpinned her hat, stabbing the pin back in through the straw crown with a little more vigour than Florence thought necessary. 'Anyhow, what he's doing is far more dangerous than anything I'll be facing in France. At least I'll be behind the front lines.'

'Those front lines move constantly,' Jesse argued. 'I've read as much in the broadsheets.'

Florence sensed the tension rising rapidly between her husband and daughter. She reached out to touch Jesse's arm in an effort to calm him. She understood her children well enough to know that, like her and Jesse, they could be stubborn when confronted. 'I think Margery will have looked into this thoroughly before setting anything in place, don't you, dear?'

He gave Florence's question some thought. 'I simply worry that you might be caught up in unexpected dangers that you hadn't considered, that's all,' he said giving Margery a pleading look. 'I don't underestimate your skill for putting this idea into action.'

Margery's shoulders relaxed and Florence could see she was calming down. 'You do both think it's a good idea then?'

Florence couldn't miss the hope in her daughter's voice. She was as frightened for her as she knew Jesse to be, but she was also aware that her children were strong-minded and felt the need to make their mark in the world, just as she and Jesse had done before them. 'I think it's an excellent one.' Florence had never been prouder of her youngest daughter than at this moment. 'Those poor young men need all the comfort you can offer them. If it isn't bad enough being at the Front in those unsanitary trenches, they then have to suffer the pain and fear of being injured and cope with an arduous journey home. We can't help worrying for your safety, that's all darling,' she explained.

Margery gave a cheerful sigh. 'I am relieved. I knew you would both have reservations about what I'm intending to do, but I do appreciate your understanding. I promise I won't take any silly chances and will make sure that both my safety and that of my assistants, and of course the wounded men, is paramount.'

'We know you will,' Florence said, opening her arms and holding her daughter tightly as Margery bent to hug her. 'But you must keep in contact with us as much as you can. We are going to need constant reassurances that you are safe and well.'

'We certainly will,' added Jesse. 'However, you do seem to have thought of most eventualities. I'm sure I speak for your mother as well as myself when I say that if there's anything at all that we can do to help this venture of yours, we hope you will let us know.'

Margery stepped back and then kissed her father on his cheek. 'Thank you. I will.'

Chapter Seven

St Heliers House, December 1914

Florence had spent the previous couple of months keeping as busy as possible to stop herself from fretting about Margery's impending departure. She felt sick every time she thought of her leaving despite all the reassurances Margery had given them. It worried her too that many male members of staff had enlisted and rather more of her girls had also left to do their bit for King and country.

Not wishing to ruin any of the time she had left with Margery before her departure, Florence helped her daughter whenever possible to source all that she needed for her canteen. Florence hadn't realised Margery's need to help others was so deeply ingrained in her. She understood why she wanted so desperately to go to France and do her bit and suspected that if she was her daughter's age now, she would feel compelled to do something similar.

It turned out that although Margery gratefully accepted small donations from her and Jesse, most of the funds she accumulated for her venture were from small events she and her assistants had arranged. Florence watched in awe as week by week Margery's supply of tarpaulin tents, bedding, first aid supplies, crockery, cutlery, recipes and dried food increased and were packed and stored ready for the time when she would be satisfied that she had all she needed to set up the canteen and run it for several months.

She watched her daughter grow in confidence as time passed and her plans came to fruition and even though she would give almost anything to stop her leaving England, she had to admit to herself that she didn't think she could ever be prouder of her youngest child.

Florence sat at their long dining room table while their Christmas lunch was served. She had made a point of putting up a much smaller tree this year and keeping celebrations less ostentatious. It didn't seem right somehow to be exchanging expensive gifts and holding large parties when so many were suffering.

She watched Dorothy deep in conversation with John's beloved wife Margaret, who was sitting next to her. Florence wished her son could have joined them for the festivities but knew it had been an unlikely prospect since his brief visit home two weeks before. It hadn't stopped her from being sad when Christmas Day arrived and he was not with them. Poor Margaret, she thought, newly married and spending her first Christmas without her husband.

'John seems to be doing well,' Margaret said, 'and would have loved to have been with us today. I'm consoling myself with the knowledge that he's happy to have been given the role of Transport Officer.'

'Yes,' Jesse said, 'he'll be good at that and no doubt relish having something to organise and get his teeth into.'

Florence was relieved she had insisted Margaret come and stay with them at St Heliers House for the festivities. She hated to think of the poor young bride alone at such a time. If she herself was missing John with all that she had going on in her life, then his wife must find his absence a bigger struggle to deal with.

Florence placed Margery opposite Dorothy and next to her own younger sister, Amy. She watched Margery chatting animatedly to Amy, telling her all her news and all that they had planned for the future of her canteen. She could almost feel her daughter's impatience to set off to France in three days' time. Florence thought of all the supplies Margery had gathered waiting to be taken from an empty storeroom Jesse had allowed her to use in one of their factories. They were ready to leave and were only still in Nottingham due to Florence's insistence that Margery spend the festivities with her family. In the next couple of days, they would be loaded onto the train to go with Margery and her assistants on the ferry to Calais.

No, she thought, determined not to dwell on Margery's impending departure. She still had two of her children with her and she would focus on them and remain as positive as she could manage. She doubted anyone was truly feeling the Christmas spirit this year but the least she could do was put on a brave face and make sure that everyone in her home enjoyed the festivities as much as possible.

On the morning of 28 December, Florence braced herself to help Margery go through final checks of her personal packing to ensure her daughter hadn't forgotten anything important. She sat on the edge of Margery's bed watching as she double-checked her large carpet bag.

'I'm very proud of you, do you know that?' Florence said.

Margery stopped folding the stockings she was holding and grinned. 'Yes, Mother. You've told me many times over the past couple of months.' She returned to her checking and placed the extra pair of stockings into the bag. 'I'll be back before you know it,' she added without looking up.

Florence closed her eyes to try to contain her rising emotion. Her daughter knew her too well, despite how brave she was attempting to act. 'I know you will. And who knows, you might end up meeting a handsome soldier stopping for refreshment in your canteen?'

Margery laughed. 'I'm not looking for a husband over there. I'm going to be working, very hard too by all accounts.'

'I know you will,' Florence said, unable to give up the small hope that Margery might meet the love of her life and end up returning to Nottingham to be a housewife well away from any fighting.

Margery, satisfied, fastened her large bag, closed her handbag and rested her palms on the handles. 'Well then. That's me ready.' She crossed the floor to Florence. 'Truly, Mother. You mustn't worry about me. I believe we all have our parts to play in this war. This canteen is mine. I promise I won't do anything silly that could put me in danger. And I'll make sure to come home whenever I have the chance so that you and Father are able to see for yourselves that I'm looking after myself properly. Agreed?'

'Yes, that's fine,' replied Florence, a lump constricting her throat making it difficult to speak without showing how emotional she felt.

It wasn't really fine, but Florence knew it was the best she could hope for. She knew there was no turning back now that Margery was about to depart for France. She had failed to persuade her daughter to stay in Britain and if nothing else she was determined to show Margery how confident she was in her abilities. Letting her know how frightened she was for her simply was not the way she intended to leave things between them on this last morning they would be sharing for along time. Florence was determined to put on a brave face. She would have more than enough time after Margery's departure to give in to the tears that kept threatening to escape.

Florence stood. 'I'll go and ask Meadows to come and fetch your bags and take them out to Father's car. Then we can leave for the station.'

Florence left Margery's room. The tension of trying to remain cheerful when really what she needed to do was have a good cry was exhausting. She made her way down the stairs to find Meadows. When she couldn't find him anywhere, Florence walked to the kitchen hoping Mrs Rudge, their cook, might know where he might be. She opened the door and immediately saw Meadows, his face ashen, holding what looked like a telegram. Something was obviously very wrong.

Mrs Rudge, Meadows and the two maids in the kitchen with them turned wide-eyed to stare at her as she stood in the doorway.

'Whatever's the matter?' Florence asked, walking across the terracotta tiles to speak to them. 'Has something happened, Meadows? You look incredibly pale.'

Meadows held out the telegram in his hand. 'It's my sister's boy, Lady Boot. She was recently widowed when her husband died in an accident. This says that her boy has been wounded. He's in a hospital in France.'

Florence's heart ached for Meadows and his unfortunate sister. 'Do you wish to go to her, Meadows?'

'I would appreciate the time to do so, Lady Boot. She hasn't asked me to come in her telegram but I'm all she's got apart from her son and I know she'll be in a dreadful state.'

'Then you must pack whatever clothes you need and go to be with your sister now. You can travel with Margery and me to the station. You can catch a train from there. We're leaving in twenty minutes though, so you'll need to pack immediately if you're to be ready in time.'

He closed his eyes. 'Thank you very much, Lady Boot. That's extremely kind of you.' He forced a smile in her direction. 'I'll fetch Miss Margery's cases down to the car and then pack my things. It won't take me a minute.'

'If you're sure you have time, Meadows,' Florence said, unsure whether to allow him to bother with Margery's cases when he had to sort himself out to come with them. 'I can ask George to take the cases.'

'No, honestly, I have more than enough time for both, I won't need to take much with me.'

The drive to Nottingham Station was a sombre one. Florence had intended being chatty and at her most cheerful for Margery's sake, but now that Meadows was accompanying them, albeit in the front with their driver, Alfred Parry, she didn't think it appropriate.

'Do you think his nephew will be all right?' Margery whispered as the car made its way down the roads from The Park.

Florence shrugged. 'I do hope so.'

'You never know,' Margery said louder so that Meadows could hear. 'Maybe your nephew will travel via my canteen on his way home from France?'

Florence wished Margery hadn't said what she did. None of them knew yet whether the boy would survive his injuries. But Meadows seemed happy at her suggestion when he turned around to face them as well as he could from the front passenger seat. 'Thank you, Miss Margery. I'd like that very much. I'll say as much to my sister.'

Florence realised that any hope of a positive outcome was better than none. The efforts she and Jesse had been making to do their best to support those fighting for their country needed to be increased, she decided. By tomorrow, she would have two children in France fighting for what they believed in and with every second that passed on the way to the station Florence felt a deeper compulsion to do whatever it took to ensure she brought them home safely.

Parry parked the motor and helped Florence and Margery out.

'Don't wait for us, Meadows,' Florence said, aware that he might have to run ahead to catch the next train to his sister's hometown. 'Please send my and Sir Jesse's best wishes to your sister and I hope that any news about your nephew is positive. I'll see you when you return to St Heliers House.'

He scooped up his bag and slung it over his shoulder. 'Thank you, again, Lady Boot. I promise I'll be back as soon as possible.'

'I'm sure you will. Now off you go. You don't want to miss your train.'

Parry called for a porter to come and take Margery's carpet bag. Florence went with Margery to check that the supplies had been successfully loaded and then to buy her ticket. She was almost relieved to discover that they only had a few minutes until the train departed and that it was already waiting for passengers to board. Although she hated to see Margery leave, she wasn't sure how long she would be able to keep control of her emotions, especially now the time had come for her daughter to leave Nottingham.

The porter followed them to Margery's carriage and helped load her larger bag. Florence heard several female voices calling for Margery and turned to see four other women waving and hurrying towards them, each with happy, excited expressions on their faces. How thrilling it must be for them to set off on this new adventure, she realised, feeling a little placated by their cheeriness.

Florence took Margery by the shoulders and bent forward to kiss her on her cheek. 'I see your friends have arrived. I'll let you join them on the train and say my farewells here.' Annoyingly, her voice broke slightly, and Florence had to swallow to gather herself.

Margery pulled her into a hug. 'I'll be fine, Mother. Please don't fret about me. You have more than enough to attend to with your own work.' She moved back slightly but kept her voice low. 'We'll both be so busy that the time I'm away will fly by. You wait and see.'

Florence hoped so very much. 'Yes,' she said, determined to sound as convinced as Margery did. 'And think of all the tales we'll have to share when you're next home.'

'I was thinking the very same thing.' Margery kissed her once more on her cheek just as her four friends reached her side. She introduced each of them to Florence, who recognised the two friends from Margery's schooldays.

'Off you go, then, girls,' Florence said, her throat aching with misery as she gave them a cheery wave. 'Go and make that canteen of yours a brilliant success.'

The women laughed and boarded the train. Margery waited while the porter closed the carriage door behind her and slid the window down to give Florence one last wave. 'Bye-bye, Mother. Please give Father my love and, don't forget, I'll see you both very soon.'

Florence heard a whistle in the distance and the next thing she knew the train was slowly moving forward, building momentum as it began rolling along the tracks out of the station. She stood and waved at Margery's ever decreasing figure, unable to focus on her properly as her eyes swam with unshed tears.

Chapter Eight

5 April 1915

Florence stared down at the tiny baby girl in her arms. 'Nancy Jessica Bruce,' she repeated, gazing at Dorothy and Wilfred's first child – her and Jesse's first grandchild – who had been born four days before. She wiped away a tear from the side of her right eye and wondered when her children had grown up into the adults they were.

'Mother, are you crying?' Dorothy asked, looking, Florence suspected, as if she was also about to shed a tear.

'I was just thinking how enormously proud of you I am. You're such a clever girl and baby Nancy is such a bonnie little thing.'

'Thank you.'

Florence carefully passed her granddaughter back to Dorothy's open arms and watched her daughter cuddle her baby as if she had been doing it for months rather than a mere few days.

She wished her other two children could be here now, so that they could all celebrate this exciting birth. The house seemed much emptier without Margery's bright personality and John not bringing his young wife for family meals or stopping by on his way home some evenings to sit with her and Jesse. Each day now held a sense of dread and fear for her, however much she tried to push it away: the constant roll call of the dead that seemed to take up more space in every issue of the broadsheets; the drawn faces of her staff, both at the Boots stores and factories and at St Heliers House; the returning wounded as well as the constant lamenting she heard whenever she ventured into the town – all were a constant reminder of what every family in Britain and no doubt the continent now faced.

Florence pictured Margery, working so hard to cater for the thousands of wounded soldiers who passed through her canteen, and John, her beloved son, on a battlefield somewhere. She realised sadly that the majority of people who believed that the war would be over by Christmas had been wrong and she had been right when her instincts had told her to fear that the war had a long way to go yet. She wished more than anything that both her children had chosen to remain in Nottingham where it was safer.

She wondered if her concern for her family showed on her face in the same way as she had seen it on many other mothers' and fathers' as the months passed by. Jesse had been spending longer hours in his study at home each night as they both desperately tried to come up with new ideas to help support the war effort. However much work it took for them to help bring about an end to the war and quicken their children's return home, Florence knew she and Jesse were determined to do it. As soon as the thought appeared in her mind another took its place and frightened her. What if her best wasn't good enough? What if she didn't manage to do enough to save her children? The thought was too horrible to contemplate and made her nauseous.

If only John had chosen to stay here and help run the Boots business, she thought, unable to ignore her concern for her son but aware that his conscience wouldn't let him do anything else but enlist. He was such a decent man. She would have been proud of him whatever he had chosen to do. It seemed that now – unsurprisingly, Florence thought – he was also turning out to be a devoted husband and would soon become a father for the first time. Only four months now until his lovely wife Margaret brought their first-born into the world. What an exciting but extraordinary and emotional time it was, Florence thought. She wondered if she would ever get used to the range of emotions that hit her each day.

She recalled their last conversation when he had tried to soothe her concerns. 'You have enough to keep you occupied, Mother,' he had told her, hugging her tightly before leaving. 'Finding ways to cope with all the shortages in the shops and here at the house, you probably won't have a moment to notice I've gone.'

He had been right only insofar as she had a lot to focus

her attention on, she decided later that day as she sat and leaved through the pages of the first issue of *Comrades in Khaki*. This was their most recent project, an internal Boots magazine that they had begun publishing, and she enjoyed reading through it. *Comrades in Khaki* was to be printed and distributed to all Boots employees from that month onwards. Florence hoped they would be able to keep publishing one issue each month for as long as possible. Jesse had been concerned that as the war progressed, there might be a shortage in paper, which she knew would affect them being able to publish the magazine, but she was hopeful that it wouldn't be the case.

This first issue – the April issue – was about to be distributed, and as she reread the brief letter of greeting Jesse had written – and which he would write for each issue – she smiled, prouder of him than ever. Jesse never let his ailing health hold him back. His misshapen hands made it difficult for him to eat now and almost impossible for him to write but he continued to do both despite everything.

She turned the pages and her smile disappeared, the ache in her heart increasing as she read the 'Boots Roll of Honour' listing the names and regiments of their brave Boots employees who had fallen. The anxiety on the faces of those she worked with was a constant these days. The names of sons, fathers, brothers and uncles represented not only those she had come into contact within Boots stores and factories but the many people in the country who were doing the same thing and were also paying the ultimate price. Too many young lives ended already. She sighed, close to tears; these names were of people she knew. Florence pictured her son in his uniform and said a prayer that he would come out of this terrifying war safely. How much longer would she and all mothers and fathers have to live in a perpetual state of fear for their loved ones' safety?

Florence needed to finish reading through the issue. She focused her attention back on the magazine, once again, with its photographs and illustrations that helped bring the news included within it to life. She had discussed and seen all the features prior to them being printed but seeing the finished article in her hands made her eyes fill with tears. To read the letters sent to them from their staff who were now fighting at the Front, and the obituaries of others who had been killed, broke her heart. But it wasn't only bad news that they published: she enjoyed reading the reports of employees' activities, included in the magazine to reassure the troops that they were being supported by those at home by way of fundraising, as well as what Boots itself was doing to support the men and their families.

She finished reading the final paragraph on the last page and turned the issue over to gaze once more at the front. Florence was looking forward to reading the May issue, when they would be praising Margery's and her assistants' continued hard work running the canteen. She had hoped to include something about Margery in the first one but Jesse had rightly suggested that maybe they should not make the first issue about their own children but keep the feature on Margery for the next issue.

The thing John had not been right about though was

that she would be too busy to have time to fret about him and his safety. He and Margery were never far from her mind and she knew from conversations she had exchanged with Jesse that he was feeling exactly the same way.

Towards the end of the month, Florence and Jesse were riding in the car to work. He was quieter than usual and had been sombre since reading his morning broadsheet. She glanced at the back of Parry's head. Not wishing their driver to be able to hear them speaking, she kept her voice low.

'You've been out of sorts since reading your paper this morning, Jesse,' she said, straightening the blanket over his knees. He hated her fussing, but she refused to let him catch cold and insisted he kept warm, especially on cooler mornings, like this one. 'What's the matter?'

He gave her a sideways look, seemingly unsure whether to confide in her. This could only mean one thing, Florence thought, her mood dipping. Jesse had thought of another idea that would mean more work for them both.

She nudged him gently with her elbow. 'You may as well get it over with and tell me now,' she said. 'At least then, I'll have the rest of our short drive to mull over how I'm going to put the plan into action, or at least my part in it.'

'It's just that I didn't want to concern you overly.'

Now she really was worried. If Jesse was worried about upsetting her then that could only mean one thing was on his mind: their son's safety. Her thoughts immediately flew to John and she took a breath to steady her voice. 'Go on. What's happened?'

'A couple of French divisions were attacked at Ypres a few days ago with tonnes of chlorine gas. Sooner or later, our boys will be attacked, too.' She leant slightly forward, snuggling closer to him to comfort both Jesse and herself. 'It's lethal,' he added, quietly turning his head to stare directly into her eyes so Florence could not fail to understand the desperate need for whatever it was Jesse was about to announce they begin producing. 'Our boys don't have any protection against gas. Not really.'

Florence blanched. The thought of losing her precious boy to this invisible killer made her feel lightheaded. She tried to remain calm; panicking and becoming hysterical would do nothing to help John. She prayed Jesse had a plan. Now she understood. 'And you want to come up with a way of producing something that will protect them from this gas, don't you?'

'Yes,' he said firmly. 'I'm told that flannel helmets are being worked on, but I believe those won't be as effective as necessary and we will need to think about what we can do to provide some way of protecting the men at the Front. We'll need to start production as soon as we possibly can.' Florence nodded her agreement. 'The first thing I'm going to do when I reach my office is find out the design we need to follow, if there is one. Then we need to source the materials to make it.'

Florence felt her need to help swell inside her. 'We must work out where we have space to set up a department.' She gave it some thought but had no idea at that moment where they could make space, or indeed how much space they might need. 'We'll need staff to work on the product. I'll start working on recruitment for this new department.' She looked at his face filled with concern. 'You were right to decide this, Jesse. We have to help protect our boys as well as we can.' She didn't add that by doing so they might also one day keep their son safe, too. 'We'll do this, don't you worry.'

He kissed her on the cheek. 'You understand me so well, Florence. And you feel as deeply as I do when expansions need to be made in the company to incorporate new ideas.'

'I think in this case especially that we have little choice but to put this in place.' She shuddered. 'To think of someone coming up with such an insidious substance to use against other men, young men. It's shocking.' It truly was, Florence thought. How many more vile ways would the powers that be come up with to kill and maim her own children, and those of her friends and colleagues? What was the world coming to? What sort of nightmare future were her children and grandchildren going to have to face?

Chapter Nine

May 1915

A couple of weeks later, Miss Tweed asked to speak to Florence about taking a week's holiday. 'It's my sister, Lady Boot. She's asked me to go and stay with her for a few days. Her husband died last year, and she doesn't want to spend her birthday alone. I said I'd speak to you and ask you if it was all right for me to go.'

Florence looked at the tiny woman standing on the other side of her desk and wondered how on earth she would ever cope if Miss Tweed left her employ. Maybe this would be a good time to see how well Miss Tweed's assistant Gladys Lightbody coped without her at the office.

Florence smiled at her secretary and wished she wouldn't look quite so concerned. She had never refused any of Miss Tweed's requests and she wouldn't do so on this occasion, either. 'Yes, of course. You must be with your sister. In fact, please go down to Number Two department and choose a gift for her from my husband and I, if you would.'

Her secretary's eyes lit up and she beamed back at Florence. 'That is most generous of you, Lady Boot. Thank you, on both accounts. I'm truly grateful. I know my sister will be, too.'

'Please speak to Miss Lightbody about your holiday. I'm sure she knows your routine. It will be good practice for her to learn the ropes so that you don't have to worry about this place when you're away.' Florence held up a finger to stop Miss Tweed from denying that would be the case, and laughed. 'Don't try to deny it, I know that you think about this place almost as much as I do. And I value your loyalty, but I'm glad that you'll be taking a week off for a holiday.'

Miss Tweed returned Florence's smile. 'I'll speak to her. Would you like me to send Miss Lightbody in to speak to you about this?'

Florence gave the suggestion some thought. 'Yes. That's a good idea. In fact, why not send her in right away. We're so busy that I want to be certain that she knows what I'll expect of her.'

Ten minutes later, Florence finished explaining what was happening to Miss Lightbody. 'Miss Tweed assures me that you will cope. I do believe that after working beneath her for the past two years, you will be more than capable.'

Miss Lightbody clasped her hands together in front of her skirt. 'Yes, Lady Boot. I'm grateful to you for giving me this opportunity,' she said, but then looked down at the desk, seeming troubled.

Florence could see the girl was wanting to say something else but unsure whether to do so. 'Is something the matter?'

Miss Lightbody looked back into Florence's eyes for a moment before nodding.

'Then, I think you had better tell me what it is, don't you?'

'Yes, Lady Boot.'

Florence waited and, then, when the girl still didn't seem able to find the right words to say to her, it dawned on her that Miss Lightbody was building up to giving in her notice.

'You're leaving Boots, isn't that it?'

Miss Lightbody gasped. 'How did you…? That is, yes. I hadn't quite got round to speaking to Miss Tweed about it yet and when I tried to speak to her before coming in to see you, she said there wasn't time and that I could tell her whatever it was that I needed to speak to her about after I'd spoken to you.'

Florence listened to the girl rambling on, feeling sorry for her, but at the same time trying to control her own rising panic. She had always thrown herself into work whenever times had become stressful but, since the war had begun and infiltrated her Boots stores, Florence's mode of escape had been taken from her. There was no escaping this war and its effect on everyone, she now thought miserably.

'Are you leaving to work in munitions, as others have done?'

She shook her head. 'No, nothing like that, Lady Boot. My Cyril… he proposed to me on his last leave and, as soon as he's next home, we're getting a special licence and will be married.'

Florence was happy for Gladys, but, aware that she would no longer be working for them once she was a married woman, knew she would need to begin looking for the girl's replacement immediately.

'Will you be able to cover for Miss Tweed while she's away in June?'

The younger woman bit her lower lip for a second, looking stunned to be asked such a question. 'Oh, yes. I can't see that my Cyril will be able to come home before then. I just wanted to let you and Miss Tweed know, out of courtesy, that I will be leaving sometime soon.'

Florence felt her shoulders relax slightly. So, her departure wasn't imminent, she thought. 'That's good news. I'm glad we have time to find your replacement so that you can train them up at least for a short while before you leave us.'

'Yes, it will be my pleasure. I'm sad to be leaving Boots. I've been ever so happy working here for you, Lady Boot. You and Sir Jesse have been incredibly kind to me over the past two years and I'll never forget it.'

Florence's heart constricted. She loved being able to help these young people in anyway she could and never wanted any thanks for it, but it was always touching when one of her staff mentioned how much her and Jesse's kindness towards them had meant.

'And I'm sure we'll never forget all your hard work for us, Miss Lightbody.'

After Gladys had left her office, Florence knew that she had no time to waste to find a replacement for her. These were difficult times indeed, for everyone. With more and more men enlisting and women joining up or going to work in munitions factories, it was becoming harder each week to find the staff she and Jesse needed to run their ever-increasing business.

She couldn't help worrying that Jesse was doing far too much. His health was constantly declining, but he refused to take things easier and allow for how his body was coping.

'I know they need these new products at the Front, Jesse,' she argued one evening when it was just the two of them sitting quietly in the living room. 'But you have to be aware of your own wellbeing if you are to continue finding ways to help others.'

Jesse grumbled something she couldn't make out then looked over at her. 'I have no choice, my dear. None of us have the luxury of time at our disposal and if I am to find ways to supply things the soldiers most need then we have to work tirelessly to find ways to develop what's required.'

Florence understood what he was saying and also felt the need to help the brave men and women who, like John and Margery, so far from home, were fighting for their country, *but* she couldn't sit back and watch Jesse killing himself. 'That's as maybe,' she said, trying her best to keep her voice level and not give away how much emotion she was holding back, 'but, if you continue the way that you are now, then you will be no use to them, not if your health breaks down completely,' she added quickly, trying to soften the meaning in her words.

Jesse lowered the book he was reading onto his blanket-covered lap. 'Do you know how disgusting the water is that those poor men in Flanders have to drink? I'm sorry, my dear, but I simply cannot rest until we have provided them with some kind of steriliser. And I'm told that their uniforms are infested with lice.'

She had heard the same thing, from John in his most recent letter, and found it almost impossible to imagine her son having to face such conditions day after day. How could he possibly stand it? She shuddered. Florence had heard from a member of staff how her brother had to run a lit candle up and down the seams of his uniform, hearing the lice pop as they exploded in the heat. It was the only measure they had to cope with infestations, and a temporary one, for the lice returned the following morning.

'Yes, I know,' she replied, wondering why she was even trying to encourage Jesse to lessen his workload. Had he ever listened when she had tried to do this before? No. It was only making her anxious speaking to him about it now. However, she loved him dearly and, even if there was little hope of her achieving any changes in his daily routine, she had to try to make him listen to her, at the very least.

'We need a vermin powder and also an anti-fly cream,

especially for the hotter months,' Jesse continued, reaching out for her to take his hand. 'I'm sorry, my love. I know how you worry about me, but this is who I am and, at my great age, I am unable to change.' He grinned at her then, cheekily.

Florence shook her head, smiling slightly. He might be old now, and sick, but he still had that boyish side to him that she couldn't resist. 'I suppose you're going to continue to increase the laboratories and production side of the business until you're able to deliver these items in a number that you believe is acceptable, aren't you?'

He shrugged. 'I think you know me well enough to be aware that you've answered your own question.'

Florence realised he was right and that was exactly what she had done. Standing, she kissed him on his forehead. 'I have to be going. I've lined up several interviews for more girls to add to the number I've already approved to come and work in our gas-mask department.' She thought of all the respirators she suspected they would need to make. 'I think I'm going to have to employ quite a few hundred of these girls to allow us to manufacture enough of them. It's going to be quite a task, especially as so many women are joining the FANY's and the Voluntary Aid Detachment, hoping for a little more excitement.'

'I have the utmost faith in you, my dear,' he said, smiling. 'You'll find all the girls we need, I know you will.'

'Do we have an idea yet of how these are to be made so the necessary supplies can be sourced?' She knew that Jesse would have already thought of this but was interested to hear his plans more fully.

'It's a simple enough respirator,' he said, his enthusiasm increasing with every word as it did when he explained things that he was passionate about. They'll be made up of cotton wool and crêpe that we will have treated with chemicals. I can't deny I'm excited about this new product, Florence.'

'I can see that,' she said, smiling, happy as always to see the light in his eyes shining brightly.

'And, yes, you *will* need to bring in quite a few new members of staff, if we're to keep up with the numbers needed at the Front, but I know you'll find a way.'

Florence nodded. She was fighting this dreadful war in the only way open to her, by helping Jesse find ways to ensure that Boots could deliver everything possible to help the war effort.

Florence and Jesse were horrified to learn of the sinking of the Cunard liner RMS *Lusitania*, after it was torpedoed by a German U-boat off the coast of Kinsale on its way to Liverpool from New York.

'Over one thousand people perished, according to the paper,' Jesse said, his voice sombre. He shook his head sadly. 'Not to mention all the supplies that have been lost that they were delivering to Britain. Sometimes I despair,' he admitted quietly. 'I can't help fearing what is to become of us all.'

'I've no idea,' Florence said, miserably. She pictured her and her children on a similar voyage, grateful their journey had taken place in more peaceful times and that they hadn't had to face such terror.

'I wish John and Margery were here now,' Jesse continued. 'I struggle a bit to think of them on the other side of the channel, especially as the news seems to become worse with each passing day.'

'I feel the same way,' she admitted, thinking of all those families and loved ones grieving those lost off the coast who would now be receiving telegrams giving them the worst news possible. It was all too heart-breaking. 'It seems that no one is safe right now.'

Chapter Ten

4 June 1915

Florence made the necessary arrangements with an agency to find a replacement for an assistant to Miss Tweed. Now that Gladys Lightbody was leaving Boots to be married, their excellent team would be splitting up. It seemed that every part of her life was now filled with worries. Florence left the two women to work through as much outstanding administration as possible during their last day in the office together.

Later, Miss Tweed came to Florence's office to take dictation. Always highly efficient, her speeds impressive, today she seemed to falter a couple of times, which was very unlike her, Florence thought, concerned.

'I'm sorry, would you mind repeating that last sentence, Lady Boot?'

Florence looked up from her notes and frowned. 'Is everything all right? You seem a little distracted today.'

'Do I?' Miss Tweed patted her immaculate bun absent-mindedly.

'Yes, that's the third time today you've asked me to repeat something. It's very out of character for you and makes me worry that something is amiss. I do hope you know you can confide in me, if ever you have something on your mind that's troubling you?'

Florence watched Miss Tweed thinking. She seemed to be considering whether or not to say something. 'Please, tell me whatever it is that's worrying you. Maybe I can help find a solution.'

Miss Tweed looked down at the dictation she had taken and, just when Florence thought she was about to ask her to continue with the letter, she replied, 'It's only that I feel I'm letting you down badly, leaving you to go to visit my sister. Miss Lightbody is to be married and will be leaving your employ and I worry that you have too much to deal with as it is, without me taking time off work while you find her replacement.'

Florence was touched but not surprised by her secretary's thoughtfulness. She rested her right hand on her chest. 'That's just like you to think of others' happiness before your own. However, I won't hear of you thinking about anything other than having a pleasant time with your sister while you're away. You deserve a holiday more than most. I hope that although your time with your sister will be marred no doubt by the loss of her husband, the two of you will be able to enjoy each other's company while you are there.'

Miss Tweed's shoulders relaxed visibly. 'Thank you. You're very kind. But I don't mind delaying my trip to see her until you've found Miss Lightbody's replacement and I've had time to train her.'

Florence shook her head. 'No. I won't hear of you doing any such thing. You're to go and forget everything at Boots and make the most of your days staying with your sister in Hull.'

'Thank you,' Miss Tweed said shyly. 'that's very kind of you.'

But Florence wasn't going to have the kindly woman say any such thing. 'It is not. You deserve this week off and to enjoy it.'

With that, Miss Tweed left to type up the letters while Florence checked through the advert that she had requested to be run in the Nottingham papers for the new scent she had been instrumental in naming, Lareine's Jersey Castle Eau de Cologne. Jesse had suggested that she call it after something in Jersey and Florence's first thought had been the two castles that the island was so proud of, Elizabeth Castle, just outside St Helier Harbour, and Mont Orgueil, known to islanders as Gorey Castle, as it stood high on a granite and grass mound overlooking Gorey Harbour and the picturesque bay of Grouville. It was a connection to her much-missed island, and she was proud to introduce it to the store. She hoped it sold well and, having tested the scent samples as it was produced, she felt sure it would do so.

She took the draft advert through to Jesse's office to show it to him. Entering, she smiled at him and placed the sheet of paper on his desk. 'What do you think?' He studied it briefly and then, looking up at her, didn't smile as she had expected him to. 'What's the matter? Don't you like it?'

Jesse rubbed his chin with his twisted right hand. 'It's not that I don't like it,' he said. 'I know you've worked hard bringing this cologne to fruition, but I've been thinking lately that maybe it's time we withdrew the trinkets and stock like this we sell. Should we not be removing these from our shelves and allowing more space for other more practical items?'

Florence wasn't surprised to hear him say as much. 'It had also occurred to me to wonder if this sort of thing is rather pointless or misplaced right now,' she admitted. 'But seeing the women in the store and factories who now, more than ever before, are living with constant fear, I believe they need something to boost their morale. Scent and little treats can help remind people of a happier time and –' she placed her hands together – 'maybe they will give them hope that there will be a time in the future when things will return to a much happier time for us all.' When Jesse didn't argue, she added, 'We might all be living through one of our darkest times in history, but women need hope, especially those waiting for their loved ones to return. I know I do.'

'Yes,' he said, thoughtfully. 'I see your point.'

'I think it's times like the one we're all living through that make little treats like these even more special.' She waited for Jesse to consider her comments.

Eventually, he nodded, slowly. 'I think you're right.' He pushed the draft advert back across the desk to her. 'I think we need to approve this and have it published as soon as possible.'

Florence was relieved. Kissing him goodbye, she made her way to Miss Tweed's office, signed off the advert, and handed it to her.

'Once you've sent that on to be printed, you can go home. I hope you have a wonderful week away,' Florence said, smiling. 'I look forward to hearing all about your holiday on your return.'

Miss Tweed beamed at her. 'Thank you, Lady Boot. I'll look forward to telling you all about it.'

Florence and Jesse spent a relaxing weekend at Plaisaunce, their holiday home. The anxiety she felt never seemed to leave her now and once again she thought of her two children so close to the Front and an ever-threatening danger. She wished with all her heart that they were with her now, safe and happy. Florence knew she and Jesse were luckier than most to have so many happy family memories to keep them going. She never ceased to be glad that they had invested in their beautiful holiday home on the bank of the River Trent years before when their children had been small. She gazed at Jesse as he dozed in his wheelchair in the shade and recalled happier times when their children had been with them to enjoy all that this riverside home had to offer.

Her book lay on her lap as she stared out at the water as it rushed past the bank at the end of the garden and she pictured the many parties they had held over the years for their business acquaintances and staff. She especially enjoyed the sports days and the musical concerts they had put on over the years and thought fondly of the sewing circles she had held there since the war had begun. They were very lucky to be able to share their good fortune with those who helped them make it and she knew she would never tire of entertaining people, but she longed to be able to spend time as a family here once again.

On Sunday evening, they travelled in Jesse's specially adapted motor back to St Heliers House. Although she had enjoyed the peace of her holiday home, it had given her too much time to ponder and fret about John and Margery so she was relieved to be returning home and looked forward to getting back to work.

Florence joined Jesse in the dining room the following morning back at St Heliers. Meadows brought in Jesse's newspapers and set the first one down in front of him.

'Thank you, Meadows,' Jesse said. 'Any news of your nephew and how he's getting along?' he asked as he spooned a mouthful of his porridge past his lips with difficulty.

Meadows stood by the table, his hands behind his back. 'They tried to save his leg, Sir Jesse, but, unfortunately, it was too badly damaged for them to be able to do so.'

Florence was saddened to hear yet another young man would have to cope with life-changing injuries. 'Your sister must be worried for him,' she said, her heart aching for him and his family.

Meadows lowered his gaze. 'She was devastated. But I told her that at least they saved his life and, hopefully, sometime soon, he'll be on his way back home to her.'

'Yes, that's the way to think,' Jesse said with a gentle understanding. 'Stay positive. Look at me with my useless legs now. I still work and others can do, too.'

'Yes, sir.'

'Any other news to report?'

'More of those Zeppelin bombings, Sir Jesse. That's the big story of the day, it seems.'

Jesse frowned at him. 'Casualties?'

'I'm afraid so.'

Florence shuddered. It was one thing knowing that there was a war going on nearby in France and Belgium but another entirely now that they were being attacked on home soil, and from the air, too. Who had ever considered such a terrifying thing could happen? It was the stuff of nightmares and all too unnerving. 'Where were they this time?' she asked anxiously.

'Hull, Lady Boot.'

Florence dropped her fork, hardly hearing it clanging loudly as it landed on her porcelain plate before dropping to the polished floorboards. 'Hull?' she whispered, horrified. 'And people were killed, you say?'

Meadows stepped forward and bent to retrieve her fork. 'That's what the broadsheets are saying, Lady Boot.'

Florence had to battle to remain calm. She wiped the side of her mouth with her napkin as she struggled to gather herself. 'Do we know how many people and where exactly in Hull this might have been?'

Jesse cleared his throat. 'Why are you asking so many questions, my dear? Are you concerned about anyone?'

'Yes, Jesse.' She was aware her voice was high-pitched but couldn't seem to help it. 'Hull city is where Miss Tweed's sister lives. It's where she's gone to stay for the week.' She turned her attention back to Meadows. 'Please can you have a quick look at the paper and tell me what it says?'

Jesse motioned for him to take the paper. Florence listened as Meadows read the news, her heart pounding rapidly in her chest. It seemed that at least twenty people, probably more, had been killed by the thirty-minute bombing around midnight the night before.

'Thank you, Meadows,' she said, feeling sick. 'I know it's probably an odd thing to say, especially when thousands of men are being killed on the Front, but it seems incredibly shocking when men, women and children are killed in their beds. Surely, we should all be able to feel safe at home?'

'It's not a strange thing to say at all,' Jesse argued. 'It is terrifying to think that nowhere is safe any more.' He wiped his mouth and took a sip from his glass of water. 'Do you have the address where Miss Tweed is staying, so we can make enquiries about her and her sister?'

Florence tried to gather her thoughts. 'That's a good idea. I don't have the sister's address but maybe Miss Tweed's assistant, Miss Lightbody, has a note of her whereabouts. I'll ask her as soon as I arrive at work.'

She had to contain herself not to give into her concerns for her secretary while she waited for Jesse to ready himself and be helped into the motor. Florence hoped desperately that Miss Lightbody would have the address to hand so that she could reassure herself that her secretary, a woman whose friendship and confidence she valued highly, was safe and well.

'I have it here somewhere,' Miss Lightbody said as she rifled through her desk drawer.

Florence found it almost impossible to hold onto her patience. How could the girl have misplaced something she had probably only been given in the past few days? She held her tongue, not wishing to fluster her even more, and only just managed to stop herself from tapping her toe impatiently. If she was concerned then surely Miss Lightbody would be, too.

'Yes, here it is,' she said, holding up a piece of notepaper triumphantly.

Florence stepped forward and took it, reading her assistant secretary's neat script. Her heart sank. She had been right. Miss Tweed would have been staying in Hull city and not in a village on the outskirts, as she had hoped. 'Thank you,' she said aware now that her impatience had probably been obvious. 'I'll take this, if you don't mind, and return it to you once I've noted down the address.' Florence, the note shaking in her hands, went to leave the room.

'It's to do with last night's bombing raid, isn't it, Lady Boot?' the woman asked quietly, her voice filled with concern for her colleague.

Florence immediately regretted being impatient with her. She wasn't the only one fond of Miss Tweed. As far as she knew, all the other staff respected her secretary and Miss Lightbody probably more than most as she was the one who worked in the same office with her each day.

'Yes, that's right.' Florence forced a reassuring smile. 'We mustn't jump to conclusions yet, though,' she said trying to reassure her despite having done exactly that earlier. 'We should say our prayers for Miss Tweed and her sister that they're safe and well. Hopefully, we'll know soon enough.'

'Yes, I'll do that. Will you let me know if you hear any news?'

'Yes, of course I will. Now I'd better go and make enquiries about Miss Tweed.'

'Thank you.'

Florence hurried to her own office next door and copied down the address, then went to Jesse's office and handed it to him. 'Would you like to phone the police station, or should I?'

'Leave this with me. I'll contact the Hull police and try to find out whatever I can.' He looked at her. 'Are you all right, my dear? I don't want you worrying about Miss Tweed. Not yet at least.'

Florence shook her head. 'I'm fine,' she fibbed. Then, aware that he knew her well enough to see through her reassurances, she turned and opened the door. 'I have a lot to be getting on with. I'll speak to you a little later.' She stepped out into the corridor. 'Please let me know as soon as you hear any news.'

Jesse was staring down at the address. 'You'll be the first one I speak to when I do.'

Relieved that Jesse was on the case, Florence went back to her office and studied the letters piled neatly on her desk awaiting her attention. She did have a lot to do but couldn't push away the nagging feeling that the news would be bad. She had always been a positive person, but the past year had changed her outlook on life. Florence couldn't bear it if Agnes Tweed had been injured, or worse. She shook her head to try to dispel the negative thoughts. She needed to focus on her tasks in hand, but it was going to be difficult to concentrate on anything until she knew her secretary was safe.

'That's enough,' she murmured, irritated with herself. She expected Gladys Lightbody to concentrate on her work and she must lead by example. After all, what else could she do while she waited?

Chapter Eleven

The morning dragged. Florence's mind kept wandering to Miss Tweed and her sister. She prayed several times that they were safe somewhere before forcing her attention back to her work. She had given Miss Lightbody enough dictation to keep her busy replying to all the letters that had arrived in the morning post, and met with another three female staff who had come to her office to give her notice. Florence was concerned to hear that three of her girls, all cousins, were leaving to go and work in the gunpowder factory at Waltham Abbey.

'Our aunt works there,' one of them informed her proudly. 'She says we can stay with her for the time being and doesn't think we'll have any problem being offered work with her standing as our guarantor.'

Florence felt obliged as their boss to at least try to dissuade them from going but knew they would listen to their aunt over her when it came to suggestions for their futures. She realised she was probably wasting her time trying to dissuade them from leaving but did her best to tell them that the extra wage they would earn working there was for doing dangerous work.

'You could be putting your life at risk working in these places,' she had said, going on to explain how she had heard that the factories needed solid brick blast walls dividing different areas where staff worked.

Each of the women had listened politely, but Florence was sad to find that none of them changed their minds.

Two further male staff also gave notice that they had enlisted. For once, Florence was almost overwhelmed by a sense of helplessness. Usually, she could talk herself into finding a positive aspect of most situations but not this time.

She decided to go for a walk around the store to take her mind off her woes. As she crossed the second floor, she noticed that although her staff wore smiles a lot of them didn't reach the women's eyes. What were they dealing with at home? Florence pondered. Do they have a brother or cousin, or even a beloved man, fighting somewhere? Could some of them have mothers at home nursing wounded loved ones who had returned from the Front or elsewhere injured or traumatised by their experiences? Everyone was fighting their own private battle to find ways to cope with the drastic change in their worlds, Florence thought miserably. The ache in her heart at being separated from her own two children and the fear she felt for their safety never left her. It was all too sad and the thought that this could continue for months or probably even years was extremely frightening.

Florence stopped at each counter to speak to her girls. She had always enjoyed taking the time to chat to her staff, believing that if they felt comfortable with her on a daily basis then they would also have the confidence to come to her with any troubles she might be able to help them with. Now, though, with all the turmoil of the war and so many Nottingham soldiers being injured or killed, she felt it more vital than ever to keep communication open with her staff.

Florence had only had time to catch up with three of her staff when she noticed Miss Lightbody rushing towards her. She could see that her assistant secretary was doing her best to appear as if she was walking calmly although not quite managing to hide her urgency. Florence thanked the girl she had been talking to and went immediately to meet Gladys. The girl's eyes were wide and her hands balled into fists. Florence suspected Jesse must have sent her with news. She concentrated on keeping her demeanour calm. It wouldn't do for customers or members of staff to see her ruffled.

Keeping a smile on her face and her voice low, Florence asked, 'My husband has some news for me?'

'Yes, Lady Boot. He asked me to fetch you to his office as quickly as possible.'

'Then let's go. Try to act calm. Everyone seems to be on high alert at the moment, what with all the bad news that keeps coming. We don't want them to think something is wrong here, do we?'

'No, Lady Boot.'

Florence didn't want to wait for the lift. It usually had others riding in it to different floors and people generally wanted to pass the time of day with her and she couldn't bear to waste a minute that she didn't have to. She walked as quickly but as gracefully as she could towards the stairs, giving those she passed smiles and brief quips about the weather, or complimenting the item that they were buying. Gladys followed silently.

'Thank you, Gladys,' she said as she reached Jesse's office door. 'You can continue with your work. I promise that if it's news about Miss Tweed then I will come directly to your office to let you know.'

'Thank you, Lady Boot.'

Florence waited for Gladys to walk into her office and close the door before entering Jesse's room. She was happy to tell Gladys any news, as she had assured her she would, but Florence knew that she would first need to come to terms with whatever Jesse was about to share with her.

'You called for me, Jesse?'

'Yes, my dear. Please, sit.'

Florence studied his face as she did so. Ordinarily, she could read his emotions, but he was keeping them closed from her at that moment. She knew without him saying anything further that he was trying to protect her and that the news was bad.

'I'm afraid I have the worst news for you, my dear.'

Florence winced. She swallowed the bile rising in her throat and clasped her hands together trying to remain composed. 'Go on.'

'I am assured by the local constabulary in Hull that Miss Tweed and her sister were killed last night.'

Without meaning to, Florence let out a sob. 'Poor Agnes,' she cried. 'After all those years spent caring for her mother, and now this happens just when she takes a little time to go on holiday.' It broke her heart to think that Miss Tweed's few days away staying with her sister had been the cause of her death. 'This interminable war.' It was harrowing enough to think of soldiers being killed overseas but to have such a thing happen to innocent women and children on the Home Front seemed like an invasion of the worst kind.

Jesse closed his eyes and sighed sadly. 'I'm so very sorry, my dear. I know this is not what you were hoping to hear.'

Florence took a moment to be able to speak. 'It isn't. I am grateful that you're the one breaking this dreadful news to me, Jesse. Please, carry on.'

'The house they were sleeping in received a direct hit. They would have been killed instantly.' He frowned. 'He assured me that they won't have suffered, Florence. We can take comfort from that, at least.' Florence hoped he was right. 'Do you wish for me to continue?'

Florence swallowed, hoping it would help her keep breathing. No, she wanted to give in to her heartbreak at the loss of the woman who had been her right hand for so many years. She hated to hear more details, but knew that she must. 'Yes, please tell me everything.'

Jesse rubbed his face with his hand. 'However tragic this

is, my dear, at least we know they would not have suffered any pain or fear.'

Only if they were asleep at the time, Florence thought, forcing from her mind an image of a terrified Agnes Tweed with her sister before they were killed.

'How could they possibly know that the two women didn't suffer, though, Jesse? The report in your broadsheet stated that the bombing raid lasted half an hour. If the bomb that killed Miss Tweed and her sister landed towards the end of that, or even a few minutes into the raid, then, surely, they would have woken and been terrified.'

'It's possible,' Jesse replied honestly. 'All we can do now is pray that they did not.' She shook her head. 'Are you all right, my dear? I know this is the news you feared the most. I wish with all my heart that things could have been different.'

Why hadn't she allowed her secretary to delay her trip when she had offered? Florence thought miserably.

'Florence? Speak to me.'

She hated to worry him so cleared her throat and forced herself to speak. 'Thank you, Jesse. At least we now know what happened, I suppose.'

'Does she have any other family, do you know?'

Florence shook her head. 'No,' she said, almost giving in to tears but stopping herself just in time. She suspected that if she gave in to her grief over Agnes Tweed then she might find it almost impossible to stop crying and that simply would not do, not while she was at work. 'She doesn't. Her mother died a few years ago. I don't believe her sister had any children and she was recently widowed.'

'How sad. Then we will cover the funeral costs.'

Florence knew he was trying to help her and was grateful for his never-ending support. 'It was my fault,' she said, miserably, unable to shift the heavy weight of guilt pressing down on her shoulders. 'Why didn't I let her postpone her trip like she had offered to do?'

'No, Florence. You must not say such things,' he replied, his voice gruff. 'How could this terrible incident have anything to do with you?'

'But I could have saved her from all this.' Furious with her lack of control, Florence found she was unable to hold back her tears any longer and began to cry.

Jesse's voice softened. 'You mustn't think that way. You encouraged her to go because you wanted her to spend time with her sister. You know it was the right thing to do then, as you will do soon when you recover from this shock. How could you have possibly known that this dreadful tragedy would occur? You did the kind thing and insisted she go,' he said. Then added, 'Imagine if you had accepted her offer to delay her visit and then her sister had died alone? Miss Tweed would most likely have blamed herself for the rest of her life for not seeing her sister on her birthday and for not being there with her. And you would have blamed yourself for that. No, I won't have you feel any guilt. It's misplaced and unnecessary.'

He was right, Florence reasoned. However tragic this incident was, and, she thought sadly it truly was desperately unfair, Miss Tweed would have suffered dreadful guilt if she had not gone to stay with her sister this week. It wasn't much consolation, but it was something and she was going to have to do her best to hold on to Jesse's words.

'I think you should give yourself time to recover from this news,' Jesse said. 'Why don't you go home and take it easy for the rest of the day?'

Florence's first instinct was to agree. Staying in her office was only going to be a constant reminder of the loss of her friend who for years had been so much more than just a secretary to her. She had valued her very highly and more so as the years progressed. Running away from the situation was not going to help anyone, though. Florence reasoned that Miss Tweed would remain professional at all times – it was something she took pride in doing – and, today, Florence decided, she was going to continue as she did each day.

'No, Jesse. Thank you for your thoughtfulness, but I think the best thing I can do is stay here and work.'

'Hang the workload, Florence. You're always telling me how I need to put my health before everything.'

Florence couldn't miss his annoyance with her. He was right, she always said exactly that to him. 'Yes, Jesse. But when have you ever listened to me when I've tried to make you slow down?'

'That's true enough.'

She needed to keep busy. To force herself to carry on. 'Miss Tweed would be horrified to think of me shirking my responsibilities. She understood only too well the importance of what we try to do at Boots. Therefore, the first thing I'm going to do is speak to Miss Lightbody and break this horrible news to her as well as I can.' She thought of Gladys's impending nuptials. 'She's also leaving us soon, though for much happier reasons, thankfully. I need to ensure we have some form of consistency here, so I'm going to have to ask her if she can stay on a little while. I need to find a replacement for both her and Miss Tweed. It's not going to be an easy task.'

'It won't,' Jesse agreed. 'In more ways than one.'

Gladys Lightbody blew her nose once again. 'Oh, Lady Boot. I dreaded you telling me this news. Poor Miss Tweed.' She sniffed. 'It's like nothing we've ever known, is it? I mean, who ever imagined we would have bombs falling down on us from the sky? I always thought it was the soldiers and nurses who were in danger. I never expected them to be killing us in our beds.'

Neither did Florence. 'Yes, well, I think there's nothing much we can do to protect ourselves from these dreadful raids, especially when they're so unexpected.' As she spoke, she wondered what plans she and Jesse should put in place for their staff in case a bombing raid took place during a working day over one of their stores or factories. 'We need to remain calm and try to press on as well as we're able.'

Miss Lightbody pushed her shoulders back and sat up

straighter a defiant look on her pretty face. 'Yes, Lady Boot. That's exactly what we must do.'

Florence hoped she was doing the right thing by the young woman trying to keep her busy. 'However, that said, if you would rather take a little time for yourself and go home for the rest of the day, I'll arrange for a taxi to take you there.'

Gladys shook her head. 'Oh, no. Thank you very much for offering, but if you're staying here and carrying on, then I will, too. I know how short-staffed you are right now and I don't want to add to that burden.' She blew her nose again and Florence watched as the girl did her best to pull herself together. Florence waited patiently for her to speak again. 'I'm aware that with me leaving shortly to be married I'm only doubling your secretarial problems.'

Florence was well aware of that but didn't think that now was the right time to broach the subject. 'We don't have to worry about that presently,' she replied, wanting to reassure the girl as much as possible.

'I know you're trying to be kind, Lady Boot, but I would rather address this now, if that's all right with you?'

Florence confirmed that it was. Gladys obviously had something she wished to say and it would be unkind to try to stop her. 'Go on.'

'I'm going to write to my Cyril and let him know that we need to put off our wedding for a few months.'

Florence felt fresh tears threatening to appear. She swallowed them away, determined not to let her emotions show to her young employee. 'No,' she said, standing firm.

'There is a war on, as we all are aware, and I am not going to be the cause of you delaying your marriage to your sweetheart.' She had no intention of allowing Gladys Lightbody to do as she had offered. Florence knew that if she felt guilt about Agnes Tweed's visit to her sister then the thought of potentially denying this young woman any time as a bride should her fiancé be killed would be too much for her to bear. She recalled her happiness as a newlywed and had no intention of being the reason these two brave young people put off their marriage.

'But, I don't mind, Lady Boot. Truly, I don't.'

'Well, I do, Gladys.' Florence smiled at her, grateful for her thoughtfulness and loyalty. 'It's an extremely generous offer and one that I appreciate greatly. But I have no intention of accepting it. You will leave to be married when your Cyril writes to let you know the date of his next leave and that will be the end of it.'

She watched Gladys's expression change from one of determination to one of gratitude. 'Thank you, Lady Boot. Cyril did say it won't be for a few months yet, so, hopefully, I'll be here to help train the new secretary as well as I can. I wanted to give you proper warning of my intentions to leave, though, even before this horrible thing had happened to Miss Tweed.'

'It's only right that your relationship isn't put aside. We each deserve what happiness we can grasp. This is a terrible unforeseen circumstance and it's beyond all of our control, but we will have to deal with it as well as we can.' She rested her palms on the blotter in front of her on her desk.

'However, that means that we need to get to work and find your replacement.' She hesitated, needing a moment to brace herself for what she had to add. 'And that of our friend Miss Tweed. It's a ghastly business but, unfortunately, the business has to keep running if we are to help the war effort in our own way here at Boots.'

'It does, Lady Boot,' Gladys said with a determination in her voice that Florence hadn't heard before.

Chapter Twelve

29 June 1915

'I have something for you,' Jesse said, having called her into his office one morning.

Florence hoped desperately that he didn't have more bad news for her. She might put on a brave face to everyone but some days it was more of a struggle to manage it successfully than on others. She sat down on the opposite side of his desk and clasped her hands together.

'Please, hurry and tell me,' she said realising that his eyes were twinkling and that it must therefore be good news rather than bad. Her shoulders relaxed and she waited as he slowly slid a letter across the desk towards her.

Picking it up, Florence immediately noticed John's writing on the envelope. She gave Jesse a quizzical look. 'What's this about?'

He laughed. 'Why don't you read it and find out?'

Florence began to read the letter, her face breaking into a smile as her eyes scanned the words on the paper.

France
26 June1915

Sir Jesse and Lady Boot
St Heliers House
The Park
Nottingham
England

Dearest Mother and Father,

I'm writing with news that I feel certain you will be happy to receive. I am to be discharged from my duty and return home on medical grounds. I leave my battalion tomorrow and unlike many of my contemporaries my discharge is not brought about by injuries received in the field of war but due to pain caused by varicose veins in both my legs. I have written to Margaret earlier today and look forward to being with you all once again. I'm not certain when I'll arrive home. I have to admit that although I chose to enlist I soon discovered that was wasn't the glorious, heroic escapade I imagined, but a gory, noisy, chaotic nightmare that I will be grateful to leave behind.

I often think of Margery and the long hours she works to help exhausted soldiers and can't help wondering how this has affected my youngest sister. I know she is a strong and determined woman capable of all that she puts her mind to, but I hope that her experiences don't alter the way she views the world.

Enough negativity. I meant only to write and tell you of my homecoming and so I will finish on that note. I look forward to seeing you both and being back in Nottingham once again in the near future.

My fondest love, as always,
Your loving son, John

'So John's on his way home?' Florence said when she had finished reading the letter, her voice barely above a whisper in her effort not to give in to her emotions. She could hardly believe her son was coming home. The relief made her slightly light-headed. 'Poor boy having such painful legs.' Was this a new thing? she wondered, unaware that her son had ever suffered from such an affliction.

'Less painful than a wound from a bullet or shrapnel though,' Jesse said, thoughtfully.

He was right. Florence closed her eyes to give a prayer of thanks that her son's return hadn't been as a result of anything life-threatening. She felt as if she could breathe freely for the first time since the war began. Her son, for all her worries about him, had fought for his country and she hoped he was as proud of himself as she was of him. Florence rested her right palm on the letter. John had touched this piece of paper and soon she would be able to hold her son close once again. It couldn't happen soon enough.

She realised she was being selfish. John had been determined to do his bit for the war effort. 'For all his bravado,' she said miserably, 'I have a feeling that John is going to find it difficult to leave his battalion behind.' If Florence knew her son as well as she assumed, then one thing she was certain of was that he wouldn't be relaxing at home for very long.

'He'll find a way to take part in defending his country by some other means,' Jesse said, picking up on her thoughts. 'John is a determined man and not one to let something like this hold him back.'

Florence knew Jesse was right and hoped that, whatever John ended up doing, it would be here in England. She thought of John's young wife, still so recently a bride. 'Margaret must be over the moon with this news,' she said picturing John and his wife sitting together on a sofa, their baby due in only three months. 'What a relief it must be for her to know he'll be back home safe in time for his first child to be born.' She could not have asked for more, Florence mused, happier than she had been in months. 'And thank heavens he won't be able to join up and return to the Front again.'

'I dare say Margaret will be pleased.' Jesse's voice was soft as he addressed Florence. 'I think we're all grateful to receive good news after all the bad that's reported each day. I sometimes wonder what my dear mother would think of this dreadful new way countries go to war with one another.'

'I'm sure she would be as shocked as the rest of us.' Florence thought back to a letter she had received the previous week from her sister-in-law, also called Florence, who was the mother of Florence's two nephews, and frightened about her own boys joining up. 'Too many young men are losing their lives or having their livelihood taken from them after being cruelly wounded. It's all too devastating.'

Florence returned to her office and sat at her desk. It would soon be July and her birthday once again. Now she could plan for John to join in with the celebrations. This year though, for the first time in many years, she was not going to hold a grand party. She wasn't able to return to Jersey to celebrate, which she often enjoyed doing. Florence decided that she would simply hold a small garden party for her family and close friends.

As she explained her idea to Miss Lightbody, she had a change of heart. 'In fact, why don't we hold a garden fête at Plaisaunce and open the event to the public.' She was warming to the idea the more she thought about it. Her weekend home was in the perfect position on the riverside to give people a much-needed break from their daily worries. 'Everyone needs something to cheer them up and Margery needs all the funds she can get to keep her canteen going. I'll check your diary to see when you have a free day so that we can begin the arrangements.'

After a few minutes, Florence had agreed the day and, picking up her fountain pen, unscrewed the top and opened her current Boots Scribbling Diary. She loved the thought of how each New Year she would open her new diary and run her fingers down the length of the foolscap, marbled front page and wonder what events she would be writing into the diary's pages over the following twelve months.

'Seventeenth of July,' she said, locating the right page. 'Yes, we'll hold a fête at Plaisaunce. We'll go through names and make a list of people we want to invite. I always find that by including a few dignitaries in an event it gives them an incentive to invite their friends along. We'll also let them know that all the proceeds will be going towards Margery's canteen. I know people are generous with what funds they have and as this is helping my daughter give a little comfort to wounded soldiers on their way home then I'm sure they will be happy to come along and donate.'

'Yes, Lady Boot. What stalls would you like to have at the fête?'

Florence gave it some thought. She had noticed her staff struggling more than ever and it worried her. The war was taking its toll on them all, she reasoned, determined to do whatever she could to help them.

'We'll have the usual tombola, lucky dip, maybe toffee apples, jam and produce stalls,' she said, thoughtfully. 'The people with allotments or who grow vegetables in their gardens can sell some on their own stalls if they wish.' It occurred to her that everyone needed to be useful and keep busy, especially during such dark times. 'I want people to feel involved, give them all something else to think about for a short while, so we accept offers from locals and staff when they come in. I think we all need a bit of a break from the constant misery.'

'What a wonderful idea,' Gladys said, taking notes as she spoke.

Florence liked the idea the more she thought about it. 'I'll donate stock for a Boots stall,' she said, watching Gladys writing everything down. 'And we need to ensure the Boots Plaisaunce Band is available to entertain the crowd.' Wanting to include as many people in the entertainment as possible, Florence added, 'Also, please let's ask the Girls' Senior and Junior Choirs from the local school. We'll also feed everyone involved and ask them all to remain at Plaisaunce after the fête has ended and to repeat their performance for some of the departmental managers and their wives. What do you think?'

'I'm sure the pupils will enjoy putting on performances. And having to practise for the event will be a pleasant diversion away from what's probably going on at home with absent father and brothers.'

Florence agreed. 'Yes, that's a good point. The more entertainment and attractions we can bring in, the better.' She clasped her hands together. 'Margery will be delighted when she finds out what we're doing for her canteen. Now we just have to pray the weather is on our side.'

She was grateful to have the fête to focus on. At least that way, Florence thought, sadly, it would stop her from fretting about John and how changed he now seemed. Maybe he would settle back down into civilian life and find a way to put his experiences and the horrors he had witnessed into a distant recess in his mind so that they didn't constantly trouble him. At least he had his new baby to look forward to, she mused, relieved that her son had a loving home apart from her own. The love she felt certain he would feel towards his first child would hopefully overwhelm all his other emotions.

Florence woke on the morning of 17 July and without even opening her eyes knew by the sound of the wind-driven rain hitting her bedroom windows that they would not be holding the fête that day.

She groaned and opened her eyes, pushing herself up to sit, and leant against her pillows. She was going to have to contact Gladys and her assistant Enid as soon as possible to ensure each of them was ready to help cancel the long list of stallholders and entertainers, as well as the guests she had invited. She hoped the women she had arranged to cater for the event hadn't begun baking the cakes and making sandwiches already.

By eight o'clock, she was sitting in her office, Gladys and

Enid poised with pens in their hands ready to make notes. 'Before we contact everyone, we need to set a date for the postponed fête, so that you can give it to them when you cancel today's event. We don't want to have to start making all the arrangements from scratch again. Letting them know the alternative date now will save a lot of unnecessary administration.'

Florence looked to her side and checked the date she had circled earlier on her diary. 'The first clear date I have when Sir Jesse and I are free is the fourth of September. I worry that any later than that, the weather might be too inclement for us to hold an outdoor event and we don't have a large enough covered area at Plaisaunce to hold it inside.'

'Well, the weather can't be much worse than today,' Enid quipped, quietly.

Gladys gasped. 'Enid, that's enough.'

Enid seemed confused for a second before her cheeks reddened. 'Oh, I'm sorry, Lady Boot,' she said, her eyes wide as she looked from Florence to Gladys. 'I hadn't meant to say that out loud. I didn't intend being rude.'

'Well, I think that you—' Gladys began.

Florence was far too busy to want to waste time on trivialities. She could see Gladys's fury at her assistant's careless remark and didn't want them to fall out on her account.

'It's perfectly fine, Enid. You are right. The weather really couldn't be much worse than it is today. But it could be much cooler if we hold the event too late in the year.' She circled the date in her diary. 'We'll go for the fourth of September.' She clapped her hands together when both women finished noting the date. 'Off you go, then, and please hurry. We don't want anyone turning up in this horrendous weather expecting to find a fête going on.'

At the end of a long and tedious day, Florence returned home with Jesse to be greeted by Meadows, looking worried.

'Whatever's the matter, Meadows?' Jesse said as Florence unbuttoned her coat.

Florence didn't recognise the look Meadows gave Jesse. 'Is everything all right?' she asked nervously. Florence didn't think she could bear having to deal with another problem after the long day she had endured at work.

'Mr John is in the living room,' Meadows announced.

'Good grief, man,' Jesse said. 'I thought for a moment then you were about to give us upsetting news. Send in some tea. I think we could all do with a cup.'

Florence pushed Jesse's chair into the living room, desperate to see her son once again and give him a tight hug. She pushed open the door and she and Jesse entered.

'Darling, John,' she cried, hoping she wasn't dreaming only to wake and discover he wasn't really there. Her smile vanished when she looked at him properly. The man standing with his back to the roaring fire had her son's features, but there was a marked difference in him that she hadn't anticipated. She forced herself to speak, desperate to cover up her shock. 'Why didn't you send word you were coming so soon, darling? We would have left work much earlier so that you didn't have to wait for us?'

'Hello, Mother, Father.' John's lips drew back into a tight smile. Florence hated to see him looking so drawn and exhausted. 'I wanted to surprise you.'

'Well, you've certainly done that, my boy,' Jesse said.

Florence could tell by the tightness of Jesse's voice that he was as shocked as she to see how much weight John had lost and the haunted look about his eyes. What had her son witnessed to have changed so much?

'Give your mother a hug,' Florence said, walking over to him and opening her arms. She swallowed the lump constricting her throat when John closed his eyes briefly before walking into her arms and holding her tightly. 'It's so good to have you back home again,' she said. 'I've waited a long time to do this and we've all missed you dreadfully.'

'Not as much as I've missed all of you,' he whispered, his voice cracking. 'I've imagined this moment many times since being here for those few days last December. I can hardly believe I'm here with you now.'

'Why don't you sit down, son,' Jesse said. 'Rest your legs. The servants will be bringing through tea any minute now.'

'Would you like something to eat?' Florence asked, noticing the sharpness of his cheeks that had never been apparent before now.

He shook his head slowly. 'No, thank you. I've come from home, and Margaret, as both of you, I imagine, was shocked to see how much weight I've lost. She insisted we eat together before I left the house to come here.'

'Good for her,' Florence said, grateful to her daughter-in-law for taking charge and looking after him so well.

They sat in companionable silence for a few minutes, each lost in their own thoughts. Florence didn't like to probe about his time away in France. He was home now, she reasoned, relieved not to have John to worry about any longer. Although, she thought, it seemed that he would need some time to recover from his experiences over the past year.

'Was it too terrible over there?' Jesse asked, finally.

John nodded. 'Far, far worse than even the papers make out. I've seen things I never want to think about again. Although, unfortunately, I find that I can't dispel them from my mind, however exhausted I might be.'

It broke Florence's heart to see her gentle son so tormented. 'Hopefully, in time you'll be able to find a way to move on from what's happened.'

John shrugged. 'I would love to think that might be possible, but I can't imagine ever being able to do so.' He gave her a wan smile. 'Maybe I will be able to, though. I don't want you worrying about me, Mother. Promise me you won't.'

Florence didn't like to make promises she knew she couldn't keep but wanted to reassure him. John had more than enough on his mind without fretting about her too. 'Of course.'

She could see that even though her son had been lucky

enough to return home without physical scars he had borne psychological ones and those could take just as long to heal in some cases. She was relieved to think that unlike many other soldiers at least John had a loving, caring wife at home who would do whatever it took to help him come to terms with all he had witnessed. She comforted herself with the knowledge that he and Margaret also had their new baby's arrival to look forward to.

Chapter Thirteen

4 September 1915

Seven weeks later, Florence stood next to Jesse in their garden at Plaisaunce, her right hand resting on the back of his wheelchair. She watched her son standing with his arm around his heavily pregnant wife's shoulders. He seemed happy, she thought with relief. He had also begun to recoup a little of the weight he had lost while overseas and his pallor didn't have the grey he had had on his return from France.

'He's doing well,' Jesse said quietly as if he could read her thoughts. 'He's a strong chap and I should imagine all his thoughts are taken up with looking after Margaret and planning for their baby.'

Florence hoped so. She would much rather her son's thoughts were consumed by something joyful. Surely, nothing could be more exciting than their impending arrival. She turned her face up in the direction of the warm sun and closed her eyes. It was a relief not to have to postpone the fête until the following spring, or have to find somewhere big enough to hold the event inside if they had been forced to hold it during the winter months.

Florence loved September days like this one. The feeling of summer slipping into autumn gave her a sense of calm she hadn't felt for a while. Although she suspected that the evening would be slightly chilly, the day was promising to be perfectly warm enough to satisfy even the pickiest stallholder or attendee. She watched quietly as those with stalls finished neatly laying out their produce ready for her to give her short speech and declare the fête open.

Shrieks of laughter made her and Jesse turn their heads towards the pavilion, where they saw the troupe of school children from the local primary school practising a few steps to their dances. One of the teachers was attempting to tell two of the children off while keeping her voice low as she motioned for others to calm down. Florence hoped they would be quieter, especially when it came time for the servants to begin serving the cream teas and other refreshments in the pavilion a little later on.

'Well, this is a relief, I must say,' Florence said, grateful that, despite having to delay the event, everyone seemed very happy to be at their riverside home to take part in the fun of the day and raise money for Margery's canteen.

Florence recalled her delight at receiving a letter in the early post that morning from Margery.

Northern France
29 August 1915

Sir Jesse and Lady Boot
St Heliers House
The Park
Nottingham
England

Darling Mother and Father,

I hope you are both keeping well and not working too hard. As I write those words, I am imagining you both at your desks planning your next battle to devise the next product in your efforts to fight the war from Nottingham. Keep up the good work.

I'm taking a break from work to write to you because I'm aware I haven't been in contact for a while despite promising to keep in touch before leaving home. I worry that you'll be concerned for me and don't want that to happen. It is hard work running the canteen. I'm tired most of the time but sleep well each night. There's always enough food to eat, although finding the time to sit and eat can be a bit of a challenge on occasion. We are very organised though. We each have our duties although are always on hand to assist each other when necessary. All of us are grateful for the supplies you send over to us.

Dorothy wrote and told me about the fête you're holding at Plaisaunce to raise funds for the canteen and I want you to know how grateful we all are here. I'll be thinking of you on the day and hope that on this occasion the weather is kinder to you. I wish I could be there to welcome my new niece or nephew but will be thinking of Margaret and John constantly. I also know you will write and tell me about the new baby as soon as you have any news to share.

I have to admit that the sheer numbers of wounded soldiers coming through the station and stopping at our canteen can be rather overwhelming at times. They are calling this the Great War but as far as I can tell there is very little greatness about it apart from the sheer number of injuries. I cannot imagine being able to walk along a street in Britain now without coming across maimed men, and I worry how our country and its people will ever recover from something as damaging as this war. We have so many distressed and tortured souls passing through here and despite their gratitude for what we do for them, I feel like it's far too little to be of much benefit.

I'm getting maudlin now and that wasn't my intention. If I had the time I would rewrite this letter, but I really need to finish it now to catch the post and return to work. Don't worry about me though. I might rage about what is happening to the brave soldiers and how tired we all are here, but I am perfectly well, if a little distressed at times. Having listened to many of the soldiers passing through here it helps me imagine what a nightmarish time John must have had while he was serving in his battalion.

My love to you both and especially to John when you see next him please.

As ever, your loving daughter, Margery. x

'It is,' Jesse said, breaking his wife's thoughts. 'I wasn't sure we would be this lucky when I spoke to someone at the Island Street factory earlier this week. He grows carrots and was concerned the weather might not hold. But it has, and we can all relax now and make the most of all your planning.'

She smiled at him seated in his wheelchair wearing his favourite dark brown hat. 'Before we open the fête, I wanted the photographer to take a photo of you with all our guests and the stallholders who have helped make this all look as good as it does right now.'

'What about you being in the photo, too?'

'Not this time,' she said. 'I have to go and check on the kitchens where the cakes and sandwiches are being prepared. We're hoping our cream teas sell well today, they usually do. If we have a photo taken again later, I promise I'll be there for that one. We must ensure that photographs are taken of groups of guests, including the two choirs.' Jesse agreed and Florence bent to kiss his cheek. 'It's good to see you away from your desk for once. It'll do you good to enjoy the sunshine today, Jesse. You always did love the fresh air and you need to remember to take time to enjoy yourself. Life shouldn't always be about work.'

Jesse laughed. 'I do love you, Florence.'

Confused to see his amusement, she crossed her arms and frowned. 'I don't understand. What did I say?'

'You act as if I'm the only one working this hard. When was the last time you stepped away from your desk?'

Florence tried to think when that could have been but realised it had been weeks before. 'There's always so much to do though,' she said immediately realising that she was guilty of doing exactly what she accused him of. 'Fine.' She grinned at him. 'I'll take time to come and sit outside with you tomorrow when this is over. Today, I must keep on top of things. We need to make as much money for Margery's canteen as we possibly can.'

'All right, I agree. You can work, but for today only. Tomorrow we must spend the day enjoying this place. We've got a long day ahead of us and many people to speak to. Then, tonight, the managers and their wives will be here to listen to the choirs and enjoy Plaisaunce. Tomorrow, it will be just the two of us and we can quietly enjoy each other's company.'

Florence seemed happy with his suggestion. 'I'm looking forward to our time tomorrow. We could do with a day, just the two of us.'

Hearing footsteps coming in their direction along the pathway, Florence turned to see Gladys hurrying towards her, a clipboard clasped against her chest with one hand and a fountain pen in the other. She looked slightly harassed, but Florence now knew Gladys well enough to feel assured that her secretary loved nothing better than to help arrange occasions like these. In fact, Florence thought, the young woman seemed to excel at this sort of work. It was a relief, especially as Florence seemed to be spending more and more time arranging to raise money for the war effort, or for entertaining the families of fallen soldiers, or for the wounded soldiers themselves. Florence loved being able to help people in this way. She had every intention of continuing to do so for the duration of the war; she just hoped it would not continue for too much longer, for everyone's sake.

'Lady Boot,' Gladys said, slightly out of breath. 'They're ready for you to give your speech to officially open the fête.'

Florence looked over to the gate to see that the general public had been allowed to start making their way into the garden. They looked so smart dressed up in their finest clothes and wearing summer dresses and straw hats, the men in their best suits and those with children grinning down to them and speaking to them – no doubt, she thought, promising treats during the afternoon.

'Thank you, Gladys. I'll come with you now.' Florence gave George a subtle wave to let him know she would be leaving Jesse by himself, satisfied when Jesse's nurse gave her a slight nod to acknowledge that he had seen her trying to get his attention.

She knew how much Jesse hated people to think him as incapable in any way. She knew as well as anyone that he was perfectly happy to be left to his own devices but she couldn't concentrate on what she was doing if she didn't feel reassured that George was at least looking out for Jesse should he need his help for anything.

She bent to kiss Jesse's cheek. 'I'm off with Gladys now, my dear. Listen out for my speech, will you? I want to be certain that I cover all that I told you I intended doing.'

Jesse smiled up at her. 'You will. You always do everything so well.'

Florence laughed, recalling all the mistakes she had made when they were first married and how she had ended up making matters worse in those early years when she hadn't listened to Jesse's advice. 'Well, not everything.'

Florence greeted people as she passed them on her way to the small stage in front of her rose garden. Deciding to wait at the side of the stage for a few minutes, until more attendees had time to arrive, she spoke to Gladys: 'Are you happy that everything is in order?'

'Yes, Lady Boot.' Gladys lowered her clipboard and ran the tip of her covered fountain pen down her long list of notes. 'Every stall is accounted for, which is good. I was worried that some might have to cancel for one reason or another. One did,' she added, lowering her voice to a whisper. 'The poor couple who were going to be selling their jams and pickles lost their younger son last week. However, their kindly neighbour and his wife are standing in for them. They had seen how much work they had put into their products and didn't want them to lose any sales.' She looked up at Florence, her eyes sad. 'I thought that was incredibly thoughtful of them.'

Florence often wondered how anyone found the strength to continue after the loss of a loved one. She knew from experience that a kind word or a thoughtful gesture could mean all the difference in someone's day. 'It was very generous of them to give their time like that.' She glanced over at the stall in question with its bright jars of richly coloured preserves. It was obvious by the sheer amount that the couple must have put in many hours of work to produce so many. 'I'll make a point of going to speak to them. I should think that after all the couple must have done to prepare for today the thought of not selling all that they hoped would be too dreadful.'

'I ensured they had the first stall next to the stage so that people won't miss it when they come into the grounds.'

'That was very clever of you, Gladys. Thank you. I'm going to miss your conscientious attitude to your work,' she said, wanting to take the opportunity at some point during the day to thank her senior secretary quietly without Enid being around. 'You are a natural organiser and keep me very much in order. I hope you know how much I appreciate all you've done for me and for Boots. I appreciate you staying on until now. I don't know what I would have done without you.'

Gladys lowered her eyes to her clipboard and blushed. 'Thank you, Lady Boot.' She looked back up and Florence noticed that the young woman's eyes were filled with unshed tears.

'Oh, my dear, I didn't mean to upset you,' she said resting her right hand on Gladys's slim arm.

Gladys shook her head. 'You haven't, Lady Boot. Not at all. It's just that I have enjoyed working for you so very much. I am looking forward to being Cyril's wife, but I'll miss working at Boots. I've learned an awful lot, you see, and you've always been so kind to me.'

Florence hoped it was the case. 'You have been a treasure, Gladys. However, it's now your time to marry your fiancé.'

'Yes, you're right.'

As locals made their way into the garden and the crowd increased, Florence checked her watch. 'I think it's time I welcomed everyone.'

She stepped on to the stage. The chatter quickly petered out as everyone turned to wait for Florence to speak. She never minded these events. It filled her heart with anticipation to know that by the end of the afternoon the stallholders, each of whom had made their own donation by paying a small amount to sell their wares, would return home having made money that would benefit their own families. Hopefully, too, she would have made enough from the cream teas, donations, tombola and lucky dips to be able to pass on money to Margery to buy necessary supplies for her canteen. Thanks to the weather holding, Florence was sure everyone was going to go home happy.

'Good afternoon, everyone,' she began, smiling at the happy faces gazing up at her. 'It is my pleasure to welcome you all here today to my husband's and my home for our garden fête being held in honour of our daughter Margery's canteen for wounded soldiers. I would like to thank the stallholders for their splendid array of produce, the Plaisaunce Brass Band, who will be entertaining us, along with the primary school, and everyone who has worked so hard to make today possible.' She mouthed a thank you at the crowd as a round of applause rang out. 'I hope you all have a splendid afternoon here on the riverside. So, without further ado, I declare this garden fête open.'

Cheers and applause filled her ears. Florence raised her hands to wave to the jolly attendees. She looked for Jesse to the side of the crowd and spotted him smiling at her. This was looking like being a perfectly wonderful afternoon and she was sure it would be one that she remembered and cherished for a long time.

The only thing that marred her happiness, Florence mused as she left the stage to go and check on the food preparation in the kitchen, was the need for Margery's canteen, and that her daughter was still in France. She was also sad that that Gladys was to leave soon. Florence was happy to know Gladys was to finally be married and become Mrs Marsh, but she was going to miss the dedicated girl.

The following Monday, Florence was standing in her office bidding Gladys a sad farewell. She thought back to Gladys's first day working at Boots and remembered a timid girl who she hoped would be able to cope with Miss Tweed's exacting standards. She was proud to see how confident and capable the young woman had become. Florence was happy to note the difference that Boots had made to this young woman's life.

'You've been an asset to the company,' Florence said as she handed Gladys the leather-bound Bible she presented to all her girls before they left the company to be married. 'I'd like you to know how much I've valued all that you've done for me.'

'That's very kind of you, Lady Boot. I appreciate it.'

'Not at all,' Florence said, always finding these moments sad. 'I'm especially grateful for you stepping up after we lost Miss Tweed and helping train the two new girls who have taken both your places.' Florence walked over to her office door, so Gladys wasn't embarrassed about how red her cheeks had gone. 'I'm sure you don't want me keeping you any longer from being with your dear Cyril.' She opened the door. 'Well, the very best of luck to you, Gladys. I hope that you and Cyril enjoy a long and happy marriage together.'

'Thank you very much, Lady Boot,' Gladys said, her voice quivering with undisguised emotion. She stroked the Bible lightly. 'I'm going to treasure this gift forever.'

Florence's heart felt as if a hand was clasping it tightly. She was always saddened to lose one of her dear girls, but she would especially miss this sweet, red-haired girl who had been such a stalwart when she needed it most. 'I'm glad that you like it, Gladys. I've added a postscript to my usual inscription in the front. Now,' she said before her own emotion got the better of her, 'off you go. You'll be missed here, but I'm sure you must know that already.'

'Thank you, Lady Boot. I do.'

Florence stepped out into the hallway and watched Gladys walk away. Gladys turned to wave, and Florence went to raise her hand in response when Enid Grimes, Gladys's replacement, stepped out of her office, blocking Florence's view of the departing girl.

'Oh, Lady Boot,' she said, startled. 'The first three girls coming for interviews for the Gas Mask Department are waiting to see you. They're in my office. Would you like me to show the first one in, or wait a while?'

Gladys disappeared around the corner and Florence shook her head. She needed a distraction from her emotions, and this was perfectly timed. 'No, Enid. Show the first woman through to me.'

Chapter Fourteen

27 September 1915

Florence stood next to Jesse as they gazed down at the baby girl in John's arms. She felt comforted to see him there with his little family and wondered how many children he and his lovely wife Margaret would go on to produce.

'Barbara Jacqueline,' Florence repeated almost to herself. 'What a very pretty name and for such a beautiful baby. I think it suits her very well.'

'As do we,' John said. 'In fact, it was Margaret's idea.' He looked down at his wife and bent to kiss her forehead. 'I don't think I've ever been as happy as I am now.'

'Nor me,' Margaret said gazing up at him.

Seeing the pair so happy together made Florence's heart swell with joy. After all the years she had fretted about John and his occasionally rocky relationship with Jesse, it was a relief to see him so settled and in love with his wife and baby girl.

'How are you enjoying serving with the Reserves?' Jesse asked.

John shrugged. 'It's not the same as being at the Front but –' he hesitated, gazing down at his baby daughter snuggled happily in his arms – 'I'm happy enough doing what I can.' He looked at Jesse. 'Did you hear that Viscount Chetwynd is building an arms factory at Chilwell?'

'Yes,' Jesse said, solemnly. 'He was given the go-ahead in August. I don't like to think of the thousands of staff they're going to need, and hope we don't lose many of our girls to their factory. Munitions is a dangerous business.'

'As do I,' Florence said, thoughtfully. She had been waiting to find out if any of her girls would be leaving to earn the extra money that working at the arms factory would bring them. She hoped there wouldn't be any, but she knew the attraction of extra wages to poor families, especially those with husbands and sons either at the Front or invalided out who needed all the financial support they could get.

'How are your new manufacturing processes coming along?' John asked his father.

Florence knew Margaret didn't mind them chatting about business, even at a time like this. She rolled her eyes heavenward to indicate her amusement at how typical it was of them to take this opportunity to chat about the latest company projects. 'Sorry,' she mouthed.

Margaret reached out to take Florence's hand. 'It's no

matter. Honestly, I'm just happy to have him back here with me.'

'What was that, darling?' John asked glancing from his wife to Florence and back again.

'Nothing for you to worry about,' she assured him.

John looked briefly at her and then turned to look at his father, waiting, Florence presumed, for him to answer his question.

'We have developed seventeen analytical tests,' Jesse said, the excitement obvious in his shining eyes. 'I'm proud to say that our aspirin is the purest on the market and we're already sending stocks to British field hospitals along with our new water-sterilising tablets. We've found that even the tiniest concentration of it can kill cholera, typhoid, dysentery and other bugs in around thirty minutes.'

'Are you serious?'

'Yes, deadly.'

Florence saw Margaret wince. The last thing a new mother needed to hear about was deadly organisms. She needed to change the subject. 'We received another letter from Margery, yesterday,' she said, focusing her attention on Margaret.

'Oh? How is she?' The baby woke and began to grumble. Margaret held her hands out to John to pass baby Barbara back to her.

He did as she asked and settled back onto his chair next to her bed. 'Did Margery or I remember to tell you that I stopped at her wooden hut on my way home?'

'Wooden hut?' Florence recalled reading in their

company magazine about Margery's canteen and was surprised to hear it described as such. She was disappointed that neither of her children had thought to mention their meeting to her before now. 'No,' she said, wishing she had the chance to visit her daughter and see her in action. 'Why didn't one of you tell us?'

'I suppose because we've all had so much going on that we must have forgotten.' He gave his mother an apologetic smile and she immediately forgave him the omission. He had indeed had far more pressing matters to contend with, she thought, glancing at her tiny granddaughter.

'Let the boy speak,' Jesse said, gently, reaching out for her to take his hand.

'Go on, then. I want you to tell me every detail.' She sat back in her chair and waited to hear his news of Margery. She was missing her daughter very much at the moment. Probably because, Florence thought, it was such a special time for the family having John back and two grandchildren now in the family. It made her want to group her flock together once again, home and safe where she could look out for them all. She realised John had begun reminiscing about his meeting with Margery and focused on what he was saying.

'She's a hard worker,' John said as if he had only just realised. 'And what's more she's very organised. The others who work with her are also kept on their toes, night and day. I'm not sure how they keep it up week after week.'

'I suppose they're spurred on knowing that they're

making a much-needed difference to all those soldiers,' Margaret suggested.

'Yes, you're probably right,' John replied, thoughtfully. 'There are seven of them and they work from a wooden hut, which was built for them in the stationmaster's garden by the engineering section at the station. They seem to have all they need to run it. There's a stove, their food and drink stores, and a supply of drugs. As you can imagine everything is immaculate. As the trains arrive at the station the ladies serve drinks and food, dressing wounds with fresh dressings, that sort of thing.'

Florence was fascinated. 'They are providing an invaluable service by all accounts.'

'They certainly are. Everyone seemed to have a role to play. Even for me who wasn't wounded or in pain, I found it comforting to stop there for a bite to eat, a cup of tea and a soothing word. It wasn't too bad either.' He glanced at Florence. 'The food, that is. They don't only serve British soldiers as you can imagine but also French soldiers and refugees passing through the station.' Florence listened with interest, proud of both her children for all they had achieved in their own ways. 'I have to admit I was extremely impressed with my little sister. To think she came up with this idea, sourced all the supplies and found the women who now help her run it. It's a triumph. The difference in the men's spirits from when they arrived to when they left was remarkable,' he said, dreamily, as if he was back reliving his time there. 'Everyone who visited left revitalised.' He looked from Florence to Jesse. 'I know you're both enormously proud of Margery, but you would be especially so to see her in action in her canteen.'

'I wish I could see her there,' Florence admitted. 'She did write to say that between the beginning of February and mid-March this year they had served almost twenty thousand people. I think that's a remarkable achievement for only seven women.'

'They must be exhausted,' Jesse said thoughtfully. 'I hope she doesn't overdo things.'

Florence caught John's amused reaction to his father's comment. 'I'm sure she won't,' Florence said, hoping to reassure him.

'Margery really was incredible. It was as if she had done this for years, not only a few months.'

Florence was deeply touched to hear him talk so proudly about his little sister. 'I'm relieved she's doing well over there. She would have hated for the canteen to have been a failure in any way.'

'Well, it's certainly not that,' John said with a laugh.

'They have nursing skills too, didn't you say, John?' Margaret asked as she cuddled her baby.

'That's right. Some of the women were already medically trained, and Margery said that she and the others have undertaken training from them to be able to help with changing bandages and generally doing small things to help make the soldiers as comfortable as possible.' He looked at his parents. 'She was impressive. Really, very good.'

Florence was delighted to hear such praise for her

daughter. It was satisfying to know that Margery had found work that meant so much to her and that made such a difference to others who needed it. 'I knew that whatever she put her mind to she would make a good job of it. Margery's always been determined; all three of you are.'

Florence noticed Margaret stifle a yawn. Then, straight after, the baby began to wail. 'I think she's hungry,' Florence murmured to Margaret. Then, in a louder voice, she added, 'We should be going. I think you three need to be left in peace to enjoy a little time together.'

Florence and Jesse said their goodbyes and she called Arthur in to help take Jesse out to settle him in their motor. Once the car was making its way along the road Jesse turned to her. 'Do you know, Florence, despite none of us being soldiers on the Western Front, we're all of us doing something to fight this war.'

Florence gave his comment a little thought. He was right. She was grateful to have the opportunity to be able to help support the war effort through her work at Boots. There was so much going on each day, with the constant adapting and upgrading how they produced products in the factories and employing extra staff to work in those departments. Already they had needed to change the production of their respirators drastically since reports had come back saying that the ones that had been sent did not deal as well with gas attacks as the British Government would like.

Florence found it difficult now to recall a time when she hadn't worried for each of her children, especially since the start of the war. Like Jesse, she knew that it was their concern for their children that spurred them to keep going.

'You've been working far too hard, lately,' she said softly. 'I know you wanted to push for those new respirators to be ready for production but now that's done, I hope you'll take things a little easier for a few days at least.'

'We've both been pushing things too far. I must admit I am feeling the repercussions of it.' He frowned at her. 'It couldn't be helped though. Soldiers at the Front and our Margery can't decide that they're too tired to do what's needed. We've needed to resolve issues with these box respirators. There always seems to be more to learn. Who would have imagined countries fighting with chemicals rather than bullets and bombs? It's horrifying.'

'But the respirators have been cleared for production now,' she said, trying to calm him. 'I think you need to let the staff do their job. We don't want Margery returning home to find us both ill from overwork.'

He sighed. 'I find it difficult to step away from a project, don't I?'

Florence lifted his twisted hand and kissed the back of it. 'You do. But then you've always found it hard to let others do their jobs without your input.' She thought of Margery insisting on working next to her assistants in the canteen. 'I think we're all a little like this in our family. You have the best staff though. You need to trust them to do the work you employ them for. It will leave you time to focus on new ideas and taking time out for rest.'

He nodded. 'We're starting off by making seventeen thousand each week, did you know that?'

'No,' she laughed, unsurprised that already he had gone back to thinking about the new respirators. 'No doubt you'll be expecting an increase in those numbers soon, too.'

'Yes. We'll need to find ways to make many more than that if we're to keep up with demand.'

'What am I going to do with you, Jesse Boot?' She sighed. What indeed? she thought, staring into his eyes, and knew that, however much his determination to keep working frustrated her, this was the man she married, and she would never be able to change him however much she tried. Just as whatever she said to Margery in reply to her daughter's letters, she could never hope to persuade her to return home until she was ready to do so. Her daughter being away broke Florence's heart; she had never imagined that Margery would remain in France for so long.

Chapter Fifteen

April 1916

Conscription had been in force for unmarried men between the ages of eighteen and forty since January and there was talk of a second act being passed at some point in the near future. This time it was to include married men. Florence worried about those male staff who had been forced to enlist and how they were faring. Each day, whenever Jesse scoured the broadsheets for the names of those who had perished on the battlefields or received word from their families of deaths or life-changing injuries, Florence's heart ached a bit more. These men should be enjoying watching their children grow, not risking their lives in muddy foreign fields. The fear of a telegram boy arriving at St Heliers bringing her news of John while he had been at the Front, and now fear of bad news about Margery, gave her many nightmare-filled nights.

'Things are getting desperate,' she said to Jesse one morning.

'I agree. I asked for the numbers to be totalled and it appears that since the war began we've already lost over four thousand employees to the war effort.' Jesse closed his eyes and for a moment Florence worried that he was having some sort of attack. He opened his eyes and Florence realised she was subconsciously on high alert worrying about John and how his time away still haunted him, and what effect the war was having on Margery's health.

He groaned and shook his head. 'I'm beginning to think that if we don't replace the men we're losing soon, we'll have a problem fulfilling our Government contracts. That's not something I can allow to happen.'

'No, you can't,' she said, unable to disagree.

'I know it's frightening, my dear, especially with all that's going on at present, but we need to be brave and press on building shops, increasing departments where necessary, that sort of thing. We're developing and producing the respirators, saccharin and water-sterilising tablets and will simply have to find the staff to do the work.'

Florence mulled over his words. Jesse was right, as usual. They had to keep going and trust that things would come right. People needed jobs now more than ever and would do so after the war ended, whenever that might be.

'I'm happy to support you in whatever ideas you come up with, Jesse. I'll also give a bigger push to finding staff to take on for the extra work we're doing now.'

'We make an excellent team, you and me.'

They did. Florence loved to think of them as a team and, as anxious as she was with all that they now faced, there was a part of her that was inspired by the urgency of all they had to contend with. 'We certainly do, Jesse.'

Florence left Jesse to focus on his work and took the lift downstairs to stroll through the store. She needed to reassure herself that her girls were coping both with their work and with any issues they might be having to deal with outside Boots. Florence had finished chatting to one of her girls when she spotted a middle-aged woman, her arm linked with a younger girl who she supposed must be around fifteen or sixteen.

Florence noticed the woman look across the shop floor at her and went to smile but the woman's attention was distracted when the girl tugged at her sleeve and frowned at her, saying something in a low voice that Florence couldn't make out. The woman then stared at Florence and, as their eyes met, there was a brief second when it seemed to Florence as if time stood still.

The next thing she knew, the woman appeared to take a step towards her before stumbling and then falling in slow motion. Florence leaped forward to try to catch her before the woman's head hit the ground as she collapsed to the floor in front of her. Someone screamed from behind her. Florence winced as the woman landed, her head hitting the carpeted floor with a dull thud. Angry with herself for not being quick enough to break the woman's fall, Florence bent down to check she was still breathing.

She heard voices calling for help then a calmer one she assumed must be one of her well-trained staff taking control of the situation. She left them to it, aware that her attention was needed by the unconscious woman. For the first time Florence realised that the woman was dressed in black. She was in mourning. Florence's heart ached for the poor, tormented soul.

Florence stood and waved to the nearest shop assistant. 'Bring me a cushion for this lady's head and keep everyone back. I don't want her to come round and find people staring at her. Then tell someone to ask Nurse Hill to come down immediately. We need her to bring a wheelchair. This lady needs to be taken to the sick bay where she can be checked and allowed to gather herself in peace and privacy.' Aware that the trauma of her loss might be the cause of the woman's collapse, Florence added, 'And you had better telephone Dr Cole's surgery. Mention that I've asked if he's able to call in to check on this lady for me, please.'

As soon as Florence was satisfied that she had done all she could to help, she turned to the white-faced young girl standing over them sobbing.

'Please don't be frightened,' Florence said, taking the girl's hand in hers. 'Is this lady your mother?'

The girl sniffed and gave Florence a guilty look. 'She didn't want to come today, but Dad insisted it would do her good to get out of the house for a change.'

Florence gazed at the unconscious woman, blissfully unaware of her sorrow for a short while at least. 'I'm sorry her visit here has ended this way.'

The girl didn't seem to hear her. 'Dad told me to bring her here, but it was my idea in the first place.' She broke into a sob, her shoulders shaking. 'I should have listened to her and let her stay at home, like she wanted. It's so hard watching her suffering so badly, though.'

Florence could feel the girl's anguish. To be mourning a loved one was horrendous enough but how many other young girls were having to witness their parents suffer in this way? She put her arm around the shaking shoulders and tried to soothe her. 'Please, don't worry. Your mother is in the best possible hands here. We have a wonderful first aid team at Pelham Street and they'll give your mother the best care and attention.'

Florence heard a male voice calling for people to move out of the way and then spotted one of the staff pushing a wheelchair towards her accompanied by Nurse Hill. Florence was grateful to have the nurse still working for them. She liked how dedicated she was and how she always managed to put those she attended to at their ease.

Someone groaned and Florence's attention returned to the poor lady at her feet. She was coming round.

'Where am I? Where's Jeanie? *Jeanie!*'

The girl crouched down next to her and took her hand. 'I'm right here with you, Mother.'

'Everything will be fine,' Florence assured her, crouching to help the woman to sit up. 'You're fine, Mrs…?' Why hadn't she thought to have asked the daughter her name? 'I'm sorry, I don't know how to address you.'

'Mrs Culley,' she said. 'Mary Culley.' She stared at

Florence, as if her sight was coming into focus. Then her mouth dropped open. 'I know you,' she gasped. 'You're... you're Lady Boot.'

Florence smiled, relieved that the woman seemed none the worse for wear from her fall. 'I am, and we're going to do our best to look after you. You mustn't worry about anything.' She waved the nursing staff over to her side. 'This lady is Nurse Hill. She's going to take you with this porter to our sickroom. She will check to make sure you didn't damage yourself in any way when you fainted. You will receive the best possible care, I promise you. We want to be certain you're well enough to return to your home. Would that be all right with you?'

She seemed to take a moment to think about what Florence had suggested. 'And my Jeanie can come with me?'

'Yes, of course she can.'

Florence watched as Mrs Culley was helped into the chair and made comfortable. 'Please make sure Mrs Culley and her daughter Jeanie are given a cup of tea and some cake before calling for a taxi to take them home.' Florence took Jeanie's trembling hands in hers. 'You see? I told you your mother would be fine. Now you accompany her and Nurse Hill. Once your mother has been checked you will both be given a nice cup of tea and some cake. You do like cake, don't you?'

Jeanie nodded. 'Yes, Lady Boot.'

'Good. Then that's settled then.' Florence gave a nod to

Nurse Hill to signal that she could take the woman and her daughter.

'Come along, Mrs Culley,' Nurse Hill said, her voice gentle. 'And you, Jeanie.'

Mrs Culley looked delighted at the prospect for a few seconds. Then grabbing hold of the arms of the wheelchair she went to stand.

'No, I don't think that's a good idea so soon after your fall, do you?' Florence asked.

'But it's too much of an imposition,' she argued quietly. 'Jeanie and me, well, we're fine to go and catch the tram. It goes near to our home, so it won't be a problem for us.'

'No,' Florence said aware that the woman was probably embarrassed by all the fuss going on around her. 'I insist you take a taxi.' It dawned on her that maybe the woman's issue was the cost of the taxi and she wanted to be clear that didn't expect her to pay for it. 'We will settle the account happily.' As soon as the woman had been handed her bag and straightened her hat, Florence asked, 'Is there anything in particular that you came to the store to buy?'

She shook her head. 'No, Lady Boot. My daughter brought me here to take me out of myself.' Her shoulders stooped slightly. 'I've recently lost my son, you see.'

Florence felt as if a hand was clutching at her heart. This woman was living her own worst nightmare. She saw the haunted brown eyes filling with tears and taking her clean handkerchief from her pocket handed it to Mrs Culley. 'I'm deeply sorry to hear about the loss of your precious son.' No wonder the poor woman had collapsed, Florence thought. She could only imagine the constant pain Mrs Culley must feel to have to keep going each day knowing she would never see her son again. 'I truly am.'

'Thank you. I heard that your son enlisted, and your daughter is also in France running a canteen.' She sniffed before blowing her nose. 'My son was a good boy. I'm not sure how I'm to carry on without him around. It's only because I have Jeanie that I don't give up entirely.'

Florence nodded, aware that she could not bear to live should she lose one of her own children.

'Now, then, Mum,' Jeanie soothed. 'there's no use talking that way. Remember what Dad said.'

The crying woman looked up at her daughter. 'Yes, sweetheart. You're right, Jeanie.'

Florence didn't like to ask what her husband had said. Nurse Hill raised her eyebrows questioningly at her and Florence realised it was time the poor grieving mother was given a little privacy and that cup of tea she had promised her. She rested her right hand on the woman's arm. 'If you're ready, I think it's best if you go with Nurse Hill for your cup of tea now. And, if there's anything at all that I can do for you or your family in the future, please, don't hesitate to ask me. I'm here most days.'

Mrs Culley reached out and took Florence's right hand in both of hers. 'I've always heard you were a kind woman, Lady Boot. You don't know how much good it does my heart to find out for myself that it is indeed the case. We need more good women like you in this world.'

'You're too generous,' Florence said, feeling a little

embarrassed at such praise, especially as she was lucky enough to have her son back in Nottingham once again.

'No, I'm not. You're the one who's been kind.' She gave Florence a teary smile. 'Thank you for your thoughtfulness to me and my Jeanie. It means a lot, it really does. I know I'll never get over losing my boy but knowing he died to fight for his country and people like you helps me a little.'

'It's the very least I can do. Please take good care of yourself, Mrs Culley.' She turned to the girl, who, she was relieved to see, now seemed a little calmer. 'And you too, Jeanie. I can see you're a good girl too and will ensure that your mother ventures back out again once she's feeling ready to do so.'

'Yes, Lady Boot,' Jeanie said, giving Florence a slight bob as if she wasn't sure whether or not a curtsey was called for.

Florence watched them go, her heart heavy to think of the pain Mrs Culley would endure for the rest of her life. War was a great leveller, Florence thought as she continued to the next counter. Her title and wealth would not protect her children from a bomb blast or a sniper's bullet. The thought of her children being hurt made her shudder but the comradeship she felt with other mothers like Mrs Culley as they shared their fears for their sons made her feel a closer connection with the women than she had ever felt before.

She wished she could do something to help Mrs Culley and her family, but what? Florence moved on to speak to one of her girls who had caught her eye and was waiting for her at her counter. Then after passing the time of day with several customers, she continued with her walk through the store until she heard a small girl's voice.

'Mummy, why is that lady's face yellow?'

Florence heard the mother hiss a sharp retort. Then, noticing Florence had seen them and no doubt heard the girl's comment, she gave Florence a horrified glance, grabbed the girl by the wrist and marched her away and out of the shop.

Without turning to look at the woman the little girl had commented on, Florence knew that she would be one of the many thousand munitions workers from the Chilwell Arms Factory that had been built the previous year. Not wishing to make the poor girl feel even more uncomfortable than she probably already did, Florence walked off in the opposite direction. She had seen enough of these 'canary' girls in the shops in recent months.

She had been as shocked as the little girl the first time she had witnessed the unusual yellow skin; in some cases, even the hair had turned green. She had asked Jesse about it and he had explained that it was the chemicals some of the women worked with filling shells and that the toxic substances were to blame for the change in colour to their skin. She had always understood that working with explosives was going to be dangerous but never thought that the women could also be poisoned by the materials. She hoped there were no long-term effects and that at some point the women's skin would return to its original hue.

Florence noticed the time on the large wall clock and decided to return to her office. She still had to check the next issue of *Comrades in Khaki*. As she hurried up the stairs to her office, stopping and chatting briefly to members of staff and a few customers, she couldn't help feeling sad that the shortage in paper meant that this would be their penultimate issue.

The magazine had been massively successful in maintaining contact with ex-Boots employees fighting in the war. Jesse insisted, quite rightly in her opinion, that Boots would cover the cost of producing the magazine so that all proceeds from its sale could go to the Boots Sick and Wounded Fund and that if there was no need for that money they would pass it on to the National Fund. She had been proud of being able to advertise for various good causes raising money for the wounded and the poor and featuring, among other things, articles and photos of their Boots Plaisaunce Band and their appearance raising money at various events.

Florence reached her office and sat at her desk thumbing through the publication with a heavy heart. She had been told many times over the past year since the first issue was brought out how much people relished reading every morsel of information in the magazine. She couldn't help feeling bad that by stopping the magazine the war funds they supported through advertising payments would have to find another source. What would the aspiring poet soldiers do with their poems now that they could no longer submit them for consideration to *Comrades in Khaki?*

She reread the letter from her and Jesse to the men sharing their regret that they had to discontinue the magazine, then the 'Boots Roll of Honour' and the 'Letters from the Front'. One letter was from a soldier who had spent ten months on the British Front and another from a motorcyclist writing about a lucky escape of an air pilot. She was particularly saddened by the photo of a young rifleman who had fallen in action. Florence couldn't help wondering about his family or those of the wounded soldiers depicted in a photo taken at the Harborne Hall Convalescent Home being entertained to tea by her and Jesse.

There was so much heartache all around them, Florence mused. She wondered how Mrs Culley was getting along and wished there was something she could do to help the family. Losing a son was devastating enough in itself, but if he had been sending his pay home to his parents maybe they had been relying on him returning after the war to continue contributing to their household income.

She rubbed her eyes, tired and feeling rather emotional after witnessing so much sadness in one day. There must be a way she could help this family, she thought. Then, recalling that Jeanie had said she was fifteen, she wondered if maybe she might like to come and work at Boots. She sat up and checked the time. If she hurried to the sick bay, then maybe she might still catch Mrs Culley and be able to speak to her about offering her daughter a job.

She hurried out of her office and made her way there, relieved to find Mrs Culley sitting next to her daughter, looking much more relaxed and a little happier as she ate a slice of chocolate cake. They heard Florence enter and both placed their forks down on their plates and went to stand.

'Lady Boot?'

Florence waved for them to stay seated. 'I'm sorry to burst in on you both like this, but I wanted to ask if Jeanie has a job yet?'

Mrs Culley frowned. 'She did, until last week when she took a day off to sit with me and her boss fired her for taking time off without prior request.'

'He did what?' Florence was horrified. How could someone be so unfeeling? 'Did he know her reasons for staying at home with you?'

Jeanie seemed hesitant for a moment before replying. 'Yes, your ladyship. I sent word with my neighbour. She works there, too, and, when she gave him my message, he said for her to tell me not to bother going back.'

Florence scowled. She wished she could ask the name of the girl's ex-boss and go and give him a piece of her mind. How could anyone be so cruel to a family who were grieving? If he was that nasty, she mused, then he couldn't have been very pleasant to work for.

'Does that mean you're looking for work then, Jeanie? Or are you wanting to spend more time at home with your mother at the moment? I understand if you do want to. I'm just asking, if that's all right?'

'We don't mind at all, Lady Boot,' Mrs Culley said. 'I'm not so bad when I'm at home and, yes, Jeanie is looking for work. May I ask why?'

Florence clasped her hands together. 'From what I've

seen of your daughter, Mrs Culley, Jeanie seems a thoroughly caring and loyal young lady. I'm always looking for girls with her quality to come and join us at Boots. We have a relatively new department where we make the masks and respirators for the brave boys, like your son, who are fighting for us all. I wondered if she might like a job there? She might not be able to join up, but she will be doing a valuable service working in the department.'

Jeanie's eyes widened and she stared at her mother. 'Mother? Could I?'

Mrs Culley smiled properly for the first time since Florence had met her. She glanced at her daughter and then looked back at Florence. 'She would like that very much, Lady Boot. As would I. When would you like her to start?'

'As soon as Jeanie chooses to, Mrs Culley.' She gave her offer some thought. 'I tell you what. Why doesn't Jeanie have a couple more days at home with you and begin her new role here at Boots on Monday?'

'Thank you so much, Lady Boot. This job will make all the difference to Jeanie,' she said, her voice cracking with emotion. 'To all the family.'

'I'm pleased to be able to help in some way. And if I'm honest, Mrs Culley, your daughter will be helping me by coming to work for me. So, it works both ways.'

Jeanie giggled and hearing the joy in the grieving girl's voice cheered Florence immensely. 'Right, I had better return to my office. I will bid you a good day, Mrs Culley. Also to you, Jeanie, and please report to my office first thing on Monday morning. I'll take you to where you'll be working and introduce you to your manager.'

As Florence left the two women and returned to her office, she couldn't help thinking how very lucky she was to be in the privileged position of being able to make a difference to another person's life. It was something that she was incredibly grateful to be able to do.

Chapter Sixteen

July 1916

A cold, dull and very miserable June finally gave way to warmer weather the following month. Florence sat in Jesse's office with two of their senior chemists going through final paperwork for the production of their approved medications for venereal disease. She still found it strange that one of their biggest products, apart from aspirin and water-sterilising tablets, was for sexually transmitted diseases.

She supposed it made sense that with so many men away from their homes, probably for the first time ever experiencing freedom away from their parents' eyes, combined with the fear that they might not live to see the following week, they would take comfort in professional women in the French and Belgian brothels. She just hadn't thought about the consequences of those visits and that so many of them, apparently one fifth of all soldiers, needed medication to cure the infections that they had picked up.

Jesse had tried to insist that Florence not be involved in this particular project due to its less than savoury connotations, but Florence had brushed aside his concerns. This had been a big project and she was determined to keep working as closely to Jesse as she possibly could. He suffered incessant pain now from his crippling rheumatism and she needed to watch over him to ensure he didn't do too much. He still insisted on being taken to each of his shops to check on them and could still do this himself since having his motor car constructed especially to his specifications. He was the man she admired most in the world, but sometimes she wished that he would take things a little easier and allow others to do more for him.

'Jesse, I'm in my fifties now and have been a chemist's wife for long enough not to be fazed by much. This is a medical issue, after all. And one that it appears is having a detrimental effect on too many of our fighting men. And I, for one, am determined to do all I can to help solve the problem.'

Now, though, as she sat across the table from the three men, she couldn't help hoping that they had indeed come up with the perfect product to help the afflicted soldiers recover as quickly and as thoroughly as possible. Each of them would need to return home with their heads held high or return to fight for their country without wasting any more time than was necessary.

Once the final signature had been added to the

paperwork Florence excused herself and returned to her own office. She looked at the pile of letters received in the morning's post waiting for her attention. She sat down, tired and emotional, and knew that if Miss Tweed or Gladys Lightbody still worked for her then they would have brought her a cup of tea by now. Gladys's former assistant, Enid Grimes, wasn't working out at all satisfactorily. Not only did she not possess the same instinct as her predecessors for picking up what was needed, but Florence had noticed that she seemed a little overwhelmed at times. She wasn't surprised; hers was an incredibly busy office with her workload increasing by the week.

Enid's assistant had given notice the previous week to join the FANYs and Florence knew that neither she nor Enid would be able to cope without decent secretarial support. She had wanted to give Enid a chance to settle into the role as her senior secretary and had misguidedly hoped that over time she would become familiar with how everything was run. It was more than a year since she had taken over Gladys's role and painfully obvious that the poor girl still felt out of her depth. Florence didn't want to ask her to leave but she did need to do something to rectify the situation. And rather than find a replacement for the assistant, Florence decided that maybe Enid would be more suitable in the supportive role. She had no choice but to demote her and find a new senior secretary to come in and work for her.

Florence called Enid into her office, deciding that she had little time to waste if she wanted to arrange the girl's replacement. Enid entered, her face pale and hands clasped together.

'Please, sit down, Enid,' Florence said, her voice deliberately gentle. When Enid was sitting, Florence began. 'You're a hard worker, Enid, and I'm grateful to you for all that you've done over the past year.'

Enid gasped. Her right hand flew to her mouth. 'You're firing me, Lady Boot?' She leaped to her feet. 'Oh, I knew you would have to. Wasn't I just telling my sister yesterday that I thought this would happen?'

Florence's mouth dropped open in shock. She had supposed Enid was expecting something to have to change but hadn't thought the timid girl would react in such a dramatic fashion. Florence waved for her to sit down.

'I have no idea what you were saying to your sister. Please, don't take on so, Enid, it really isn't the way I expect my staff to behave.' She waited for the girl to take her seat once more.

Enid stared down at the floor shamefaced. 'I'm so sorry, Lady Boot.'

'There really is no need for you to be alarmed. I am not asking you to leave.' She waited for Enid to take in what she had said. 'However, by what you've just said, it appears that we are both of the same mind. You are obviously finding it difficult to cope in your current role. Do you agree?'

Enid's eyes filled with tears and she nodded slowly. 'Yes, Lady Boot.'

Florence relaxed slightly, relieved that Enid was now

listening to what she was trying to say. 'I do appreciate all that you've done for me this past year, but I believe you are much better suited to an assistant secretarial role.'

Enid gave a relieved sigh. 'I think you're right.' Her eyes strayed to her lap.

Florence hated having to lower the girl's expectations of a future at Boots, but it couldn't be helped. There was far too much at stake and too many staff members' livelihoods had to be looked out for. She needed to be firm and find the most appropriate way to make her own office work efficiently if she was going to keep working at the level that she now faced.

'I would like you to carry on as you are for the time being,' she said, giving Enid a reassuring smile when the girl looked up at her. 'And, in the meantime, I'll search for a new senior secretary to come in and look after my administration. I think that once these changes have been made you will probably find your work much easier. That in turn will make your working day a more pleasant one. Don't you think?'

Enid's shoulders lowered and she appeared to relax. 'Yes, Lady Boot. I'm sorry I didn't cut the mustard. I did try my best, though, I promise you.'

'I know you did, Enid. Please don't worry. We will sort this out and I think that with a new set-up everything will run much more smoothly.'

Enid smiled and thanked Florence again before leaving her office. Now all Florence needed to do was to find someone she could rely upon to step up to the role as her senior secretary. She sighed. If she had failed to find the right woman before, how could she hope to find her now?

Enid brought Florence in a cup of tea and a biscuit. Florence thanked her and as she sat back in her chair and sipped her tea, she stared out of the window at the pouring rain, trying to feel more positive than she felt.

Then it dawned on her. Her old friend Lily Buttons! Hadn't she instinctively known exactly what Florence needed and when? Lily was organised and incredibly hard working. Maybe she should ask her to come and help for a few months while she looked for a permanent replacement? Florence wasn't sure if her old friend would accept the offer, but it was worth a try.

She decided that the best way to approach Lily would be face-to-face in the informal setting of her pretty cottage rather than sending her a letter asking her to meet in the office. She sent a note down to Lily asking if she could call in on her that evening after work. Florence knew how Lily liked to walk home alone each day so decided that she would call in on Dorothy and baby Nancy first to give Lily time to take it easy after a long day in the store. She could go to her home afterwards and put forward her proposal.

She arrived at Dorothy's home happy to see her eldest daughter cuddling her enchanting daughter. They sat in Dorothy's living room; the light seemed to fill the room despite the miserable weather. Florence was amused to watch the little girl taking shaky steps from her mother's outstretched arms into her own. It was strange to think that so many years had gone by since Dorothy was doing the same thing between her and Jesse.

As she sat forward in the armchair and reached out to catch Nancy should she fall, Florence felt as if she had been transported to when she had been a young mother. Jesse and she had worked hard then, too, she recalled, and had relished the chaos of each day as their children fought and played, bringing the house alive with their chatter. It dawned on her suddenly how much she missed those times.

'You're such a clever girl,' Florence said, grabbing hold of little Nancy when the cherubic child stumbled as she neared her. She swooped her up into her arms, making the little girl giggle with delight.

Florence sat Nancy on her knee and bobbed her up and down as she and Dorothy caught up on what each of them had done that day.

The front door banged shut and the captain called from the hallway. 'Where are my best girls?' Florence heard him say before she heard his footsteps coming towards the living room. She waited for him to enter the room. 'Wonderful to see you,' he said, walking over to her to kiss her cheek. 'Have you seen how clever little Nancy is with her walking now?' He bent to ruffle his daughter's hair. The little girl reached her arms up for him to lift her. Once she was in his arms, the captain kissed her forehead and tickled her.

Florence's heart swelled to see Dorothy with her small,

happy family. 'I'd better be on my way,' she said picking up her purse.

'Please don't rush off on my account,' he said, walking over to Dorothy and slipping his free arm around her waist. 'You're more than welcome to stay for dinner.'

Florence shook her head. 'I'd love to, but I have a prior engagement.' She looked at Dorothy. 'I'm going to ask Lily Buttons to come and work as my secretary for the time being until I can find a suitable replacement.'

'She'll be very good,' Dorothy said. 'You always did say that Lily seemed to know exactly the right thing to do.'

Florence laughed. Her daughter was right. 'Well, I'll just have to hope I can persuade her.'

She kissed Dorothy and Nancy goodbye and went out to her car hoping that by approaching Lily she was doing the right thing. What was the worst that could happen?

Chapter Seventeen

Florence linked arms with her dear friend and breathed in the fresh scent of the vast array of summer flowers blooming on either side of Lily's cottage garden. After a miserable, wet morning, the weather had brightened to a warm and humid afternoon.

'This place always makes me smile,' Florence said, stopping to admire the bright colours all around them. 'You've done a marvellous job here, Lily.'

'It's not really all down to me. My brother loves to garden and is always out here pottering. I'm grateful for it, too. I prefer to sit on my porch in the shade and gaze at it. It reminds me of some of those gardens you could see along the road in front of those pretty Victorian terraced houses, going towards Havre des Pas beach in Jersey.'

Florence pictured the tall white bow-fronted houses, some of which had been guest houses and others private homes. Many had made the most of their small front gardens for passers-by on their way to the seafront to admire.

Lily gave Florence's arm a gentle squeeze. 'I'm looking forward to finding out what you're planning.' Florence frowned at Lily, unsure about what she meant. Lily gave her a knowing smile. 'I know you've come to ask me something, I can sense it. Let's sit out here on the porch and I'll fetch us tea. Unless you'd rather have a glass of lemonade. My sister made some fresh this morning. It's a little tart but perfect on a hot day like today.'

Florence realised she hadn't tasted lemonade for a while. 'I'll try your sister's drink,' she said. 'Thank you.'

'Take a seat here.' Lily indicated two rattan chairs facing the pretty garden. 'I'll be back in a jiffy.'

Florence sat, relieved to be in the shade once again. She gazed out over the colourful garden with its dahlias, poppies, hollyhocks, various types of roses, sweet peas growing up a small cherry tree and other flowers making up the delightful display and couldn't help thinking how the weather had changed from earlier in the day.

Florence heard Lily's footsteps coming out onto the small porch and looked up. She was carrying a small, lacquered tray with two glasses and a jug of the pale drink. Setting it down, Lily took the crocheted cover with its beaded sides from the top of the jug and poured them a glass each, handing one to Florence. 'Try that. If it's too tart for you I'll make tea.'

Florence took a sip. One of her eyes winked

automatically at the sharpness of the drink, but it was delicious.

'Too much?' Lily asked, taking a sip of her own.

'No, I like it.'

Lily grinned. 'Really?'

Florence laughed. 'When have you known me to not tell you the truth?'

'Good point,' Lily said, returning Florence's smile and sitting on the other chair. She placed her glass on the table and turned to Florence. 'Right. Now, are you going to tell me why you're here?'

Florence smiled at her. Lily knew her so well. She loved that her friend felt comfortable enough to be straight with her and tease her about things. Florence explained how, since Miss Tweed's tragic death and Gladys leaving to be married, she hadn't been able to find anyone to replace either woman.

'I know Miss Tweed was a force to be reckoned with and I had been concerned about her asking to retire for a couple of years,' Florence admitted. 'I hadn't expected Gladys to be able to completely fill her shoes, but she was very good. In fact, I hadn't realised quite how proficient she was until Enid took her place.'

'But she's been with you a while now, hasn't she?'

'Yes, almost a year.'

Lily narrowed her eyes. 'How exactly do I fit in?'

Florence knew to come straight to the point. Lily didn't need a build-up to hearing news and she had already gone some way to do that. 'I need you to step in as my senior secretary.' She raised her right hand. 'Only for a few months until I find someone to replace you.'

Lily didn't reply immediately. 'But what about poor Enid? I can't be responsible for some other woman losing her job.'

Florence shook her head. 'You won't be.' She went on to relay her earlier conversation with Enid. 'So, you see, you would be helping both of us out by coming to work for me.'

'But why ask me? I haven't done that sort of work for so long I doubt I'll know what to do now.'

'Nonsense. You know me. You know how I like things done and apart from Jesse you're the most organised, hard-working person I know.' She decided to change tactics. 'I promise it will only be for a short while. You can help Enid and she'll keep you up to speed with all the things that need doing each day.' Florence took another sip of her drink. 'I will begin looking for a replacement immediately, but it's difficult finding office staff, or any staff to be honest. So many young women want the excitement of working more directly for the war effort, and I can understand that, what with the increase in wages.' She watched as Lily thought about her proposal. She hadn't immediately refused, and Florence knew that meant that Lily was considering accepting.

'Who will cover for me while I'm upstairs working for you though?'

'It will be good training for your assistant, don't you think?'

Lily looked out over her garden thoughtfully. 'It would

make a change, I suppose.' Florence watched her silently. 'And I'm always happy to help you out. Yes, go on then. I'll do it, but only for a few months at the most.' She paused. Florence knew this was to reaffirm her last comment, so nodded her acceptance. 'I love working on the shop floor,' Lily continued. 'I don't want to be away from my department for too long. What if they get used to not having me there?'

Florence took Lily's nearest hand in her own. 'I can't ever see that ever happening. The staff at Boots have great respect for you, Lily. The women in your department most of all.'

Lily sighed. 'I hope you're right.' She placed her free hand on top of Florence's. 'Then we are agreed? I'm happy to come and work as your secretary for a few months only.' Her eyes twinkled in amusement. 'No more than three at the most.'

Florence removed her hand and picked up her lemonade, smiling at her friend. 'Anyone would think you didn't enjoy working by my side.' Florence laughed to show she was joking. She was well aware of Lily's loyalties to her but knew her heart had always lain with her job dealing with customers. 'Yes, I'm happy to agree to any terms. Three months at the most then.'

Florence breathed a sigh of relief and beamed at her generous friend, delighted. She reached out her hand and took Lily's again. 'Thank you, Lily. I was hoping you would do this for me. How soon can you start?'

Lily laughed. 'Will Monday be early enough?'

'It will.' Now, thought Florence, all she had to do was to start looking for Lily's replacement as her secretary. She didn't want to take advantage of her good friend's kindness. Finding a new senior secretary wasn't going to be easy, as had been proved to her when she had taken on Enid. The right woman must be out there somewhere though. She simply needed to find her and persuade her to come and work for her.

Chapter Eighteen

Early hours, 25 September 1916

Florence and Jesse had spent a fun afternoon with Margaret and her two daughters in the warm living room of her house. As she changed for bed Florence thought back to how sweet the two little girls were and wondered if John and Margaret would be happy to leave their family at two, or maybe try for another child at some point.

Florence cleaned her teeth and after kissing Jesse good night went to her own room and got into bed. She really should turn out the light and get some sleep, she thought, but for some reason sleep evaded her. She picked up her latest book from the lending library and opening it, took out the bookmark and began to read.

Sometime later, Florence was distracted by a deep droning sound. She stopped reading and listened. It wasn't a sound she thought she had ever heard before and for a few seconds Florence prayed that it wasn't the thing she dreaded most. A distant wailing pierced the night air making her jump up. She immediately realised that the siren was alerting them to a Zeppelin attack. The deep sound of the air machine was getting louder. She thought back to the Zeppelin attack on Nottingham in January the previous year and realised in horror that one of the monstrous machines was coming their way.

She snapped her book shut and threw back her bed covers. Sliding her feet into her slippers, she grabbed her dressing gown and tied it as she ran down the corridor to Jesse's room next door. Before waking him, she pulled on the cord by his fireplace to call for his nurse George. He was always alert and would come racing up the stairs in a panic to see what the matter was.

'Jesse?' she said, gently trying to rouse him by pushing his shoulder with one hand and turning on his bedside light with the other.

'Wha—?' He gazed at her bleary-eyed for a second before trying to sit up. 'What's happened? What's the matter?'

She didn't want to make him panic, but knew that if there was to be a bombing raid then the last place they needed to be was upstairs in their bedrooms. 'Can you hear that sound?' she asked, as she pulled back his covers and took hold of his ankles, pulling them round so that his feet were on the floor. She took his slippers to put them on his feet as Jesse listened carefully to try to hear the sound that had caused her such alarm.

'I do. Heaven help us, I think that's a Zeppelin.'

'I think so, too.'

'We need to get everyone down to the cellars straight away.' He put his hands on her shoulders. 'Have you called for George, or Meadows?'

Florence went to take his dressing gown from where it lay over the back of his chair. 'They should be here any moment. I thought I'd come and wake you first though. We can't waste any time.' Even without concentrating on the sound now she could hear the clear dull sound of the Zeppelin. Her head pounded as she helped him on with his dressing gown.

Just then, the door opened, and George ran in, closely followed by Meadows. 'Are you all right, Sir?'

'Did you hear the Zeppelin, too, Lady Boot?' Meadows asked, keeping his voice low, as George lifted Jesse out of his bed.

'Yes,' Florence said, waving for him to following her onto the landing. 'And I must admit that it's unnerved me somewhat. We need to ensure all the servants are woken and taken down to the cellars immediately. Can you do that for me, Meadows?'

'Right away, Lady Boot.'

'And tell them to bring a blanket from their beds, it'll be cold in the cellar and we've no idea how long we'll have to remain down there.'

Without another word Meadows ran to the end of the

corridor to the door that led to the back staircase and up to the servants' quarters in the attic. The only servants who had rooms downstairs were Mrs Rudge and Meadows.

Florence went back into Jesse's bedroom to see if Jesse was nearly ready. 'Let me know if you need me to do anything to help, George.' She grabbed the eiderdown from his bed.

'No thank you, Lady Boot. You just lead the way downstairs if you would. We'll follow you down there in a jiffy.'

She hurried down to warn Mrs Rudge. The sound of the Zeppelin was now so loud that Florence assumed it must almost be overhead. She doubted that anyone could sleep through the noise and thought of Miss Tweed and how there was no way she would have been able to sleep through the bombing that had stolen her and her sister's lives.

She forced herself to concentrate. There was nothing she could do now to help Agnes Tweed, but she could help save members of her household. As Florence pushed the baize door open, she heard the first panic-stricken voices of Ethel, the under housemaid, and Mavis, the kitchen maid, immediately followed by Meadows snapping at them to be quiet.

She rushed to the kitchen, stepping on a corner of the eiderdown that had slipped from her arms and almost falling. Florence grabbed the back of a chair and righted herself. She noticed that Mrs Rudge was already setting up a tray with a large jug on it and several glasses.

'Mrs Rudge,' Florence said concerned they might be caught in the kitchen if bombs began falling. 'There's no time for refreshments. Get down to the cellar, now.'

The next moment, Meadows burst into the kitchen, glanced from Florence to Mrs Rudge and, taking in the scene, took the tray from Mrs Rudge's hands. 'I'll take these. We need to hurry.'

Mrs Rudge stepped back for Florence to follow Meadows and as Florence passed her she noticed her cook pick up a tin of biscuits. How typically thoughtful of her, Florence thought, comforted to know that her staff always had everyone else's best interests at heart.

'George is bringing Sir Jesse down,' she said as Meadows opened the door to the cellar and they all filed down, followed by her maids and the first footman.

George switched on the light. Thankfully, Florence thought, they had set up blackout curtains in all rooms even down where they were now in case this sort of thing happened during a dinner party and wine still needed to be brought up from the cellar.

How naïve we were, Florence thought, finding a space where she settled down Jesse's eiderdown for her to sit next to him when George brought him down to join her. She turned her wedding ring round her finger anxiously awaiting their arrival. Where were they? Surely George should be here by now?

'Meadows?' she said, about to ask him to go and see if George needed any help with anything. Then, hearing footsteps, she turned to see George at the cellar door.

Meadows handed the tray to one of the maids and ran to help his colleague.

'We're fine,' George said taking each step tentatively as he carried Jesse carefully down to them. 'Where would you like to sit, Sir Jesse?'

Meadows ran up the stairs and closed the cellar door. Florence noticed him glare at two of the maids who were snivelling in the corner, no doubt terrified of losing their lives, she thought, feeling deeply sorry for the young women.

'I have a place here for you, Jesse,' Florence said, sitting and patting the eiderdown next to her.

'This will do as well as any,' Jesse said, giving her a reassuring smile. 'I must say I didn't expect my night to be interrupted in such a way when I retired to my bed.'

A couple of the servants tittered, no doubt, Florence thought, relieved to be able to release some of their current emotions.

Once Jesse was settled, she forced a smile, determined to put her servants at ease as much as she possibly could with the heavy dull thrum of the Zeppelin engines sounding closer than ever now. 'We must all try to be brave,' she said, hoping her own fear didn't show in her voice. 'Hopefully, we shan't be down here for very long and can return to our warm beds.'

'What's that you have over there, Mrs Rudge?' Jesse asked watching her setting out the biscuits and drinks on an old sideboard.

'Cook has cleverly thought to bring us all—' Florence

realised she didn't know what was in the jug. She gave Cook an inquisitive look. 'I'm sorry, what was it that you've brought for us?'

Mrs Rudge clasped her hands together in front of her looking pleased to have her thoughtfulness acknowledged in front of everyone. 'I have some nice cool milk and biscuits for everyone.'

'Well,' Jesse said, smiling. 'I, for one, am incredibly grateful. I find that now I'm fully awake I'm rather thirsty and as you know, Mrs Rudge, I can always enjoy one of your tasty biscuits.'

Florence put her arm around Jesse's waist. She knew she could always trust him to try to take charge of a difficult situation as he was now. She was relieved her children and grandchildren weren't with them right now and hoped that their homes were safe enough away from the route the Zeppelin pilot had planned to follow. But if she had to meet her Maker then she would want to do it by Jesse's side. She hoped that their being down here with the entire household gave the servants some solace.

'Mavis,' Mrs Rudge said, spotting her kitchen maid ashen-faced in the corner next to Ethel. 'You can come here and make yourself useful. Hand out glasses of milk. And, Ethel, you can take the tin of biscuits around. It'll do you both good to keep busy. It's no good fretting about something we cannot do anything about.'

'And we should all be safe down here,' Florence added, her last word barely leaving her lips when the whole house shuddered at a nearby explosion.

Ethel screamed and almost dropped the biscuit tin. William, the first footman, leant towards her and took the tin from her grasp. 'You go and sit back down. We don't need you dropping these, especially not if we're to sit here for hours and they're all we're going to have to eat.'

Florence didn't like him snapping at the frightened girl but didn't say anything. She assumed that although his reaction was one of anger it was most likely his way of expressing his own fear. Right now all she wanted to do was cling on to Jesse but it wouldn't be seemly so she sat as decorously as she could manage with just an arm resting lightly around his back and the other on his left arm.

'I wonder where that landed?' Jesse whispered. 'I hope no one's been hurt.'

'So do I.' She willed the Zeppelin to pass over soon so that they could all relax once again. How many other people were trembling in their homes right now? she wondered. She had heard that Londoners had taken to going in the Underground stations during Zeppelin raids. She wasn't surprised. It seemed like an excellent idea to her right now.

There was a collective groan as the house shuddered once again as another nearby bomb exploded.

'I think that was slightly further away,' Jesse said. 'What do you think, Meadows? George?'

'Yes, Sir,' they both agreed.

What a relief, Florence thought. She waited for another ten minutes then, unable to sit still any longer, said, 'I think we can probably return to our rooms now. At least we know the drill if there's another raid tonight.'

'I doubt there'll be another following the same route though, don't you?' Jesse asked. 'Why waste bombs on targets you've already hit?'

He made sense. Florence watched as George carefully lifted Jesse and with Meadows's help took him back upstairs.

'Off you go, everyone,' Florence said. 'Back to your beds. Try your best to get some sleep.'

She watched them leave the cellar, but before following everyone else, decided that this might be the only time she would have sight of a Zeppelin airship. She glanced at the door again to check everyone had gone and then, unlocking the door to the back garden, opened it, and stepped tentatively outside.

Florence followed the sound of the airship and peered up into the night's sky. She gasped. Light from the ground shone up at the enormous silver cigar-shaped Zeppelin. It was like nothing she had ever seen before. Oh, she had seen pictures in newspapers like everyone else, but until now, Florence thought stunned, she had never appreciated the sheer size of the things that caused so much terror to the people of Britain. She watched for a few minutes before stepping back inside the cellar.

'And I never want to see another one again,' she said to herself, shocked by the experience she had just had.

She closed the back door and locked it, then, seeing that one of the maids must have taken Jesse's eiderdown back upstairs, followed the others out of the cellar. Mrs Rudge was putting the milk jug away and wiping the sides. Florence suspected this was her way of calming down after the frightening evening she had just experienced.

'Please don't worry too much, Cook,' Florence said. 'I'd rather you returned to your bed and managed to get some sleep tonight.'

Mrs Rudge stopped cleaning. Then, wiping her hands on a hand towel, she sighed. 'You're right, of course, Lady Boot. I think I'm just a little overwrought, that's all.'

'Then you definitely need to go back to your bed.'

'Yes, I think I do.'

'Good night, Mrs Rudge. And thank you for all that you did tonight. I really appreciate it.'

Florence left the shaken woman and went back upstairs to Jesse's room, where he was already in bed, his eiderdown back on top of his bedclothes, waiting for her to wish him good night.

'Well, that was a new experience, wasn't it?' he asked, his eyes twinkling mischievously.

Florence suspected that now they were all safe and well he was finding the unexpected adventure rather exciting. She went over to him and kissed him. 'Yes, it was. And it's not one I care to repeat.'

'I'll agree with you there.'

As she settled down in her bed Florence couldn't help thinking of the people that might be caught up in the frightening bombing raid. Her thoughts straying to Agnes Tweed and her sister, Florence prayed that no one had been injured or killed this time. She had been lucky so far that no one in her family had been hurt, or worse. She shuddered at the thought and quickly pushed it away. It dawned on her that while she had been fretting about John and Margery away at war, the rest of her family and her granddaughters were no longer as safe as she had imagined now that the war had come to Britain. She stared at the walls, the rose-patterned wallpaper she loved so much impossible to see in the darkness. Would this war never end? she wondered anxiously. And, if it did, would her family survive it intact?

Chapter Nineteen

Florence arrived at work the following morning. She had gone ahead of Jesse for once, wanting him to sleep a little longer while she stopped by Margaret and Dorothy's homes to check that they and their little girls were safe and well. He needed to catch up with a little of the sleep he had lost the night before. Relieved to know that those closest to her were fine, she rushed to the Pelham Street store to check that there had been no damage caused by the bombing raid seven hours earlier.

Florence stepped out of her car and stood facing the shop front, studying it to see if there was any obvious damage to the red-brick building. She sighed with relief, noting that there didn't seem to be anything.

She entered the store and, as she walked past the counters and bid her staff her usual good mornings, couldn't help sensing that the mood was rather sombre. She wasn't surprised. After all, she thought, most of the area must have had their night's sleep interrupted. She herself felt a little worse for wear after the frightening sight and sound of that enormous airship and the bombs exploding.

She supposed Jesse would be reading out reports from the newspapers later in the day and hoped that there hadn't been any fatalities. Florence reached her office to be met by Enid ready with a cup of tea and the early morning post opened and sorted by her assistant secretary, ready for Florence to read through and draft her replies.

'Were you disturbed by that horrendous raid last night?' Florence asked, taking off her coat and hanging it up then unpinning her hat and doing the same with that. She sat at her desk and waited for Enid to finish placing the tea and post on her desk and reply to her question.

'We were, Lady Boot,' she said.

Florence noticed dark circles under the girl's pale eyes. 'Sit down, Enid,' she said gently. 'Are you all right this morning?'

Enid gave her question some thought. 'Just a little tired, that's all.'

'And your mother?'

Enid nodded. 'We're fine. Thank you.'

Florence knew something was wrong and that Enid would never like to burden her with anything from her personal life. She wished it wasn't the case. She valued Enid's loyalty even if she had not turned out to be as efficient as either Miss Tweed or Gladys, and wished she was more comfortable confiding in her.

Surely, her instincts were not wrong on this? 'I can tell

there's something the matter though,' Florence said. 'Please won't you tell me what it is? Maybe I can be of some help.'

Enid pressed her right hand against her chest. Florence wasn't sure if it was to steady herself or because she had a lot to say. 'We're fine, Lady Boot, but our neighbours four doors down were killed in the raid.' Florence frowned. 'That is, the husband and son were. The mother and daughter were taken to hospital with cuts and bruising and I believe they'll be all right.'

'Physically, maybe,' Florence said thoughtfully. 'I'm not sure what this sort of shock will do to their minds though. Do you know if they have somewhere to go and stay? If they have any other family who can take them in?'

'I've seen an older lady and another woman Mrs Cooper's age coming to the house on Sundays and high days sometimes,' Enid said. 'I assumed they were Mrs Cooper's mother and sister, or maybe they were related to Mr Cooper's side of the family. I'm not certain.'

Florence was determined to help in any way she could and her first instinct was to go and visit the woman in hospital, but as she thought about doing so it occurred to her that maybe this grieving widow would not welcome a stranger, however well-meaning, to visit her at her hospital bed.

'Enid, how well do you know your neighbours?' When her secretary seemed confused, Florence added, 'That is, would you feel comfortable going to visit Mrs Cooper in the hospital to speak to her on my behalf?'

Enid seemed surprised at Florence's request. Then,

gathering herself, she nodded. 'Yes, I'd be very happy to do that, Lady Boot. What would you like me to say to her?'

Florence thought for a few seconds. 'I think the first thing to do is to send my commiserations for her terrible loss. Then maybe take her some flowers and fruit from Sir Jesse and me. Mostly I'd like you to ascertain if they have anywhere to go after she and her daughter are discharged from hospital.' She watched Enid noting down all she was saying. 'Also, if there's anything at all that they need.' She sighed, trying to keep her emotions in check. The thought of losing a son and a husband was almost too terrible for her to contemplate. 'Maybe to gauge if she needs help paying for the funerals. That sort of thing. Whatever you think. Please let me know and we can talk about it tomorrow and then work something out.'

Enid laid her right hand on her chest. 'Oh, Lady Boot, you really are the most generous person. Truly.'

Florence didn't want appreciation for what she was doing. 'Not at all. I'm just in the lucky position of being able to help others when they need it most. It will give me an awful lot of satisfaction to know I've helped Mrs Cooper and her daughter. She won't be the only one benefitting from whatever it is that I do for her.'

'Still, though,' Enid said, uncharacteristically speaking without being asked for her opinion, 'I think it's a wonderful thing for you to do. So very caring.'

Florence raised her hand and shook her head. 'Nonsense. Now, if you find out the visiting hours and then, probably not today as it'll be too soon and her family will probably want to go and see her, but maybe tomorrow or the next day, if you visit her then you can tell me what you think.'

Florence was shocked to discover that there was nothing about the bombing in the local papers. 'How strange,' she said to Jesse over a light lunch that she had arranged to be delivered to his office at midday. 'You'd think there would be columns of reporting about what happened last night. It must have affected many people.'

'I thought the same thing,' Jesse said, wiping his mouth after finishing his chicken salad. 'But then I suspect the government might have put an embargo on the story.'

'But why would they do that?' It didn't make any sense, she decided.

'I don't know but I would think that the shock of being bombed in our beds is enough to terrify the population. Maybe the government think that to read about the horrors in the papers will lower people's morale. They could be right.'

When he put it like that, Florence mused, she could understand the motive behind the restrictions. 'But how are we supposed to know who has suffered at the hands of these bombers and be able to help them?'

'I have no idea, my love.' He smiled at her. 'I believe though that the local grapevine will soon tell us all that we need to know. People talk regardless of what the newspapers do or do not report.'

'Yes, that's true.' She was relieved. It might take days but they would end up hearing at least some of what had occurred the previous night and then they could create a plan for helping any families or individuals that needed them to do so.

Half an hour later, Florence welcomed Lily into her office. She could see that her friend was concerned about something. 'Please don't tell me that one of your girls has been hurt in that awful raid last night.'

Lily tilted her head. 'Only one and she has a few cuts, nothing more. She is very shocked though.'

Florence motioned for her friend to take a seat and called for Enid to bring some tea for them. 'Tell me.'

'The house where she boards has been badly damaged by one of the explosions. I'm told that no one was hurt but she's having to move out because the property will need extensive repairs before it's habitable again,' Lily explained. 'I gather that no one was killed and that she is able to move in with her brother's family but she's rather shaken.'

'Have you sent her home to her brother's?'

'I have.'

'Good. If you let me have the brother's address, I'll call in on her and take a hamper of food for them.'

'That's very kind of you, Florence. I'm sure they'll be grateful, what with the shortages and having an extra mouth to feed.'

Florence listened to her friend but was more focused on the dark circles under her eyes than on what she was saying. 'And you, my friend, how are you keeping?'

Lily sighed. 'I'm fine, although a little tired. My sister is now engaged to be married and was still out last night when the raid occurred. I'm afraid I was rather frantic worrying about her, but she finally arrived home shortly after it ended. I have to admit I lost my temper with her a little.'

She looked so sad that Florence wanted to console her. 'Well, that's hardly surprising. You must have been beside yourself with all that destruction going on and not knowing where your sister was.' Florence reached out across her desk and patted her friend's hand before sitting back down. 'I'm sure she'll understand once she has time to reflect on what she did and how that must have made you feel.'

Lily sighed miserably. 'I do hope so. We usually get along ever so well, and I would hate for that to change.'

'Your brother, how is he?'

'He's fine. I don't think he'll ever marry and to be honest it's pleasant sharing the cottage with him. I know I was never interested in marrying but it is nice to have someone to talk to and share supper with each evening.'

Florence realised she had never spent evenings alone. Or at least not completely alone. Even if Jesse had been unwell and upstairs eating supper in his room, she had asked for hers to be served in there, too, so that they could spend the time together.

'I'm glad you have some of your family living here with you, Lily. We all need family sometimes, or close friends with whom we can spend time talking about our days.' She thought of all the women who were now alone since their husbands had been killed since the beginning of the war. How strange life was sometimes, she marvelled. Last night they were all hiding in a cellar to try to avoid mass slaughter and today she was back at work trying not to fret about her daughter working hard to look after the many wounded soldiers who passed daily through her canteen, while at home her other two children were raising their small families. The range of emotions coursing through her was tiring but she was relieved and happy.

'It makes me wonder at life sometimes,' Florence admitted, thoughtfully.

'What exactly?'

'How no matter what horrors some are experiencing, or how close to death others are, life simply goes on.' Florence shook her head. It really was quite exhausting. 'I'm grateful my children live nearby and that I am able to visit my granddaughters when I wish to.' She then pictured Margery working hard in her canteen, surrounded by soldiers who were in pain and desperate to return home. 'It's such a strange time right now, isn't it?'

'You're not wrong there, Florence.'

The next day, Florence went to Jesse's office before leaving to go and visit Lily's shop assistant with a hamper of food.

'I've been told,' Jesse said, 'that when the sirens began most of the city immediately turned off lights yet for some strange reason the railway companies didn't do so.'

Florence thought of the passengers travelling. 'Maybe it was because they were concerned that passengers might fall and hurt themselves if they couldn't see where they were going?'

'Whatever their reasoning,' he said, 'it meant that the Zeppelin pilot could see them and then knew they would hit their target when they dropped their bombs. The porter also told me that bombs were dropped on Eastcroft, through the Meadows to Midland Station. They hit Haddon's factory in Carrington Street and a warehouse in Lister Gate before making their way to Victoria Station, where, thankfully, the damage was restricted to broken windows.'

Florence was shocked. To think that the airship could do such damage and from the sky too. How could they ever be safe from such a monstrous event?

'I'm also told that the Methodist church on Canaan Street was set on fire by an incendiary bomb. So much destruction.'

'It is shocking, but bricks and mortar can be replaced,' Florence said, thinking how devastated she and Jesse would be should one of their properties be destroyed. 'What about the people? Were there any casualties that you know of that we might be able to help?'

Jesse rubbed his tired eyes with the back of his hands. 'I'm told that there have been a few, yes. All we can hope is that they were asleep and didn't suffer.'

Florence thought again of Miss Tweed and her sister as she had done just after the bombing. She thought it highly improbable that anyone could sleep through a bombing but didn't want to upset Jesse further by suggesting that might be the case. She gave his shoulder a comforting squeeze. 'I'm sure that if we do hear of anyone we can then decide if there is a way that we could help them, or at least send them whatever they need to help them in some way.'

He raised his hand to rest lightly on hers. 'You're a thoughtful person, my dear. These are such troubling times. I can't help thinking how lucky we are to live in such a big house with a cellar where we can go at a moment's notice with our servants.'

'Yes, we are very lucky.' As she spoke, a thought occurred to her: 'We don't have any instructions in place for the staff to follow should there be a daylight raid. We need to work out what each of our shops or factory managers must do to ensure our staff and customers are kept safe should there be one. Don't you agree?'

Jesse opened his mouth to speak then closed it again. 'I do. I can't believe I hadn't thought about doing this already,' he said. 'I'll start making plans while you are out and then we can discuss them later and put them in place as soon as possible.'

The following day, John visited his mother and father at Pelham Street. Florence took one look at him and knew he had come to tell them something they wouldn't like. Her heart pounded rapidly. 'Nothing's wrong with Margaret or any of the family, is it?' she asked before he had time to take off his coat.

He shook his head and kissed her on the cheek. 'No, it's nothing like that.'

'But it is something for me to worry about, isn't it?' She prayed he would disagree, but he simply waited for her to take a seat next to Jesse. 'Go on then, you'd better get this over with before your father or I send ourselves mad panicking over what news you have for us.'

'Yes, do tell us,' Jesse said, irritation obvious in his voice.

'I'm returning to France.'

'What?' Florence couldn't believe what she was hearing. 'But you've been demobbed. Your legs? You can't possibly go back there.'

John pulled back a chair on the opposite side of Jesse's large desk and sat. 'I'm not fighting and will be away from the front lines,' he said, calmly.

His words reassured her slightly but the thought of her son going away again was almost too much. She waited for him to continue.

'I've been given a managerial role at General Headquarters and I'll be leaving in the next week. I'm sorry I didn't say anything about it to you before, but I wanted to be certain first that I was ready and had completed all the training that I needed to do.'

Florence thought back to John's absences and realised she had assumed they were to do with work so hadn't bothered to question them. 'But why would you want to go back there when you can stay working for the company?' She felt breathless at the notion of losing him to the war once more.

'Because as much as I know I'll miss you all, I know that this war won't last forever and I want to be certain that when it is all over I can feel satisfied that I did all I could for my country.'

Jesse mumbled something Florence couldn't quite make out and then added, 'But you can do that from the safety of Nottingham, son. You do valuable work for Boots. Doesn't that mean anything to you?'

John scowled. 'You know it does, Father. But I have to go where my conscience takes me. You've both always instilled that in me, Dorothy and Margery, haven't you?'

He was right, Florence realised. How could they expect him to go against the very virtues they had both brought him up to follow? 'Yes, you're right,' she admitted. 'But it won't stop your father and me from worrying about you.' Florence wondered how much more she could stand of this interminable war. How was she going to bear to lose her son, yet again, to the war effort?

'You have to do as you see fit,' Jesse said. 'Naturally, your mother and I will be worried for you until you return, but we can't argue with what you're doing.' He turned to Florence. 'Can we, dear? Although I know we both wish to.'

'When do you go?' she asked, hoping it wouldn't be too soon.

'Tomorrow, I'm afraid.'

It was too soon, but what could she do? Florence hated the thought of him leaving again but to drag it out would be painful, she knew that much. She stood and opened her arms. 'Then, I wish you well,' she said, 'but you have to promise me that you will stay safe and come back to us as soon as you possibly can.'

'I will be back before you know it,' he said.

Florence knew that was impossible but hoped it wouldn't be too long until John returned home. She couldn't believe the war was taking her son from her again. How long could his luck possibly last? Dare she hope that her own good fortune would last long enough for him to return to them unscathed once more?

Florence thought of other women bidding farewell to their sons as she was doing now, and how they had struggled with their loss when those sons had failed to return. Could her turn be coming?

Chapter Twenty

October 1916

The following week, Florence was about to meet with the manageress of the Gas Mask Department when Lily brought in an envelope. 'Joseph Meadows delivered this letter from your home a moment ago. He said you would want to read it immediately as it's from Margery.'

Florence smiled, gratefully. 'Thank you for bringing it in to me.'

As soon as she was alone, she slid her silver letter opener through the fold at the top and withdrew a sheet of paper. She unfolded it and gazed at her daughter's neat handwriting.

30 September 1916

France

Sir Jesse and Lady Boot
St Heliers House
The Park
Nottingham

Darling Mother and Father,

I'm writing in the hope that you are both well and not too shocked after the Zeppelin bombing in Nottingham the other night. I heard the news from one of the other girls whose parents had written telling them about the incident and then John wrote to me to let me know you were both fine. He said that he suspected you wouldn't mention it to me hoping not to worry me. Please don't be cross with him for doing so, I'm glad he did. We hear news from home all the time and I would rather know what happened and that you were both safe than not hear anything at all and make up my own assumptions.

It's strange to think that all this time you've been concerned for my welfare and now the danger is coming closer to home and the tables appear to have turned somewhat. I'll have to trust that you are both safe and know that you will have already made plans for what to do in case of another similar attack. I love my work but miss you both all the time and it's at times like these when I truly wish I was back at home with you and seeing for myself that you are both safe and well.

I know you will want to know how I am. All I can say is that we've had a difficult time of it lately. The number of injured men seems to continually be on the increase and we are rather more stretched than we're used to being. I don't know if I'm being more sensitive than usual but it's troubling me more than ever to see so many men, especially those of my age and younger, with life-changing injuries. I worry that the futures they might have once imagined will now no longer be possible. However, when I become morose I remind myself that I am one of the lucky ones and it's my job to help soothe and cheer them.

Before I forget, I want to thank you for the extra supplies you shipped to us recently, they were much needed and their arrival very timely.

We have had to move our canteen several times since we first arrived in Northern France. The front lines move often and we have to move with them to stay out of harm's way and also to be as much help as we can. The result is that I'm rather tired and although at times it's difficult to keep my spirits up, I'm rarely alone long enough to ponder on the situation and whenever I'm down one of my colleagues will find a way to cheer me up.

They're a good bunch and we are all very supportive of each other, so please don't fret on my account.

I can hear another train pulling into the station bringing more soldiers. They'll be needing our attention so I had better press on.

My love to you both.
As ever, your loving daughter, Margery

Florence breathed in the scent of the paper, hoping it would bring her closer to her daughter, but couldn't pick up anything familiar. Then, folding the letter, she placed it back into the envelope and put it into her bag to show to Jesse later. Margery was right. It was strange that after all this time worrying about their daughter, Margery was now concerned for their welfare. Florence determined to reply to her letter as soon as her next meeting was over. She didn't want her daughter to worry about her and Jesse needlessly.

She checked her hair was neat and left her office for the factory to meet her manageress. It was something she liked to do as often as possible, believing that visits to her staff encouraged her girls to remember that she was working as hard as them. They needed to push themselves to produce as many of the small box respirators as they could, and her continued presence and support always seemed to help achieve the numbers that were necessary each week. Jesse was busy working on the emergency bombing raid plans which were coming together well. He had the senior managers from each shop and factory working on their own plans to send them to him as a matter of urgency.

Florence spotted one of the newer recruits to whom she had given a job only a week before. 'Good morning.' The girl looked up at Florence from under her eyelashes and said something she could barely hear. 'Tell me, how are you getting along in here? I hope the girls are all looking after you and helping you settle in?' Florence gave a friendly smile to the other women. 'I'm told this is one of the busier departments to work in and that the production is increasing most weeks.'

The girl barely looked Florence in the eyes but nodded. 'It is busy, but I'm really enjoying being part of the team I work on, Lady Boot. Thank you.'

'Good, I'm glad.' Florence gave an approving look at the manageress. 'All seems to be running very well here, as usual.'

'It is, Lady Boot. The girls are all hard workers.'

Florence noticed that the new girl was still waiting for permission to return to work. 'Thank you. Please carry on with what you were doing.'

They walked on to the next row of women working hard, their fingers quick and dextrous as they put together the pieces on the station where they were standing. Florence bid a few of them a good morning and passed the time of day before continuing with the manageress.

'I note from the reports that this department's output is extremely high. I must commend you for that. Thank you. These masks are desperately needed by our boys at the Front and the sooner we can provide our Forces with them, the fewer men will be killed in gas attacks.'

'Yes, Lady Boot. I think the reason these girls work extra hard is because a lot of them have loved ones fighting. It's an added incentive and those that don't, well, they simply want to do as much as they can to help the war effort.'

'Well, they're all doing a marvellous job.' She stopped at the door before leaving. 'Girls, I want to thank you for all your wonderful efforts,' she said wanting to induce them to achieve more. 'Reports coming from this department are truly first class and my husband and I are grateful to you all for your hard work to support Britain's war effort. You might not be able to fight on the battlefields, but you are playing a vital part in what you do. Thanks to you and your efforts many men will be returning to their families who otherwise might not, and I thank you for all that you do.'

'Thank you, Lady Boot,' one of the girls called out. Then another and another, until all Florence could hear were the women cheering for her. Her throat tightened to hear them thanking her when all she had done was give them the chance to produce vital war supplies and praise their efforts.

Florence visited a couple more departments and then returned to the Pelham Street store. As she neared the staircase, she overheard one of the girls saying something and caught the name 'Lightbody'. Florence recognised the voice as Bridie, one of her younger girls and, by the sombre tone in Bridie's voice, Florence gleaned that whatever she was saying, it wasn't happy news. Florence immediately called her over to a quiet area.

Bridie looked unsure why she was receiving Florence's attention but walked over to her side. 'Yes, Lady Boot?'

'I overheard you mention the name Lightbody just now.'

Florence kept her voice low so that no one could hear what she was saying.

'Yes, that's correct.'

'If it's not too much of a personal issue, may I enquire what it was you were discussing?' Wishing to make herself clearer, she added, 'That is, were you referring to Gladys Lightbody, by any chance?' Florence waited for the girl to reply and hoped that Gladys was all right.

'Gladys is one of my neighbours,' she said quietly.

'She is?' Florence could tell Bridie wasn't sure how to put across what she had been saying to her colleague moments earlier. 'Please, go on.'

She watched for a few seconds as the girl gave some thought to what she needed to say. 'It's just that Private Marsh, that's Gladys's husband, Cyril, was killed a couple of weeks ago.'

Florence gasped, horrified to think that Gladys's life as a wife had lasted such a short time.

'I'm sorry, I can't help thinking of her as anything but Gladys Lightbody. She'd be mad if she knew. She did love her Cyril so.' Bridie cast her gaze down at the floor. 'They were devoted to each other, those two. Cyril was the only man for Gladys, my mum says. Thankfully, they were living with her widowed mum, so Gladys has someone to look after her.' She looked back up at Florence, her eyes filled with unshed tears. 'Oh, Lady Boot, it's horrible to see her so broken. I'm sorry, I know I shouldn't have been talking about her during work hours, but I'm that worried for her. I was hoping my colleague might have an idea how to help Gladys.'

'Not at all, Bridie. I'm glad you were speaking about Gladys. She needs her friends right now.'

Florence thought back to the happy girl she had bid farewell to after presenting her with a bible only the year before. Her heart ached for Gladys and all the wives like her who had lost their men. She rested a hand on Bridie's shoulder to comfort her. 'You leave this with me,' Florence said quietly. 'I'll pay Gladys a visit this afternoon and see if there's anything at all that I can do to help.'

The girl brightened visibly. 'Oh, would you Lady Boot? I know a visit from you would cheer her up no end.'

Florence sighed. 'I'm not so sure about that but, if there is anything I can do to help her, I certainly will make sure that I do it.' She smiled at Bridie. 'Thank you for confiding in me. I'm grateful to know how things stand. Now, I'd better get on.' She spotted two customers at the counter and indicated them with a tilt of her head. 'I think that, by the looks of things, so must you.'

Bridie rushed off and Florence hurried back to her office. She closed the door and leant against it for a moment, shaken to think of Gladys's monumental loss.

Moments later, when Florence was seated back at her desk, Lily knocked once and walked in carrying a cup of tea and two digestive biscuits. She put down the cup and frowned. 'Is something the matter, Florence?'

Florence lowered her face into her hands and closed her eyes for a few seconds. Then, opening them again, she looked across to her friend. 'It's Gladys Lightbody: I've just been told that she's lost her husband.' She struggled to believe that the young woman was now a widow. 'I keep thinking how excited she was to be marrying her Cyril. This war is making widows of far too many young women. So many haven't even had a chance to start families.' Anger coursed through her. 'It's all so cruel and heart-breaking.'

'It is.'

'I'm going to see her this afternoon, to make sure she's coping. Would you mind going down and preparing a hamper for me with food, a tonic and maybe a few books from the lending library? I'll take them to her this afternoon.'

'Of course,' Lily replied. She walked to the office door, her step faltering before she opened it.

Florence noticed and wondered what was worrying her. 'What's the matter?'

Lily looked over at her for a couple of seconds and then shook her head. 'It's nothing. I'll go and arrange that hamper for you now.'

Florence wasn't sure what Lily had been thinking, but soon forgot about her reaction and going to her cabinets searched for Gladys's home address. She decided not to send notice ahead that she would like to see Gladys, in case her ex-secretary panicked about Florence visiting her at home.

She knew from experience that many of her staff found it disconcerting if Florence popped in. Some of them were embarrassed by their homes, but Florence hoped that she soon put them at their ease. Hadn't she been raised in a small flat above a shop? She hadn't always been a Lady and even if others didn't know or forgot her roots, Florence never did. She was proud of her parents and where she had come from and certainly would never judge others by their misfortune or even their fortunate start in life. No, Florence thought, she judged people by how they acted and how they treated others. If they were decent, caring people then they were acceptable as far as she was concerned.

Florence told her driver the address of the house she was visiting and spent the short drive to Gladys's home thinking through what she wanted to say to the young widow. All she really wanted was to find a way to help Gladys in some way, however small. The car stopped in front of a tiny terraced house.

'This is it, Lady Boot.' Her driver got out of the car and opened Florence's door. Then, lifting the hamper from the back, he followed her the couple of steps to the front door.

Florence knocked and, seconds later, she heard footsteps and the door was opened by an elderly lady who Florence assumed must be Gladys's mother. The tired eyes opened wider when she spotted Florence standing on her doorstep.

Florence was used to this reaction. She extended her gloved hand for the woman to shake. 'Good afternoon. Mrs Lightbody, I presume?'

'Y-yes, that's me.' The woman frantically wiped her hands with her apron before reaching out and taking Florence's hand in her trembling one.

'I'm Lady Boot. Your daughter Gladys used to be my

secretary.' She kept her voice quiet, not wishing to disconcert the woman.

'Yes. I, er... Is there something I can do for you, Lady Boot?'

'I apologise for coming to your home unannounced. I hope you don't mind, but I was hoping to have a quick word with your daughter? Would that be all right?' Florence realised she might have to admit to knowing Gladys's sad situation. 'One of the girls at Pelham Street alerted me to Gladys's dreadful news and I wanted to convey my and my husband's condolences to her.'

Mrs Lightbody's eyes welled up. She stepped back and waved Florence inside. 'What am I like, leaving you standing on the doorstep and not inviting you in? Please, do come in and I'll call for Gladys.' She seemed to notice the driver for the first time.

'Please, don't mind my driver. He's only stopping long enough to carry a small hamper of things I thought you and Gladys might make use of. Just a small gesture from my husband and I.'

Mrs Lightbody visibly brightened. 'Well, I must say that's very kind of you, Lady Boot. If you'll both please follow me through to the parlour, I'll call for Gladys.'

Florence walked into the room with its dark Victorian wallpaper and sat down on the sofa when her hostess indicated for her to do so. She watched the woman leave the room and asked her driver to leave the hamper on the table. As soon as he had done so, he left the house to wait outside for her in the car.

Florence studied the room. It was spotless and she couldn't help wondering how often it was used. Not very, she thought, imagining the family gathering here on holidays and high days. Such a waste of an extra room in a small house but everyone seemed to keep their front rooms for best.

She heard footsteps and Gladys's voice murmuring something to her mother.

'Lady Boot,' Gladys said, her eyes puffy as she tried to give Florence a welcoming smile from the parlour-room door. 'I'm sorry, you find me in a little bit of a muddle. I hadn't realised you were coming by.'

Her mother entered after her. 'Lady Boot has kindly come to see how you are, Gladys. Look at the gift she's brought you.'

Gladys's red-rimmed eyes moved from Florence's to the hamper. 'That's very kind of you, Lady Boot. Really, it is.'

Her mother looked from one to the other of them. 'May I offer you tea, Lady Boot?'

Florence was so taken aback by the change in her once vibrant secretary that she took a moment to be able to answer.

'That's very kind of you, Mrs Lightbody,' she said. 'But, no, thank you. I don't wish to intrude on you both for long. I have to be elsewhere this afternoon but wanted to call in on my way there.'

'I'll leave you both to it, then. Thank you again for your thoughtfulness,' Gladys's mother said. 'We really do appreciate you taking the time to come and visit us.' She gave Florence a brief nod and left the room, closing the door quietly behind her.

Florence turned her attention to her ex-secretary. It was heart-breaking to see how her sorrow had diminished Gladys so badly. The already slim girl was now a bag of bones and Florence hoped that some of the tasty treats Lily had included in the hamper might encourage her to eat. For once, Florence was lost for words. She thought of John's wife and how badly she would take the news that John wouldn't be returning and wished for the hundredth time that he hadn't returned to France. Poor Gladys represented all the women that must be going through heartache at the moment. Florence wondered when she could expect to see her son again now that he was back in France. All she really wanted to do was go home to her room and sob for the future this poor girl and thousands of others had lost. But, she thought, this visit wasn't about her, it was about Gladys.

As much as she didn't want to bring up the death of Private Marsh, she had little choice, if she was going to try to find a way for the girl to move on. Then it dawned on Florence what Lily had been about to say to her in her office. She could offer Gladys her old job back. She would be entitled to a small Army pension for the loss of her husband, but Gladys would need more than that to be able to take care of her and her mother. Florence would see how their conversation went and work out whether she should make Gladys the offer of work.

Florence cleared her throat. 'I was dreadfully sorry to

hear about your tragic loss, as are your friends and colleagues at Boots. How are you doing, Gladys?'

Fresh tears ran silently down Gladys's face. For the first time, Florence saw that Gladys was gripping a handkerchief in her hands. She watched as the girl dabbed at her eyes then wiped her nose.

'I'm so sorry, Lady Boot. I know this isn't the way to behave in front of a Lady, but I can't seem to help myself.'

'Now, don't you worry about that, my dear. You cry, if that's what you need to do.'

Gladys sniffed. 'Thank you. You're always so kind. My mother and I are extremely grateful for the hamper. I can imagine it's full of beautiful and tasty things.'

It was. Florence had checked it and repacked it before leaving her office. She had also gone down to the shop floor and picked up a few extra treats to add to it: a box of soaps, cold cream and some hand cream. However dreadful the world was, a beautiful scented cream always seemed to help her, if only minutely.

'It's my pleasure.'

Gladys looked at her hands. 'I know I must look dreadful to you. I've found it difficult to eat since,' she hesitated, 'I heard the news about my Cyril. I know that sitting here wallowing each day doesn't help.' She looked up at Florence and for the first time Florence saw a determination behind the blue eyes. 'I've always been so busy, you see. It was one thing giving up work to be a wife, but now I feel like I'm just whiling away my days, and to what end? It isn't like I have anything to plan for, not now

Cyril isn't coming back to me. I may as well force myself to accept that, but I think it would be easier if I had something to keep me busy.'

Florence wasn't sure, but she suspected Gladys was asking her for a job. 'Do you want to return to work so soon?'

Gladys shrugged. 'I do, but Mum keeps telling me it's not necessary. She insists we'll find a way to manage.' She shook her head. 'Mum's rather old-fashioned, you see. She believes I should be in mourning for at least six months.'

Florence believed that everyone had their own way of coping with grief. 'And what do you believe?'

Gladys brushed away a stray tear from her gaunt cheek. 'I want—' She stopped. 'No, I need to go out to work, Lady Boot. Half the time, I feel as if I'm losing my mind being enclosed in this house day after day.' Florence wasn't surprised. If she lost her precious son and had to spend her days sitting at home she would lose her mind, too. 'I'm used to working with people. I need to find a job.' She took a deep breath. 'I know it's impertinent of me to ask when you've been kind enough to come and pay us a visit, and with a beautiful gift, too, but do you mind me asking you?'

'If I can find you work, you mean? Of course I don't.'

Gladys closed her eyes and sighed heavily. 'Thank you. Really. You don't know how much I appreciate you saying that. I don't mind what it is, or even the wage, I just need to keep busy.'

Florence understood. She might not have suffered a loss like Gladys but whenever her life had taken a turn for the worse – when John had run off to Canada that time, his return to France more recently, Jesse's bouts in hospital when his health failed him, Margery leaving for France to run her canteen – Florence had always been able to cope by focusing all her attention and energy on her work.

'You might not believe me when I say this, Gladys,' Florence began, 'but I did only come here to see how you were and bring the hamper to you. However, I would dearly love for you to return to work, as my secretary.' She raised her hand on seeing Gladys's surprise. 'Only if you feel you're up to it, that is. If you'd rather I find you an easier job, then I'm happy to do that.'

Gladys's mouth fell open for a second. 'I don't understand. What about my replacement?'

'Enid is a decent, hard-working girl, but she is much happier in an assistant secretarial role and has found it rather difficult to keep up with all I've thrown at her since you left.'

Gladys gazed at Florence, thoughtfully, her eyes brighter than they had been. 'Then who is acting as your secretary right now?'

'Someone you know. Miss Buttons, from Number Two department. I asked her to step in after Enid spoke to me about how she was struggling, and she kindly agreed. Miss Buttons prefers working on the shop floor. She is desperate to return to running the department.'

'Are you telling me that I could have my old job back, Lady Boot? Right now? And I wouldn't be stepping on anyone else's toes? Because I would hate to do that.'

'That is exactly what I am telling you, Gladys.' Satisfied that she had at least brightened the young widow's world for that day, Florence stood. 'I'll leave you to think about my offer. I think you had better discuss it with your mother, first. I don't want to cause any friction between the two of you. Let me know what you wish to do when you're ready.'

Gladys got to her feet slowly as if in a trance. 'I can't tell you how happy you've made me, Lady Boot. I don't need to think about your offer. The answer is yes, and I'll start as soon as you like.'

Florence smiled. 'I am very happy to hear that. However, I think it might be better if you spoke to your mother first.'

Gladys shook her head. 'It'll be fine. My mother is only trying to be protective of me. She knew how much I loved working for you and how sad it made me to have to leave. I'll explain how much I want to go back to working for you at Boots and I know she'll give me her blessing. I know she will.'

'Then, shall we say that, unless I hear otherwise, I'll expect you to start next Monday? Unless, of course, you'd like a bit longer?'

Gladys didn't attempt to hide her delight. 'No, that's more than enough time. Next Monday it is.'

As Florence sat in the back of her car on her way home, she thought of how delighted Gladys had been to be offered her job back. She knew that Lily would be relieved to know she could return to her colleagues in her own department, and Florence could relax her search for Lily's replacement and focus on the many other items waiting for her in her diary. She gazed out of the window at the passing pedestrians and vehicles and felt a tug to her heart as she thought how poor Private Cyril Marsh's death had meant that her own working day would improve drastically. It didn't seem fair somehow, and despite having no hand in his demise Florence couldn't help feeling a pang of guilt.

Chapter Twenty-One

December 1916

The past few months had been traumatic for all of them. Who could have foretold that we would still be suffering such global hardships? Florence thought, struggling to come to terms with the fact that yet another year had almost passed them by. Those of her family who were in Nottingham had left the day before after joining her and Jesse at St Heliers to celebrate a quiet family Christmas. Initially, Florence had expected Dorothy, her husband and baby Nancy, as well as John's wife Margaret and their baby daughter Barbara, but at the very last minute, as they were bidding each other a good night to leave the drawing room to retire to their bedrooms on Christmas Eve, John arrived at St Heliers to surprise them, having returned from France.

Florence had just reached the third step on the staircase going up to her room when she, Margaret and Dorothy heard the distinct sound of a car engine drawing up outside the house. They glanced at each other questioningly and then Florence looked down to the hallway where George was about to pick Jesse up from his chair to take him upstairs.

'Who on earth could that be?' Florence asked. 'It's nearly ten o'clock.' Her heart raced as it dawned on her that whoever was here could be bringing bad news. She turned and ran downstairs, reaching the door just before Meadows arrived and the doorbell rang.

'Thank you, Meadows,' she said raising her chin and bracing herself to greet whoever was on the other side of the front door.

Meadows pulled open the door. 'We weren't expecting you, Mr Boot.'

Mr Boot? Florence gasped as Meadows stepped back and John walked in, a wide smile on his gentle face.

'John?' Margaret whispered. Florence made room for her to greet her husband and smiled at Jesse.

'Well, this is the best Christmas present I think any of us could have asked for,' Jesse said, his eyes brighter than usual.

Margaret moved to the side and Florence smiled as her son grinned at her. 'Merry Christmas, Mother. I thought you wouldn't mind an unexpected arrival for the festivities.'

Florence opened her arms and drew John into a tight hug. 'My boy,' she said. 'I don't think I've ever received a more welcome gift than your arrival. Now I know, we'll all have an absolutely wonderful Christmas.'

She watched John as he greeted his sister before putting his arm around Margaret's waist and kissing her cheek. She knew his happiness to be with them was genuine but could not miss the slightly forced cheerfulness and wondered what he might have gone through in the few months since she had last seen him. For now though he was back home and safe. The relief of not having to worry about him even if only for a few days was immense and Florence knew that for the first time since John had told her he had enlisted she would be able to sleep deeply.

'It's marvellous to be back here with you all,' John said. 'Are you all off to bed now?'

'We were,' said Florence, laughing, 'but I doubt that any of us are in a rush to get to our beds just yet. Come through to the living room and I'll ask for some food to be brought to you.'

Having John with them to share their festivities had been the best present Florence could have ever hoped for. The only other gift she would have wished for was if Margery had come home with him. Florence recalled the surprise and then seconds later the joy on John's wife Margaret's face when she turned to see who had arrived at the house so late.

Now, though, they had all finished celebrating their third Christmas during wartime. Florence hoped there wouldn't be a fourth. As with the previous two Christmases Florence had made a point of keeping the celebrations low-key and the presents to a minimum. It didn't feel right somehow having fun and spending a lot of money treating themselves when so many others around the country and elsewhere were grieving for their lost loved ones, sitting by hospital bedsides or waiting for news of those missing in action.

Florence had insisted on holding a muted affair, especially with Margery being away. Thinking of her working so hard in her canteen in Northern France worried her terribly. As much as she was proud of her youngest child, she wished she would consider returning home to Nottingham. If only she could persuade Margery that by helping tens of thousands of wounded soldiers and refugees she had done her bit now, and that maybe it was time to return and find work to do on safer ground. Margery had always been a hard worker when she was at Boots. Florence knew she had enjoyed the camaraderie working in one of the factories. If only her daughter would consider setting up a canteen at a British station, it would be much safer and closer to home. Even as she thought of suggesting her idea to Margery, Florence discounted it, aware that it wouldn't have the same satisfaction for Margery as her work on French soil.

With Christmas now over, Florence was looking forward to the next celebration they were to enjoy as soon as the New Year had begun. She gazed at the letter in her hand addressed to Jesse from King George the Fifth. It was odd to think that the king had placed one hand on this same piece of paper that she was holding in order to sign his signature. To think that her darling Jesse, who had dedicated his life to providing many thousands of people with medicines and other items that they needed, was to become a baronet the next month. It was tremendously exciting, and Florence couldn't help feeling immensely proud of her husband.

Florence sighed. She was in her fifties now and Jesse in his late sixties. She had assumed that Jesse being knighted for his achievements seven years earlier by the then King, Edward the Seventh, would be the highest accolade bestowed on him. Florence had taken a little time to get used to being called Lady Boot. It had been strange to think of her husband as Sir Jesse then, but now he would be Sir Jesse Boot, Baronet. It was a lot to take in.

She thought back to when she had spent her younger days serving customers and dusting shelves as an assistant in her father's shop in Queen Street in Jersey, and how it would never have occurred to her that she would mix with a baronet and his wife, let alone be those people. She gave a laugh, amused at how much her life had changed – beyond anything she had ever dreamt her future to be. At times like these, if she sat quietly and took herself back to those carefree days, she could still almost summon up the young girl she had been, with all the hopes and dreams she had imagined for herself.

How much she had learned over the years since meeting Jesse. She thought of Jesse's reaction to reading this letter and discovering the new honour being bestowed on him.

'Can you believe it, my dear,' she recalled him saying on opening the envelope. 'I'm to be recognised by a second king. And when you think where we've both come from and how far…' He had gone quiet momentarily, his eyes misting over. Then added, 'My mother would be so proud of me right now.'

Florence had kissed him. 'Your mother would be proud of you every day of your life, Jesse. You were an exemplary son. Think how many people, me included, have benefited from all that you've worked to achieve.' She pictured her dear Jesse going to ask for her hand in marriage thirty-three years before and how nervous he had been. Now he was this important man and still he was the same Jesse to her.

'Look at us now,' she murmured to the empty room. Jesse had always been ambitious and never failed to work as hard as he could, which, she thought, was far too hard most of the time. But on the eleventh of January he would be honoured for a second time and her heart swelled with pride for him.

How many thousands of people had he helped over the years simply by employing them in one of his five hundred and sixty plus stores? She thought of the hundreds of thousands of customers to have shopped at their stores or benefitted from the medicines sold in their cash chemists – and now those in the Forces being treated by those medicines, the men in trenches now having a way to sterilise dirty water so that they could drink it safely and those brave men saved from gas attacks by gas masks made at Boots.

Yes, she thought, she was immensely proud of Jesse's hard work – and, if she was honest, hers, too – over the years, finding ways to help others and provide them with medication and pretty things.

Jesse was asleep upstairs, and the staff were downstairs eating their supper. Florence generally enjoyed quiet moments like these, but tonight she couldn't settle down to the book she had chosen from the lending library several days before. She missed having her children living in the house. At least at Christmas John and Dorothy had brought their daughters to play at the house and she and Jesse had sat watching their brood, her hand on his twisted one, enjoying being taken back to a time when they had their own small babies, with so much of their future waiting for them to grasp it and make of it what they wanted.

What to do now though? She wasn't tired, despite having been up since five that morning when Jesse had woken her suffering from a coughing fit. She needed to feel close to one of her children. The two closest to her were in their homes with their families. She would write to the child she currently worried about the most and the one furthest physically from her.

Florence walked the few steps over to the small desk underneath one of the side windows, lifted the lid and took a sheet of paper and a fountain pen from inside, then, lowering the lid quietly, sat down to write to Margery.

St Heliers House
Nottingham
28 December 1916

Dearest girl,

We all missed you here this Christmas and hope that you were able to take some time during the day for yourself. I expect you received the small package of gifts that we sent on to you. You might have received them a little earlier than necessary because we wanted to be certain they wouldn't be delayed past Christmas and so decided to post them to you ten days before.

The Christmas cake and Christmas pudding were your father's idea. He insisted you should have them even if you decided to share them among the visiting soldiers and only ate a mouthful of each. He said they would give you a taste of what we were eating at home, to transport you back to being here with us, even if only in your mind.

The enclosed bundle of socks and scarves I thought you could pass on to any soldiers who needed them and the other box of medicines and bandages we thought might be put to good use at some point. The leather gloves were for you and your assistants and the coat and footwear we hope will help keep you warm through the winter months.

I'm hoping that this is the last Christmas we have to spend apart, or in particular that you have to spend overseas. Remember that if you ever wish to return home but still want to continue helping soldiers then I can always find you a place in our Gas Mask Department. We're making a huge number of masks each day and constantly supplying the British Forces with them.

The most exciting thing has happened to your father. He received a letter from the King advising him that he is to receive the honour of Baronet on the eleventh of January. I am arranging a party to celebrate the honour for the day after we return from Buckingham Palace. I would love it if you could be here as a surprise for your father but completely understand if that is not a possibility. I know how vital your work is especially now that the numbers of wounded soldiers continue to mount by the day. Please therefore don't feel pressurised by me to come back if it's not something you feel you can do. I am only making the suggestion in case you are able to come home then.

Other than that, there is little to report. Dorothy and John's little girls are growing each day and it's a joy to have them in the house. It takes me back to when you three were little and scampering around. The servants love them and spoil them with treats if we're not careful. Secretly, I love that everyone is always so happy to see them here.

Work is busier than ever, as I'm sure you can imagine. Everyone works tirelessly as always at Boots, whether in the stores or the factories and I think we all enjoy knowing that we are each playing our part in keeping the vital supplies available to everyone who needs them.

Florence covered her mouth as she yawned. It was too late for her to still be up when she had to rise before six o'clock the next morning to help Jesse get ready for his daily massage. She didn't want to finish off her letter yet, but if she was to ensure Meadows posted it first thing in the morning then she needed to sign off and seal it in an addressed envelope ready to go to Margery.

Well, my darling daughter, I hope you are looking after yourself as well as those passing through your canteen. Write back whenever you have the chance and remember always how much we love you and miss you.

Love always,
Mother X

Chapter Twenty-Two

12 January 1917

Florence shivered as she walked from the kitchen, where she had just gone through final details with Mrs Rudge for the low-key party that evening. They might not be able to have a splendid array of food and decorations such as they would have enjoyed prior to the war, but it was enough to know that they could mark the day in some small way.

She knew the weather was seasonably cold but that was no reason for the temperature of the inside of St Heliers to be as low. Why hadn't one of the servants lit the fires yet? It had been a relief to arrive home the previous evening after visiting London for Jesse to receive his baronetcy from the King, and enjoy peace and quiet after the excitement and ceremony of the previous couple of days.

London had been busy as ever although Florence was

certain there seemed to be more ex-soldiers begging on street corners than the last time she had visited. Then again, maybe she was just more aware of them for some reason.

She was relieved that Jesse had coped well with the travelling and she looked forward to celebrating his new honour with their family and a few friends with a small gathering she was arranging at home later that evening. Typically, Jesse had wanted to invite more people, but she was not going to chance his health declining further than it already had by letting him get carried away with visits from friends.

Florence made her way to the library to work on a report she had promised Jesse about their female staff situation. It was still proving difficult to source male staff but thankfully that wasn't Florence's concern so much as placing the women who applied for work at Boots in the area where they would be most suited and content.

She worked for a couple of hours and double-checked her figures before blotting her latest notes. Sitting back in her chair she looked outside at the grey day and thought back over the previous two weeks and her excitement at having John home for Christmas, Dorothy giving birth to her second daughter nine days before, and Jesse's big day.

It had been thrilling for all of them to have him around to celebrate with their father. She just wished that Margery could have been there with them this evening so that Jesse could have all his children with him at such a special time.

Harriet, her lady's maid, knocked on the library door

and entered. Florence wondered for a second why she was carrying her coat and hat.

'Is it that time already?' Florence asked, realising she must have been working on the report for far longer than she had imagined.

'Yes, Lady Boot. You were to leave at ten to eleven to go for coffee at your son and daughter-in-law's home. I thought I should come and remind you when I spotted Mr Parry waiting outside the front door with the car.'

Florence placed her report in a folder and stood to put on her hat and coat. 'Thank you, Harriet. I don't know what I would do without you.' She buttoned up her coat and put her hat on her head, pinning it in place. 'I don't think Margaret will be pleased if I'm late.' She indicated the folder. 'Please, will you take this to Sir Jesse's study. He'll be waiting for it and I don't want him to have an excuse to leave his warm office to come searching for it.'

As Parry drove the car carefully along the icy roads Florence looked forward to sharing the event of the previous day with John and Margaret. She would have loved to invite the two of them up to London for the ceremony or at least to enjoy a celebratory meal with them afterwards but Margaret was heavily pregnant and looking forward to the birth of their second child in the next week or so. She couldn't ask John to leave his wife at home while he had the chance to spend time with her, especially when he would be returning to France sometime soon.

She arrived at their pretty home and was welcomed in by John.

'Quickly, let's get you inside where it's warm,' he said, linking arms with her.

Florence thought he seemed a little more animated than usual but put it down to so many exciting things happening to them as a family in the past couple of weeks.

'We're through here in the living room. Margaret's waiting with cocoa for us all.' He lowered his voice. 'She thought it would be the perfect drink to have in front of the fire on such a grey and miserable day.'

Florence thought it was an excellent idea. She always enjoyed a good mug of cocoa and realised that now John had mentioned it she very much looked forward to drinking some.

Their maid joined them in the hallway and gave Florence a curtsey. 'Please, may I take your coat and hat from you, Lady Boot?'

Florence took them off and handed them to the girl who, like John, seemed to be exceedingly more cheerful than usual. 'Thank you.'

She followed John into the living room where Margaret was seated looking rather uncomfortable now that she was almost nine months pregnant. She walked over to her daughter-in-law. 'How are you?' Florence asked, sitting next to Margaret on the cream sofa.

'I barely recall how it feels to be comfortable,' Margaret groaned. 'This baby can't be born soon enough.'

'I can imagine,' Florence said sympathetically, recalling how cumbersome it was to be heavily pregnant.

'You won't mind if I don't accompany John to St Heliers

tonight for Sir Jesse's party, I hope?' Margaret winced and moved one of her hands to her back. 'It's just that I'm so tired by early evening.'

'Not at all. It's horribly cold out there apart from anything else and you'll feel far better staying here where you're warm and able to rest.'

'Thank you. John said you wouldn't mind but I wanted to be certain.' She moved slightly on the sofa cushion. 'Nanny is bringing Barbara through to see you after we've had our drinks. She's a bit of a handful at the moment, always running about the house and up to mischief.'

'Yes,' said John, laughing. 'She rarely wants to sit still and is into everything if we let her.'

Florence thought fondly of the toddler who was now sixteen months old. 'She always was an independent little thing.' Florence pictured the dear little girl, who seemed to have learned something new each time she saw her.

Florence was about to ask if they had settled on any baby names when she noticed John's eyes dart to the back of the room followed by the door opening and a couple of light footsteps. The expression on John's face was odd, so concerned about what he had seen, Florence turned in her chair and gasped. She could not believe her eyes.

'Margery?' she asked her voice shaky with emotion. 'I can't believe you're here.'

'Hello, Mother,' Margery said with a laugh. 'I wanted to surprise you and John kindly agreed to help me.'

'Well, you've certainly done that.' Florence stood on shaky legs and held her arms out for Margery to step into them. 'Oh, my darling, it's so wonderful to see you again.' She held her daughter, happy to be in her embrace once more.

Margery raised her hand and wiped a tear away from Florence's cheek. She hadn't realised she was crying until that moment. 'I'm sorry,' she said, her legs feeling like they were made of jelly. 'I'm going to have to sit down again.'

'I do hope I haven't given you too big a shock?'

'Not at all.' Florence patted the seat next to her. 'Come and sit with me and let me look at you.' She studied her daughter's face. She had lost weight and there were dark circles under her eyes, but Florence hoped that she could soon rectify both if she could persuade her daughter to rest and enjoy Mrs Rudge's cooking for a few days. 'You look well.'

Margery laughed. 'Shouldn't I?'

Florence shook her head. 'No, it's just that I wasn't sure how you were faring as far as having enough time to rest between shifts.'

'Why don't we all sit back down and catch up with each other,' John said, walking to the bell pull and ringing for one of the maids. 'I think it's time they brought in our drinks.'

Florence couldn't think straight. 'When did you arrive? You look too rested to have come this morning.'

'Yesterday afternoon. I was longing to see you and Father, but John said you weren't returning from London until later and suggested I spend the night with them to catch up on a little sleep. He thought it best if I travel with him to the party at St Heliers this evening to surprise Father. What do you think?'

Florence pictured Jesse's delight to have all his children with him. 'I think it's an excellent idea.' She reached out and took Margery's hand in hers. 'It's exceptionally good to see you again. This is the best of surprises.'

It truly was, Florence decided, as she listened to Margery telling her how she and the other women at the canteen had spent their Christmas. 'It was strangely festive,' Margery said. 'And it made us all very satisfied to think that we had given those men a taste of the Christmas that they were missing with their families in Blighty.'

'I couldn't be prouder of you.' Florence sighed. 'Of all of you.' She looked from one to another of them, grateful to have such caring people in her life.

'Does Dorothy know you're here?'

Margery shook her head. 'No, she doesn't. I gather from Margaret that you're going on to visit her for a light lunch today and thought I might accompany you. It will be fun to see my sister again and her new baby, Charity.'

'That's a wonderful idea,' Florence said knowing that Dorothy would be as thrilled to see Margery as she had been and especially delighted to introduce her sister to her second daughter, who had been born on the third of January.

'I hear Charity's second name is Florence,' Margery said. 'After you. That must have delighted you, Mother.'

'I was touched, I have to admit it. I'm excited to be there when you meet your new niece for the first time.' She couldn't wait, and enjoyed knowing how special it would be for Margery to spend time with her sister's new baby.

'It's been an exceptional few days for our family,' John said. Then going to stand next to his wife and resting his hand on her shoulder, added. 'And it's not over yet. Soon, Mother, you'll have a fourth grandchild.'

'You're all so very clever,' Florence said, sitting back down. 'You've all made your father and me so very proud. Each one of you.' She smiled at Margaret.

Florence couldn't wait until the evening for Jesse to be reunited with his youngest daughter. It was a relief to spend time in Margery's company again. They had so much to catch up on that they couldn't cover in letters.

'How do you find Margery, Florence?' Margaret asked smiling.

'A little thinner than the last time she was home,' she said relieved that Margery hadn't lost as much weight as she had dreaded she might. 'But you do look well, darling, I'm happy to say.'

Margery laughed. 'It's good to see you again too, Mother.'

Florence shook her head. 'I was a little fearful, especially after the miserable weather we've been having lately, that you might have caught a chill, but told myself that your nursing friends at the canteen would know how best to care for you if that did happen.'

Margery gave Florence's hand a gentle squeeze. 'I'm fine, Mother. You really don't need to worry about me so much.'

Florence couldn't help staring at her daughter. She had longed for this moment and could hardly believe it was now here. 'Your father is going to be delighted to see you and John this evening. Especially you, as I think he worries about you as much as I do, although he keeps his concerns more to himself than I can.'

There was a knock on the door and, before John could answer, it opened and a toddler ran inside to join them.

'Look at you,' Margery cheered as little Barbara giggled and stumbled, making them all gasp, but grabbing the edge of a chair and managing to right herself before Nanny could reach her.

'She is a little menace,' John said, laughing.

Margery sighed. 'I didn't realise toddlers were so terrifying to watch. Mind you, I couldn't miss coming home for this, now could I? Anyway,' she continued before either Florence or Margaret could reply, 'I thought it about time I came home to be with my family.'

Florence cooed at Barbara as she picked her up and settled her on her lap. She bobbed the little girl up and down making her giggle loudly. 'I'm glad you have. Now that we're here together, tell me how it really was for you over there in France.' She pulled a face at Barbara. 'It must have been rather shocking for Aunt Margery coming face to face with so many injured soldiers, mustn't it?'

Margery frowned and glanced at Margaret, who was laughing at Barbara's reaction to her grandmother. 'Um, it was.'

Florence hated to think that her daughter was keeping

distressing memories from her. 'Margery? You can tell me anything you know. In fact, I wish you would share your experiences with me. I can see that they've had a profound effect on you and I believe that by sharing them you will find the weight of their burden a little lighter.'

Margery watched her thoughtfully for a moment. 'I can't imagine I'll ever be squeamish again. We all found it rather more difficult than any of us had imagined, but when one of us was glum the others did their best to boost their spirits. We've been fine, for the most part. I think the most difficult thing, after we had all got used to dealing with exhausted men, a lot of whom were in pain, was the shocking tiredness we all felt most of the time.'

Florence could see she was underplaying the trauma of what she had witnessed. 'Glum? I imagine you all felt far more troubled than that.' She tried to picture her fair, gentle daughter coping with whatever she had faced.

'It's all right Margery,' John said. 'I've seen for myself how nightmarish things can be over there. Nothing you can say will shock me, I can promise you that.'

'Your mother's right,' Margaret said. 'John has told me some of his experiences and I promise you I would rather you share with us than try to keep everything to yourself.'

Margery looked from one to another of them and Florence could see she was trying to make up her mind whether to confide in them. Her eyes moistened and she turned away briefly and wiped her eyes, before facing them once more with her chin raised and a determined expression.

'We all agreed to put on a brave face when we saw our families,' Margery admitted. 'You're right, John, when you said it was the stuff of nightmares over there.' She gazed over their heads at the window. 'I've seen men with bandages covering most of their faces and it haunts me to think what's underneath the dressings. So many with missing limbs and others with wide eyes and a faraway look who seem unable to communicate with anyone.' She stared at her hands. 'I can't see how those worst affected men will ever be able to move on from what's happened to them.'

For a few seconds no one spoke. Then, John walked over to his sister and slipped his arm around her narrow shoulders. 'I can't either,' he said. 'But you need to focus on how you and your friends giving them brief respite by letting them have a taste of home will help each and every one of them.'

Margery's eyes filled with tears and Florence thought her heart would break. 'But we give them so little and they're all so grateful.'

'What you give them,' John argued, 'means an enormous amount. Even those men who can't see you can hear your gentle voices and the kind way in which you address them. They taste familiar food that will remind them of the home they're returning to. What you do is help them move from their experiences in France and Belgium and give them a touch of Blighty. It's worth so much and you should all be very proud of yourselves.'

The tears in Margery's eyes spilled over and down her cheeks. 'Do you really think so?'

'I might not be injured but I have my own demons from my time in France and I know that passing through your canteen was like a breath of fresh air for me and the men I was travelling with. So, yes, I do think what you do makes an enormous difference to these men.' Florence watched as her son took his handkerchief from his top pocket, shook it out and dried his sister's tears. It gripped her heart to see her oldest and youngest children comforting each other.

Little Barbara blew a raspberry and Florence widened her eyes at her granddaughter before tickling her, grateful to be able to do something so that her children didn't notice how emotional their conversation had made her.

After a couple of minutes, Florence looked up and saw Margery watching baby Barbara. 'How selfish of me,' she said, shocked to think that she hadn't given her daughter a chance to hold her niece. 'I'm so sorry.' She pulled a funny face at the toddler. 'Do you want to go and sit on Aunt Margery's knee now?'

The little girl turned her upper body towards Margery and held out her arms to be lifted up.

Florence watched as Margery carefully took the child in her arms and hugged her.

'She's so adorable.' Margery said. She looked from her brother to her sister-in-law. 'You're both so lucky to have found each other. And especially now with this little tot.'

Florence wondered when Margery would fall in love and settle down. She hoped it would be soon and that it would be with someone living if not in Nottingham then somewhere not too far away. How incredible it would be, she thought, to be able to visit Margery on any day she chose just like she was able to do with Dorothy and John?

An hour later she and Margery were in the motorcar as Parry drove them to Dorothy's home. Florence was looking forward to seeing baby Charity and trying to picture her when Margery turned from looking out of the motor car window.

'I don't think I ever told you that I met Meadows's nephew soon after I arrived in France that first time.' Florence shook her head. 'It was when his train stopped at the station and he and other soldiers travelling with him were brought to the canteen for a bite to eat and some tea.'

'Did you speak to him at all?' Florence wondered if Meadows was aware that the two of them had met.

'Yes.' Margery laughed. 'He was a little forlorn when he arrived but did perk up after a while. He told me that his uncle was a servant at my parents' home in Nottingham.'

'I'm pleased he looked you up when he arrived there. What was he like?'

Margery tilted her head to one side thoughtfully. 'Quiet, but I don't know if that is since he received his injuries or if that's his personality. It's difficult to tell sometimes. I could see hurt in his eyes.' Margery sighed sadly. 'I see that a lot but his seemed deeper somehow. I hope that when he's had some rehabilitation, he'll feel a lot better about his situation.'

'Poor Meadows has been very concerned about him and

also his sister. She was understandably upset when he was so badly hurt, but I think she's mostly relieved he was able to return home at all.'

'He was very dreadfully injured,' Margery said quietly. 'I'm not sure if Meadows or his sister will have been told the true extent of his injuries.'

Florence hated to think of Meadows having to deal with more than he already was. 'Like what?'

'I was speaking to his nurse and she said that it's not just that he's lost his leg, but they don't think he'll walk again and, apparently, there's shrapnel in his brain that they were unable to reach.'

'Did she mention the repercussions of leaving it there?' Florence asked, willing her daughter to say something vaguely positive.

Margery looked away from her and Florence could see she was battling whether to divulge anything further from the conversation. 'If it moves, even slightly, it could kill him.'

Florence exhaled sharply. 'Oh, Margery, that poor boy. Should we say anything to Meadows? As a warning?'

Margery shook her head. 'I've been contending with the same thought for days. The boy knows his prognosis and I believe it's for him to tell his family if he chooses to do so. Not for us. After all, I'm not really supposed to know anything.'

As much as Florence felt guilty towards Meadows for not tipping him off about his nephew's true medical condition, she understood that it wasn't her place to say anything. 'You're right. Then, we must not repeat what we know, however desperate we are to tell Meadows.'

As difficult as it was probably going to be for Meadows's nephew, at least he had a family, Florence decided. She wondered how men without families coped when they returned, having had to deal with so many changes. She knew that no matter what troubles she witnessed outside in the streets or the issues she was always working to resolve at the company, she was lucky enough to have her close family to return to. She hoped never to forget how blessed she was to have such a loving family. They had the joy of a new generation of Boot family members now and she and Jesse would always know that whatever successes they had or hadn't attained, their biggest achievement would always be their family.

Coming across so many customers and staff who had suffered life-changing losses was always something that made Florence remember with gratitude how lucky she was to still have not only her husband by her side but also her three children. To think that while her family was growing others were having to contend with theirs being depleted… It broke her heart. How much longer would they all have to continue living with the constant threat of loss? She couldn't see that this war would end any time soon but prayed that it wouldn't be too long before things changed and all the men and women fighting away could return home and the death and injuries would stop.

After lunch at Dorothy's, Florence had Parry dropped Margery back off at John and Margaret's home, then made her way to the office to dictate a few letters to Gladys. It was a joy to have the girl back working with her even though each time Florence saw her she couldn't help feeling a pang of sadness that the kind young woman should now probably be welcoming a new baby into her life rather than having to get used to being a widow and losing the man she had loved so deeply.

She closed her eyes, reminding herself that she had a party to return home and start overseeing the preparations for. She had arranged a cake just large enough for a small slice for each of the family, guests and servants to enjoy. Florence would have loved to pay for an elaborate cake to be the centrepiece of their dining-room table but it didn't seem right to do so knowing how much food had gone up in price and how the less wealthy people in Nottingham were struggling to find enough and having to queue each day for what they needed to feed their families.

Her and Jesse's friends were aware that they did not drink alcohol and so she knew that none of them would be surprised that instead of toasting Jesse's latest honour with champagne, their glasses would be filled with elderflower juice. When Florence had announced that Jesse was to be honoured by the King, Mrs Rudge had visited her in her study when they were arranging what food and drink to prepare for the party and had delighted Florence by telling her that she had been keeping a batch of elderflower cordial that she had made up the previous summer and been storing, hoping to use for some such celebration.

'I hadn't expected it to be this though, Lady Boot. I was hoping the war might have ended by now.'

Florence sighed. 'That would be something worth celebrating. But in the absence of an Armistice, we at least have something to enjoy right now.'

Mrs Rudge had made up several large crystal jugs of her elderflower cordial together with a couple of jugs of dandelion and burdock that Jesse favoured. Apart from that, the rest of the food, Florence decided, would consist of cold meats and whatever salad they could source from their small vegetable garden and the nearest market. They had barely socialised since the start of the war. Neither of them had felt it right to do so unless they were entertaining their staff in some way or raising money for the war effort. Florence was grateful that they could afford food despite the increase in prices but never forgot that for many other families putting food on the table was a daily struggle.

Florence stood, a glass of Mrs Rudge's elderflower cordial in one hand and the other on Jesse's shoulder, watching as John took the floor to give the toast to his father.

'Father,' John said, smiling proudly and giving his father a slight bow. 'Or should I address you now as Sir Jesse Boot, Baronet of Wilford, in the County of Nottingham?'

The guests cheered and sang out their congratulations

once again to Jesse. Florence stepped forward to take a look at her husband's beaming face as he sat in his cane bath chair. He seemed so happy, not only, she knew, to have such an accolade bestowed upon him, but also to have his three children and their families and friends here to celebrate the special occasion with him at St Heliers.

Jesse raised his hand when John had finished addressing the party. 'Thank you to my son for his kind words. I'd like to thank my darling wife, Florence, without whose hard work, love and support, I'm sure I would not have received this recognition by the King. Thank all of you for coming here and celebrating with me today. I'm deeply grateful to have this honour of a baronetcy bestowed on me.' An invisible hand clutched at Florence's heart as she listened to her beloved husband speak.

'When I think back to my life as a young boy, walking mile after mile with my mother to collect herbs for our fledgling business, in my bare feet to keep my only pair of leather shoes in the best condition possible for chapel on Sunday, I can hardly believe how my life has altered beyond all recognition. I am truly blessed. With that in mind I'd like to raise a toast to the King and all his brave subjects, both the men and women abroad –' he looked at Margery and smiled proudly – 'and everyone here striving to keep Britain supplied with all that she needs.'

He raised his glass. 'To the King and his subjects, wherever they may be.'

'The King and his subjects,' the rest of them cheered as

they lifted their glasses before taking a sip and congratulating him once more.

Florence stepped forward to kiss Jesse on his cheek. 'Shall we eat?'

She took hold of Jesse's hand briefly before leaving him to chat and receive congratulatory wishes from his guests. She walked over to John's side and rested a hand lightly on his back. 'That was a lovely toast you gave for your father, thank you.'

John looked past her to watch his father enjoying the attention he was being given. 'I'm very proud of him, Mother. And you. When I think how much you've both achieved it astounds me.' He leant forward and kissed her on the cheek. 'This is a special day and I'm so happy that Margery and I could make it back here to enjoy it with you both.'

'As are we, my dear boy.'

Florence left her guests and walked through the hall, through the green baize door and down the stairs to the back of the house where the servants worked in the warren of rooms reserved for them. She could hear the chatter as she neared their sitting room past the kitchen and smiled. It was good to know that they were happy for Jesse, too.

She walked into the kitchen. Suddenly, spotting her, Mrs Rudge stood up from the chair where she was making notes in a book. 'Lady Boot, I'm sorry, I didn't hear you come in. I was miles away updating my food order book.'

Florence shook her head. 'Please, it's fine. I only came to thank you for your delicious cordial.'

Mrs Rudge's pink cheeks reddened even further. 'You enjoyed it?'

'I certainly did, as did Sir Jesse. You've surpassed yourself, Cook. Thank you. Please, also thank the servants for all their hard work. I hope they enjoy their treats this evening that you've made them.' She thought of the cake that Mrs Rudge would hand out to each of them after their supper, later.

'They will, I'm sure, Lady Boot.'

Florence tilted her head towards the clock on the wall. 'Well, I had better return to my guests and I don't want to disturb the servants while they're taking a moment to relax in the sitting room. Please thank them for me for all their hard work today, will you?'

'Yes, Lady Boot, I'll be happy to.'

Florence left the kitchen aware how lucky she was to still have so many of her staff working for her at St Heliers House. Apart from her lady's maid Harriet and Jesse's male nurse George, they had five other household staff and a driver. They had lost one kitchen maid and an under-housemaid, but she had managed to replace them after a week or so.

As she made her way up the stairs and through the baize door back to her guests Florence wondered what her younger self would have thought if she had been told that she would move on from sharing a bedroom with her sister Amy above the shop at 27 Queen Street to this huge brick house with its round conservatory, large garden and squash courts – and become the wife of a Baronet. She was amused, certain the younger Florence wouldn't have believed her and would have accused her of having read too many novels.

'Ah, there you are,' Jesse called, happy to see her. 'Where have you been? I've been waiting for you to cut the cake.'

The cake! How could she have forgotten that they still needed to cut it?

'I'm sorry,' she whispered, reaching him and giving him a quick hug. 'I forgot and went to thank Cook for all her hard work.'

'Shall we do it now then?'

Florence laughed. 'We should if we want people to have a taste before they leave.'

Chapter Twenty-Three

March 1917

Florence sat in her conservatory making the most of the watery March sunshine before going upstairs to check on Jesse, who was having an afternoon rest. The cold weather had caused him to come down with a chill and she wasn't taking any chances or accepting any argument from him. She had refused to allow him to travel to inspect several of their stores and factories for the past week, insisting he either stay and work from his study at St Heliers, or go direct to his warm office in the Pelham Street store.

Today, the weather was stormy and very wet and Florence had no intention of allowing him to leave the house at all although she did intend going to visit John's wife Margaret, who had given birth to their second daughter, Jocelyne Mary, at the beginning of the previous month.

'There's nothing needing your attention so badly that it can't wait until tomorrow or the next day,' she had insisted when she caught him with his coat on and being taken out to the car by Meadows.

'How can you be so certain of that?' he asked, an amused glint in his eyes.

Florence could tell he was up to something but knew by the look on his face that it wasn't anything he was ready to share with her. She didn't mind, she knew well enough that Jesse would tell her whatever it was when he felt the timing was right. At least it seemed to be something that was cheering him rather than concerning him.

'Just this once, I insist you do as I ask,' she said, motioning for George to come out from where he was standing by the front door. 'George will take you back inside, where you're to spend the day resting in the warmth of your study. I'll go over to the store later and can bring home any paperwork that needs looking at, but that's all.'

Jesse opened his mouth to argue but Florence waved her finger at him. 'No, Jesse. Most days, I sit back and let you do as you wish, because I know you'll only waste time arguing with me. However, today is not one of those days. I have no intention of sitting back and watching you leave the house for the day when you're still under the weather.'

He must be feeling unwell, she thought, when his reply was a gentle shrug and he asked Meadows to settle him in his study.

Florence rang the bell and when Ethel came through asked her to check Jesse's fire and to bring both of them some tea. She then made herself comfortable facing her bare garden. Florence loved the brightness of the spring and summer flowers but at this time of year there was extraordinarily little of note to gaze upon outside.

Her mind drifted once more, and she thought again of John and Margaret's new baby daughter. 'Jocelyne Mary,' she repeated to herself a few times. Another pretty name. She was relieved that John was near home, hopefully for the next few months, to spend time with his wife and newborn baby daughter, unlike so many other men whose lives had been cut short in the past couple of months.

She wondered for a moment what it was that Jesse wasn't sharing with her. As far as she knew, he shared most things. She knew he was worn out from all the extra work the company had been carrying out producing alternatives to sedatives and antiseptics to send to other companies who were under contract with the British Fire Prevention Committee, as well as rushing to launch the new water-sterilising tablets for the British Forces.

Florence was feeling a little down because of her own problems at work. She wished that she wasn't losing so many of her female staff just when she needed them most. She didn't like saying goodbye to those girls who had come to work for Boots directly from school and whom she knew a little better than the rest, like Pearl Smith, a bubbly girl always ready with a funny story. Florence had always thought that if the girl had been born closer to London's

West End she would have probably ended up going on the stage. When it came time to bid goodbye to Pearl and three others in her section that were leaving Florence could see that she wasn't the only one to be sad about losing a popular member of staff.

It worried her more than usual that most of them were being lured by higher wages to work in the Chilwell Arms Factory, especially because the job was so dangerous. She had heard from several of them when she had seen them in town and chatted to them asking how their new work was going that the risk of explosion in the factory were so high that the workers had to change into boiler suits and wear rubber boots and a hat as soon as they arrived.

It was worrying, too, when Gladys told her that one of the women she lived near who had left Boots' employ to work at the arms factory had explained that the chemicals they handled were so toxic that they had to wash their faces and arms thoroughly in washrooms before leaving for home at the end of each day.

'They do have medical inspections,' Gladys said, 'but I'm not sure how in-depth they are or how often they take place. The girls have to be extremely careful when they're working, too.'

Florence was horrified. 'Surely that level of danger can't be compensated by higher wages,' she asked.

Gladys shrugged. 'I suppose it depends on how much these women need the money. I know some just like the freedom of having more in their wage packet each week, but others need to compensate for lost wages when their menfolk leave to enlist or are killed. The army pension isn't very much, not when there are quite a few mouths to feed.'

Surely there was something she could do to persuade her girls to stay working for her? Young women shouldn't risk their lives at work. Then again, Florence thought miserably, who was she to think that way? The government needed the artillery that John had spent his time in the army transporting to the Front. How else were their forces going to be able to fight back and who was going to make them if not her girls who had left Boots to go and work at places like Chilwell?

'I suppose,' she mused, 'that however upset I might be to lose any of my girls to these places, someone has to do the work, otherwise how else are the arms to be produced and this seemingly endless nightmare brought to an end?'

Florence wondered when that might be and then tried to picture how life would be after it was all over. Already the war had continued far longer than anyone had imagined it would. She felt sure that the people of Britain would be very changed after coping with such a lengthy and difficult experience. How could they not?

Florence reflected on how up until now those with more money had been protected against the difficulties that poorer people suffered. It seemed from reports and talk that she had heard that the officers, sons of wealthier and aristocratic families, were being killed in higher numbers as they led their men over the top and into battle, coming into contact with enemy fire first. Class didn't matter though when it came to bombs being dropped from airships. Yes, she thought miserably, this war had been a great leveller to them all. For the first time in history it didn't seem to matter who you were, what your background was, if you were a mother you could lose your son at any time and the pain would always be just as acute.

Florence couldn't shift the feelings of anxiety that weighed heavily on her today, but she put a brave face on when she went to Jesse's study to see how he was feeling.

'Sit down, my dear,' he said, indicating the chair next to him. 'I have something I want to share with you.'

Florence did as he asked and hoped that whatever it was it wouldn't be more bad news. She waited patiently for him to speak.

'You know I've been holding a few more meetings with the board than usual of late?' Florence nodded. 'Well we've been discussing you.'

Florence couldn't understand why that might be. 'Me? But why? What have I done to merit such attention, especially at such a busy time?'

Jesse held his hands out for her to take. 'It's been approved that you're to become the next director of Boots.'

Florence couldn't speak. What had he just said?

'Did you hear me, my love? The Board have agreed that upon receipt of your consent they are happy to appoint you as the first female director of Boots.' He smiled at her and waited for the unexpected announcement to settle in her mind.

'Me?' Why couldn't she come up with something a little

more intelligent? Florence wondered, unable to take in what Jesse had just told her.

Jesse laughed. 'Am I to understand that you're happy about this?'

She stood and leaning forward kissed him. 'You know I am. I simply can't quite believe it, that's all. I'll need a moment to gather myself, let it all sink in.' Florence replayed Jesse's words over again in her mind. She was going to be a company director serving with a board of directors and at Boots. It was the biggest honour she probably would ever receive. 'Jesse, for once I'm almost lost for words,' she said, aware that she was probably grinning inanely at him. 'Thank you so very much for putting this trust in me.'

Jesse raised his right hand and rested it on her cheek. 'After all that you've done to grow this business over the decades. It's largely thanks to your innovative ideas and constant hard work that this company has been transformed from a chemist into the huge brand it is now. I think it's the very least I can do to show you how much I value your business brain and your never-ending support for all that I do.'

Florence didn't know of any other women serving as company directors. She thought back to that twenty-three-year-old girl working in her father's stationery shop and what she had thought to be enormous ambitions she never truly expected to realise. Now, here she was, about to be appointed to the board of directors at Boots. It was a dream come true – albeit a dream she hadn't even let materialise privately because it wasn't something she ever thought could happen.

'The day I met you in my parents' flat at 27 Queen Street was the luckiest day of my life,' she said, her voice barely above a tight whisper. 'I always knew I was lucky that you had come into my life, Jesse and I thought I knew how much you valued me, but this is something I never dared hope for. I am truly honoured. I hope you know that?'

'I do, my dear,' he said leaning forward and kissing her. 'And I can't think of a more worthy person to bring to the boardroom table. And,' he said, raising an eyebrow, 'I look forward to having you sitting in on all meetings and offering your valuable opinions.'

Florence laughed, picturing the scene. 'Even those opinions that irritate you and which you disagree with.'

'Yes, even those.' He frowned thoughtfully for a moment, a glint of amusement in his eyes. 'I say this now but imagine that I won't find it quite as funny when we do disagree in meetings.'

'Probably not.'

Chapter Twenty-Four

May 1917

As March slid into April, Florence and Jesse were cheered that the United States Army had entered the war on the 6 April.

'Hopefully, the allies will have enough military strength behind us to be able to overcome the enemy, once and for all,' Jesse said.

Florence hoped so, too. 'Yes, then the men and women who are overseas can return and we can all start getting on with our lives again.' When Jesse didn't reply immediately, she suspected something might be wrong. 'Don't you think?'

He sighed. 'I'm not so sure it's going to be that easy.'

'Why? What do you mean?'

'Think about it, Florence. Our turnover has increased

massively and that's in the new departments where we make the ventilators. What will we be able to give those employees working in there when we no longer need to produce them? And what about when the men return home and want their old jobs back? Will the women be happy to give up their new-found freedom and return to keeping home and not earning their own income, do you think?'

Florence tried to imagine what it would be like if someone took away her role at Boots and gave it to someone else simply because he was a man. She would hate it; she knew that much.

'But what can we do about it?' She thought of all the roles at Boots that were once carried out by men and were now covered by women. These absent men and, to a smaller extent, women should not be penalised for fighting for their country. But did it mean that those who had stepped in to cover for them would now have to suffer from their return to England? It seemed so, because she had no idea how else they could rectify the situation but by honouring those jobs for ex-employees on their return.

'Thankfully, we have a large number of roles for female staff,' she said thoughtfully. 'But I see what you mean. We can't expect soldiers to go and risk their lives for us for a number of years and then return to nothing, can we?'

Why was life constantly throwing up new problems? she wondered.

Jesse nudged her gently. 'Don't look quite so down. We're not there yet. We still have to find a way to win this war before this will be an issue for us.'

She returned his reassuring smile but was still troubled. 'Yes, that might be true, but it is something we need to keep in mind for when we do win the war.'

Jesse laughed and gazed at her. She couldn't miss how much love there was for her in his look. 'I love your certainty that we will do so.'

Florence shrugged. 'We have to believe it will happen,' she insisted. 'The alternative is too terrifying to contemplate.'

The following days and weeks lowered her spirits even further when Jesse sat at the breakfast table and read out snippets of news from his broadsheets. 'It seems that for every four boats importing food into Britain, there are U-boats managing to sink one of them.' He looked up from his paper and stared out of the window. 'At this rate the people will suffer greatly, or even starve.'

Another thing to worry everyone, Florence thought miserably. 'But what can we do, apart from make sure we grow as much as we can in our vegetable garden and take care not to waste anything?'

Jesse looked at her. 'We already do those things, Florence. It's not us that I worry about so much as those without gardens. How are they supposed to find ways to supplement their food?'

She didn't know. 'Can't the government do anything to help guard against this happening?'

Jesse sighed and looked back down at his newspaper. 'It seems that they are introducing a convoy system, which I hope will go some way to guard against the worst happening.' He lowered the paper to the table and stared at her. 'I thought matters had been difficult in the past when I witnessed others' suffering through poverty and even my own childhood experiences, but this war is coming down heavily on so many people, Florence. It's too cruel.'

She wondered if Jesse was referring to a blind, one-legged beggar they had seen and stopped to give money to the day before on their way to work. He could not have been much older than Margery and his life had been reduced to standing in the rain begging for money to be able to feed himself and his family. Her heart ached for him and all of those like him whose lives had been destroyed, leaving them in a living hell. It reminded her of something she had recently been told about one of her ex-employees' sons.

'I heard the other day that Nellie Blythe's son was terribly injured on the Somme last summer.'

Jesse frowned thoughtfully. 'I know that name but can't place her.'

Florence thought back to how she had tried to help the young unmarried mother early in her marriage to Jesse and had messed things up terribly for her. It had been a dreadful situation and one that she had had to work hard to rectify. 'I think it was back when we first opened the Pelham Street store,' she said, giving the matter a little more thought. 'It must have been around 1892 or '93. Do you remember, she had a son and I tried to help her but initially made matters a whole lot worse?'

Jesse thought for a moment and then nodded slowly. 'So you did. I seem to recall that you were terribly upset by the whole situation.'

'I was mortified,' she said, recalling how Jesse had tried to dissuade her from becoming involved as she had done. 'But I managed to sort things out in the end, thankfully.'

'Tell me, what happened to her son?'

Florence cleared her throat to dispel the emotion threatening to overcome her as she thought of the baby boy she had hoped to help, back when she too was a young mother. 'His right hand was damaged, so I'm told, and one side of his face has been destroyed. Poor Nellie is understandably heartbroken for him. He was engaged and his fiancée broke things off with him once she had been to visit him and saw the extent of his injuries.'

Jesse glowered across the table. 'What an unfeeling young woman she must be. He will be better off without her.'

Florence agreed. 'That's as maybe, but I don't think he sees things quite in the same way.'

'The poor man… and after all he must have done to help fight for his country.' Jesse shook his head. 'Is there no way we could help him?'

Florence would love nothing more. She wished she could recall the name of Nellie's little boy, but despite going over and over that time she had gone to Nellie's mother's house and seen the baby, just couldn't remember what it was.

'I can check to see what vacancies we have in the factories.'

'Or, if he's self-conscious, then maybe we can find work for him in one of the back rooms. Either way, we should invite him in for an interview. If we don't have a position for him then we'll come up with one.'

Florence gazed lovingly at her caring husband. 'Thank you. I knew you would want to help him, as do I. I haven't spoken to Nellie for a few years, but I'm sure she won't mind if I contact her,' she said hoping she was right. 'If she's open to it, I'll ask her to send her son to me at his convenience and see what I can do about work for him. I'm told that she desperately wants to help him find a way to leave the house and face people once again.'

'That's a good idea. The poor boy needs to find his way back to normality again, I shouldn't wonder.'

Florence gave Jesse a nod, aware how difficult it must have been for him to come to terms with his ailing health over the years. It never ceased to surprise her how, despite all his difficulties in movement, he always seemed to find a way to continue working for his business. What a shame it now was that he was too incapacitated to drive his specially adapted motor car himself. She knew Jesse was luckier than most to have been able to afford to have the car built to his specifications in the first place and at least he had a driver to take him where he needed to go so that he could maintain some of his independence. She was glad of it.

Later that day, Florence wrote to the last address she had for Nellie in her records.

St Heliers House
The Park
Nottingham
5 May 1917

13 Red Lion Street
Nottingham

Dear Nellie,

I hope you are keeping well and can hardly believe it's almost three years since you married and left Boots. I am taking a chance that you still live at the address I have for you but if not I'm hoping that it is forwarded on to you and that it finds you very soon.

I apologise for my presumption in contacting you, Nellie, and do not wish to offend by doing so. I have been advised that your brave son went to war and has returned injured and I wanted to offer any help that Sir Jesse and I might be able to give him regarding his employment. We appreciate the difficulty in some returning soldiers finding work and so offer our assistance.

Should your son wish to meet with me regarding work at Boots, then please ask him to come to my office at Pelham Street where we met and spoke with each other many years ago.

My best wishes to you and your family.

Yours sincerely,
Florence, Lady Boot

Florence sealed the letter in an envelope and placed it on the pile of signed letters for Gladys to send to the Post Office that afternoon. She closed Nellie's file and put it back in the metal filing tray for Enid to replace in her filing system. Florence hoped that the letter would reach Nellie and that either her son had already found work that satisfied him or he came to see her so that she could ensure he was given employment. How sad, Florence thought, for a young man who should be starting out building his own family to have been abandoned by the woman he had chosen to be his wife. How heartbroken must he now be to have to find a way to move on with his life just when he had imagined he would be celebrating having children and a home of his own?

Florence stood and walked over to her window and clasping her hands behind her back looked down on the busy street below. She couldn't help wondering how many of those pedestrians were going through their own heartache. It was a dark time in their history, of that she had no doubt. She wished she had the power to look into the future and see how much longer this torturous time would continue.

She turned to go back to her desk and thought of all the

men who would never return to their homes or families and those, like Nellie's son, who did return but were very much altered. She knew she had to do everything she possibly could to help Nellie's son and other ex-soldiers.

Chapter Twenty-Five

July 1917

'Lady Boot,' Gladys said, entering Florence's office, her voice low. She appeared a little shaken, which was not like her secretary at all. 'There's a young man asking to see you. He says his name is Joseph Blythe.'

'Joseph Blythe.' Florence glanced at her diary. There was no mention of Nellie's son coming to meet with her today. 'I wrote to his mother a couple of months ago, asking that he come and see me.'

'A couple of months ago?' Gladys repeated, sounding surprised.

Florence waved Gladys away. 'It's fine. Please, do send him in.'

She watched Gladys leave and braced herself, aware that he had suffered injuries to one side of his face, determined not to show any shock at his appearance when he entered.

Seconds later, the door opened once more, and Gladys stepped into the room. 'Mr Joseph Blythe, Lady Boot,' she announced before motioning for him to enter.

'Thank you, Gladys,' Florence said, standing to greet him. She was interested to see the young man she had met only once as a baby, so many years before. 'That will be all.' She looked at Joseph for the first time, shocked by the vivid red scar like a map across one side of his face. The other side was untouched and very handsome. She felt a fist grip her heart tightly and forced a smile. He was staring her straight in the eyes, his jaw clenched and his expression defiant. He obviously didn't want to be there. 'Unless you'd like a cup of tea, or some other refreshment, Mr Blythe?'

'Thank you, no.'

She asked him to take a seat and once they were both sitting clasped her hands together resting them on her desk. 'We've met before, but you won't remember it.'

Her comment took him off guard. Florence was relieved when he appeared to forget his determination to be standoffish. 'I wasn't aware that we had,' he answered, confused.

'It was when you were a tiny baby. I visited your mother and grandmother at their home to speak to them about something.'

He didn't say anything further but stared at her. Florence watched him studying her and could see he was surprised by what he found. 'My mother has always spoken very highly of you, Lady Boot, and of your husband. She said you are very kind and once helped her when she needed it most. It's the reason she managed to persuade me to come here today.'

Florence relaxed slightly. 'You're a very honest young man,' she said. 'I like that. I'm glad to see you here today and relieved that my letter found your mother. I wasn't sure if she would still live at the same address. She is well, I hope?'

'Yes, very. She's happy, which is the most important thing to me.' He looked down at his hands resting on his legs. 'At least she was until –' he hesitated for a second – 'I came home.'

Florence wondered how she would feel if this was John sitting opposite her. She hoped that people would be kind and not treat him any differently to how they would if he hadn't been injured in this way.

They sat in companionable silence for a few seconds. She liked this direct man and wanted to help him find a way to settle back into Nottingham once more, as she hoped others might do for John if fortunes were reversed.

'Now I remember,' Florence said. 'Your mother called you Joey when you were small.'

He smiled and although the scarred side of his face creased oddly his eyes lit up. 'She still does.'

'Well, Joseph.'

'Please, call me Joey,' he said, his voice losing the tightness that he it had initially held. 'I feel that, as this isn't the first time we've met, it's the correct thing to do.'

Florence was happy to see him soften towards her and lose some of his defensiveness. She wondered if this barrier he had built up against others was recent or if it was something he had always had as the son of an unmarried mother. Poor boy, she thought, he can't have ever had it easy, and now he had to contend with a scar that he had no way of covering up.

'Thank you, Joey. I suppose you wonder why I asked your mother to send you to me?'

'She thought you might be able to offer me work at one of your factories.'

'That's right. Do you have particular skills that you'd like me to consider when finding where to place you in the business?'

He thought for a moment. 'I'm strong, despite this,' he said raising his right hand to show where he had lost two fingers. 'I write well and I'm good at addition.' He shrugged. 'To be honest with you, Lady Boot, I'd just be happy to get back to normal and earn a weekly wage to help my mum.' He looked down at his hands once more. 'I think something out of the way might be best.' He looked her in the eye again. 'I don't want to put off any of the customers by them coming face-to-face with this.' He indicated his scarred cheek.

Florence hated to see this gentle young man being so self-deprecating. 'Joey, I know you have had a lot of changes to –' she hesitated, struggling to find the right words – 'get used to recently, but you have so much going for you. You need to value yourself and then others will do the same. Don't let what's happened hold you back from living the full life you are meant to enjoy.'

'Thank you, you're very kind. I know you mean well, Lady Boot, and I appreciate you trying to help me. For now, at least, I'd rather have a role behind the scenes in one of your stores or factories. If possible, that is.' He looked down at the desk. 'If I'm honest, I'd rather not go out at all in the daylight.'

Florence couldn't hide her shock. 'No, Joey. You mustn't think that way, not for a second.' He tore his gaze up once more to stare her in the eyes. 'The scars you bear are a mark of your bravery. They're not something to be embarrassed about.' She hoped she hadn't overstepped that invisible line between trying to be helpful and just being downright annoying. After all, she didn't really know him at all. 'You are a heroic young man, and don't you ever let anyone's ignorant behaviour let you think otherwise.'

He raised his eyebrows and Florence could tell he was surprised by her outburst. 'Maybe one day I'll be able to see this mess of my face in the way that you describe, Lady Boot. I do hope so. For now though, I find it difficult to ignore the shocked looks some people give me. A few have even stopped in front of me, stared and whispered behind their hands to the person with them.'

'But that's shocking.'

'I agree. I hadn't realised how cruel people could be about something like this, and at a time when there must be many other men with similar injuries walking around.' Florence had to concentrate on keeping her temper in check. 'My mother thinks that when those particular people see me, it probably reminds them that what happened to me can happen to their loved ones fighting away.' What he said made sense to Florence, but it was no excuse to be cruel to someone. She was about to say so when he added, 'Others are simply disgusted by my face. Like my ex-fiancée.'

Pain dripped from his words and Florence wanted to hug it away. His face reddened and Florence realised he wished he hadn't been so open with her.

'All I can say to that, Joey, is that some people are shallower than they should be. I think you should take as little notice of them as you possibly can.' She tried to imagine the depth of his pain when his fiancée cast him aside. 'You are worth so much more than these people who hurt you with their thoughtless actions.'

She placed her palms down on her desk, aware that the best way to help Joey was to give him some way to feel needed while keeping his mind off his pain.

'I think we need to take the next step towards making your future as satisfying as I know it can be,' she said, hoping to reassure him. 'I need to look into my files and find a couple of vacancies that I feel might be suitable for you. Do you mind returning to my office to see me again tomorrow?'

'No, not at all.'

Florence opened her diary and ran her finger down the list of appointments she had set out for the following day. She was already booked up for the day and had promised Jesse to take time out to eat lunch with him in his office. It was the only time she could adapt to fit in Joey's visit. She knew that once she explained everything to Jesse, he wouldn't mind shortening their lunch break.

'Come back at noon tomorrow. I'll go through what vacancies I've found for you and we'll take it from there. Will that be all right?'

His mouth drew back into a wide smile. 'Thank you, Lady Boot. I'll be here. I suppose I should have given you a little notice before coming today as well, shouldn't I?'

Florence laughed, presuming he had noticed the long list of appointments in her diary. 'It would have saved you coming back tomorrow, but no matter.' She stood and walked around her desk to the door. She waited for him to join her and proffered her hand for him to shake it. 'Everything will work out eventually, Joey. I know it will.'

'My mother said you were a determined lady,' he said, his smile slipping slightly. 'I hope it's not rude to say that?'

Florence thought back to the meeting she had had with Nellie and then her mother's anger in this very office and then about her visiting their home with her offer of a position of work for the young, terrified woman years before. 'It isn't. And I'm not surprised your mother did say that of me.'

She realised that he was contemplating whether or not to say something. Florence waited for him to speak but when he wasn't forthcoming, she decided to probe him slightly.

'Was there something else you wished to ask me?' she asked, hoping he would open up a little more. 'Please, feel free to ask anything.'

He glanced at the silver-framed picture of her three children with Jesse that she always kept sitting on her desk and pointed to it. 'It's just that I met your daughter, when I was in France.'

Whatever she had been expecting him to say, it wasn't this. 'You did? When?'

'On my way back to Blighty,' he said wistfully. 'It had been a long and arduous journey, and, if I'm honest –' he raised his hand to almost touch the damaged side of his face, stopping just before the tips of his fingers connected with the raised, red flesh – 'I was in a foul mood and a lot of pain. When the train stopped and we were all told to disembark to wait for the next one bringing us to Calais, I wasn't impressed. I didn't want to speak to anyone or get off the train. Word reached me and the lads I was with about some English ladies running a canteen. We decided to make the most of our wait and fetch a cup of good old English tea. I'd been desperate for a decent cuppa since leaving Blighty.'

He stopped speaking and looked at Florence, his expression sad. 'I wasn't ready to speak to no ladies, not even with a dressing covering this.'

Florence's heart ached for the young man who had gone through so much trauma. 'But you did get off and go to the canteen, I hope?'

He nodded. 'Didn't have much choice. I was taken there by the lads. They were starving and had heard from someone that the food was tasty.'

Florence thought how undomesticated her youngest

daughter had always been. 'And what was it like?'

He smiled for the first time since starting to relay his story. 'Good. Very good, in fact. It was like a tiny corner of England had been transported to Northern France,' he said wistfully. 'It cheered me up no end, despite myself.' He laughed. 'I spoke to that lady too,' he said indicating the photo once again. 'It's strange to think I've met your daughter so far from home, isn't it?'

Florence thought so, too. 'Tell me more,' she said. 'I've read accounts of soldiers passing through Margery's canteen but not spoken to one directly.'

'I think she's very like you, if you don't mind me saying so, Lady Boot?'

'I don't mind at all. In what way?'

His face reddened. 'I don't know either of you properly, but you both have the same strength about you somehow. And –' he thought for a moment – 'a kindness that a person can't miss. Although,' and he laughed again, 'I can't imagine many people would cross either of you. I think you're both rather formidable.'

Florence burst out laughing. She loved hearing someone being so honest and she imagined that her daughter would be just as amused.

'You don't mind me saying such things, I hope? I'd hate you to think me insolent.'

Florence shook her head. She picked up the photo of her three children with Jesse and gazed at Margery's determined expression. 'I hadn't noticed how alike we were before,' she said, proud to think her daughter favoured her in such a way. Placing it back down on her desk again, she grinned at him. 'I have no issue with you describing us in this way at all. In fact,' she said, 'I think you've summed us both up pretty well.'

'She's an incredible lady. Your daughter and the other ladies working with her are doing a grand job in France, Lady Boot. I have to say I felt much better after spending a short time in her canteen, as did the lads I was there with.'

'That's marvellous to hear. I'm sure my husband will be delighted when I tell him the difference our daughter's canteen made to your journey home.'

She showed him to the door. 'Until we meet here tomorrow, then, Joey.'

Gladys appeared from her office. 'Please, Mr Blythe, come with me and I'll show you out.'

Florence walked into the office that Gladys and Enid shared. 'Enid, please find me all the vacancies that you think will suit a young, fit man, then bring them to me this afternoon.'

She left Enid to her work and returned to her office and stared once more out of the window down to the pavement. A couple of minutes later she spotted Joey crossing the road and stopping to talk to an older woman. The woman reached up and placed her palm on the unblemished side of his face before the two of them turned and walked away down a side road. Florence realised the woman had been Nellie and was relieved that she would be able to help the devoted mother find her beloved son a place in the Boots company.

Chapter Twenty-Six

Florence struggled to bid farewell to yet more of her girls. It broke her heart to see them leave. Some of them had come to Boots straight from leaving school and she had thought them settled and happy in their work. Each assured her that they had been, and she had to believe them. She had hoped that as time wore on fewer would go, but with the scarcity of food and the Women's Land Army being formed, along with the many adverts encouraging women to give their labour voluntarily in the countryside, more of her girls left Boots to do just that.

She supposed it was the thought of working in the countryside as opposed to a town and being in a factory all day. Thankfully few of her shop assistants left, but she knew that if she lost many more of her women to the arms factory at Chilwell, or as Land Girls replacing the farm workers who had left their jobs to enlist, then she was going to have a problem finding enough staff to carry out the work to provide all that they made at Boots.

Only the previous month Ethel, her under-housemaid, had left to go and work on a farm, living with three other field workers. Before leaving she had, so Harriet her lady's maid had told her, been boasting to Mavis, one of the other maids, that she intended looking for a handsome farmer to marry. Weeks later Harriet told Florence, one evening as she dressed her hair for a dinner party, how differently things had turned out for poor Ethel.

'I think,' Harriet said, choosing a few metal hairpins from the pot on the dressing table, 'that Ethel was rather shocked to discover that not only were there no handsome farmers living on the farm, but few men at all. Apart from an ancient man who was the father of the farmer's wife.'

'Oh dear,' Florence said, hoping things improved soon for the naïve young girl, 'but has she made any friends among the other women she's living with?'

'I think she gets on well with one of them, but she doesn't like her Gang Leader very much, according to Mavis. Apparently, the better educated girls or more enthusiastic girls are given those roles and the one in charge of Ethel didn't take to her too well.'

Florence wondered how many other men and women had left their homes and all that they knew to race off to what they expected to be a more exciting, fun life, only to discover that it was extremely hard work and most of the time in not very pleasant surroundings.

'Do you think she'll want to return here to St Heliers, at

all?' Florence asked, concerned that now she had taken on Lena to replace Ethel she might have to find work for both of them should Ethel ask for her old job back.

Harriet shrugged. 'I'm not sure. I doubt it though. I think it would be too embarrassing for Ethel to come back after the way she boasted to Mavis about her exciting new role.'

'But she's writing to Mavis telling her how dreadful it all is now so that really doesn't make very much sense.'

'No, not really,' Harriet agreed, her voice clear although she was holding a couple of hairpins between her teeth. 'She also mentioned that she was working on the fields planting, that it's backbreaking work and how she hopes to be one of those chosen to learn how to steer the plough.'

Florence thought of the small, skinny girl and couldn't imagine her being able to work a field let alone control a horse and plough but said nothing.

'As sweet as Ethel could be,' Harriet said, 'she was always a little dreamy and unrealistic.'

'Poor girl,' Florence said, feeling very sorry for Ethel and the predicament she had found herself in. 'I hope she settles in soon and starts to enjoy working at the farm as much as she expected to.'

'As do I, Lady Boot.'

It wasn't only the garden at St Heliers that now had been turned over to vegetables. Florence noticed the last time she went to Lily's that her pretty little front garden was now reduced to a narrow border alongside the front path. The rest of the space had been put to growing vegetables, some in the beds and others in terracotta pots of varying sizes. It made sense to make the most of the outside space you had, Florence thought as she passed cabbages, carrots, beetroots and tomatoes held up by willow branches tied at the top with string. Lily had a small household to feed and what better way to supplement their meals than to grow as much as they could, especially now that as well as the food supplies dropping the prices seemed to be increasing far too quickly for everyone's liking. She wondered how the poor families without outside space were managing to cope through the crisis.

She had heard some of her girls speak about how their husbands or fathers had managed to obtain their own plot to set up an allotment. A lot of them were on land previously given over to nature or wasteland that most people ignored. Other councils set up plots for locals in the town park nearest the shops, and some even used public land, converting it to allotments so that people could grow vegetables.

Florence was relieved to see the local councils trying to help the people of Nottingham in such a way. Each afternoon as she and Jesse sat in their car being driven home from the office, she noticed the queues at the butchers, bakers and other food shops lengthening. It was obvious food was becoming scarcer by the month. It had been the case for a couple of years now and Florence couldn't imagine how people were going to keep their families nourished on an ever-decreasing supply of food. The wretchedness on the faces of those waiting for hours in line hoping to be able to buy something that they could feed to their family was horrifying.

'These people are slowly starving, Jesse,' she said, staring out of the car window. 'I don't think I've ever seen anything so dreadful.'

'I agree,' he said quietly. 'When I was a boy and we had nothing, we could at least rely on the congregation at our church to help feed us. Now though, with food so scarce throughout the country, there's none extra to supply to those who need it most.'

'At least our girls still have their cocoa each morning,' Florence said half to herself. 'It's not much but it's something.' She thought of her servants at home, each of whom, like she and Jesse, had cut back on their food intake. 'I wonder how much longer the country can go on in this way before we completely run out of food?' She shivered. It was like an ongoing nightmare that she couldn't wake up from, dragging on and on, getting continually worse in ways she couldn't have imagined.

'I've no idea.'

One afternoon, as they were driving through the town on their way home, Parry slowed the car, waiting for a vehicle that had broken down to be moved out of the way, when shouts erupted. Florence and Jesse looked out of their window towards the nearest queue where an argument had broken out. The next thing she knew, one man's fist connected with the other's jaw. He fell backwards and then several more men and women joined in.

Florence gasped. 'They're going to kill each other if they're not careful.'

'They're frightened, Florence,' Jesse said sadly. 'Those men are panicking because they don't know how to find enough food to feed their families.'

Florence's heart pounded as she tried unsuccessfully to tear her eyes away from the ugly scene. What was the world coming to if decent men like these forgot themselves in this way? It devastated her to see how the fear of not being able to provide for their families had brought them so low. People were falling apart and surely it was only going to get worse the longer this war and the lack of food continued. How soon would it be until her own family were brought to their knees?

Her vision blurred and she wiped her eyes roughly with her gloved hands. 'Surely there's something we can do to help these poor people?'

The sadness she felt at witnessing such hopelessness was almost overwhelming. She was worn out by the war, as was everyone around her. It had dragged on for so long now, changing everything they had once known. Florence wished she could see an end in sight, but there was little sign of it coming any time soon.

Jesse sighed heavily. 'I only wish we could do something, but the problem is too enormous. The government needs to step in and find a way to help this countrywide problem. Hopefully it will do something soon, for all our sakes.'

Chapter Twenty-Seven

November 1917

'Milly Jones to see you, Lady Boot.'

Florence motioned for Enid to show her employee into her office.

'Sit down, Milly,' Florence said, indicating the seat on the other side of her desk. She recognised the fresh-faced girl. She had taken a look at her records prior to the appointment and reminded herself that Milly was only fifteen when she had come to work for them two years before. 'How are you keeping?'

'Very well, thank you, Lady Boot.' Milly chewed the side of her lower lip anxiously.

Milly didn't say anything further and Florence sensed she was there to give notice. It wasn't difficult to detect the signs – she had come up against this quite a few times over the past couple of years.

'Would you like to tell me what I can do for you, Milly?'

The girl sat up a little straighter and seemed to brace herself. 'Firstly, Lady Boot, my mum said I must tell you how happy I've been working for Boots and to thank you for taking me on when I left school.' Florence didn't like to interrupt. It was obvious by the way Milly kept swallowing that her mouth was dry and that she was nervous about speaking to her. 'I'm sorry but I'll be leaving, Lady Boot.' For the first time, she looked Florence directly in the eye. 'It's not that I haven't been happy here because I have been. Very happy. It's just that, well, I…'

Florence could not bear to watch the girl suffer so badly. She raised her hand to stop her saying anything further. 'I'm sorry to hear that you wish to go. Do you mind telling me where you'll be working next?'

'I don't mind at all. My cousin helped get me a job up at the shell-filling factory. Chilwell way.'

She had been right, then, Florence thought, concerned. She clasped her hands together on her lap, not wishing Milly to see how concerned she was at hearing the girl's future plans. She wished so many of her girls hadn't been tempted by the extra wages but understood how the increase in their family income would come in handy. The arms factory offered the girls thirty shillings a week.

No doubt Milly's family, like most people in Nottingham, were panic-stricken that there seemed to be little prospect of an Allied victory, and they had to cope with increasing restrictions, constant news of more losses and the return of many wounded, who, even if they recovered, would continually struggle with the changes their wounds had brought to their bodies and minds.

'Is there anything I can do to persuade you to remain at Boots?'

Florence wondered if she would ever get used to feeling helpless when it came to situations like these. She doubted it. The company couldn't afford to increase everyone's salaries in an effort to keep the girls; there were too many staff. Florence knew now that many of the girls were leaving out of a sense of duty to their country. Didn't they realise that working at Boots fulfilled the same role? After all, the company was working hard to support the war effort and surely by working in those departments the girls were doing their part. She said as much to Milly, but her efforts proved fruitless.

Milly shook her head. 'I'm sorry, Lady Boot, but I've made up my mind.'

'I'm sure your colleagues will be sad to see you go.' She looked down at Milly's file and, opening it, read her most recent work report. 'Your manager says here in her report that you're a valued member of staff and a hard worker.' Florence closed the file. 'If you do decide that working in munitions is not for you, please do come back and see me. I'll do my best to find you work here and we'll certainly be happy for you to return.'

Milly's shoulders relaxed slightly and Florence could see she looked very relieved. 'Thank you so much. My mum was upset when I said I was leaving here and worried what

I'd do if I hated it there, so she'll be happy to hear what you've said.'

'Good.' Florence discussed Milly's notice and her last day working at the Island Street factory. Then she wished her well once again and showed her out.

She watched helplessly as Milly walked along the landing towards the stairs and prayed that the girl would stay safe. She had heard tales of girls being terribly injured and others dying of toxic poisoning in munitions factories despite the strict regulations they each had to abide by. She hated to think that one of her girls might end up permanently damaged or even losing her life for the sake of a few extra shillings a week. She despised how powerless she felt to stop them from going, but knew that now more than ever these girls' families needed the extra money they would be bringing in.

Florence's concerns for Milly were forced to the back of her mind when she returned home to an unexpected surprise.

'You'll never guess what happened today,' she said, walking into the living room expecting to find Jesse sitting by himself reading in front of the fire. Florence saw a woman stand up and start to turn towards her and by the look of happiness on Jesse's face she knew before she turned fully to face her that it must be Margery.

'Hello, Mother.' Margery grinned at her and immediately hurried around the sofa to hug Florence.

Florence's heart leaped to see her youngest child at St Heliers House. 'My darling girl,' she said, taking her in her arms and hugging her tightly. 'When did you arrive?' She let go and taking Margery by her upper arms held her away from her slightly to study her, fear seeping into her mind. 'Nothing's wrong, is it?'

'No, not at all.' Margery leant forward and kissed Florence on the cheek. 'I'm perfectly well.'

'I didn't receive word that you were on your way,' she said, trying to recall if she might have missed something. She marched over to the side of the fireplace and pulled the cord to call for one of the servants. 'Your bed isn't made up and we need to make sure Cook prepares enough supper for you.'

'Calm down, my dear.' Jesse waved for her to sit. 'Margery's been here for almost an hour and her room has been made up and Mrs Rudge spoken to. Everything is in order and there's no need for you to fret.'

Margery took Florence's hand in hers and led her to the sofa. 'Sit next to me, Mother. Tell us what's happened today. You seem a little out of sorts and I know it's not me turning up out of the blue.'

Florence realised she was acting erratically so did as her daughter suggested. Once seated she smoothed down her skirt and took a deep, calming breath.

'You're quite right. Today has been rather worrisome.' She patted Margery's hand. 'I am delighted to see you here though. How long do we have you with us this time?' she asked hoping it would be for at least a fortnight but doubting Margery would be able to take that much time away from her canteen and her colleagues.

'It's only for a couple of nights, I'm afraid.'

Florence couldn't hide her disappointment, but said, 'Take no notice of me. Two nights is far better than none. I'm simply relieved to have you here at home, for however long it might be. It's a long way to travel for two nights though, you must be exhausted.'

'I am a little. It was a rough crossing and we travelled with a boat load of wounded being brought back from what sounds like a very bloody, extremely muddy battle somewhere called Passchendaele.'

Florence had read horrifying accounts of an ongoing battle that had been raging for a couple of months on the Ypres salient. She shivered at the thought of the men Margery would have encountered on their way home.

'Oh, my poor girl. That can't have been easy?'

Margery shook her head slowly and stared at the flames leaping in the grate. 'It was… I'm not sure how to put it into words.' She looked at Jesse and then Florence and Florence could see the weariness in her daughter's eyes. 'I know I'll never again see life as I used to do. Or be able to forget what I've seen. I try to push the memories aside, but they seem to be imprinted on the inside of my eyelids so that closing my eyes doesn't help at all.' She shook her head. 'I've seen many wounded soldiers before, obviously. Tens of thousands have passed through our canteen and I foolishly believed I was finally becoming used to seeing badly injured men. These poor souls though seemed worse than any I'd met before. Many of them seem to have broken minds, as well as damaged bodies,' she said so quietly that

Florence struggled to hear her clearly. 'I can't imagine that those will ever be able to find work after the war does end. And if they can't work, how will they support themselves or their families?'

Florence wished she could protect Margery from all that she was witnessing in Northern France. 'We don't have to speak of it, if you'd rather not.'

Margery shook her head. 'I'll only become weepy if I do,' she said. 'And that's not the way to behave when I have so little time with you both.'

'Nonsense,' Florence said hoping to reassure her. 'We're here to listen to you. You must speak freely and for as long as you need about any subject while you're here.' Florence looked at Jesse to back her up. 'Isn't that the case, Jesse?'

'Yes, it is.'

Margery brightened. 'You're both very sweet, but I'd rather find out how you've been getting along and catch up with your news.'

'You go first, my dear,' Jesse said. 'My news isn't too interesting, I'm afraid. Just more of the same.'

Florence and Margery smiled at each other fondly. How typical of Jesse to want her to share the news of her day. He had seen how disturbed she had been on arriving home and knew she needed to get a few things off her chest. She told them about her meeting with Milly Jones and how she was going to join several others of her girls by leaving to work at the shell-filling factory. 'I'm concerned about their safety, that's all.'

'I understand why,' Margery agreed. 'I've heard all sorts

of stories about these places. And remember the Silvertown explosion in West Ham at the beginning of this year.'

'Yes, I recall reading about it only too well,' Florence said. 'Over seventy people killed, and hundreds injured, if I recall rightly. I just can't bear to think of that happening to any of my girls.'

'My dear, they won't be your girls any longer, not if they've left your employ,' Jesse reminded her. 'They are no longer your responsibility and I'm afraid there's nothing you can do to keep them from leaving and going to work wherever they choose.'

She knew that only too well but wished it wasn't the case. She felt Margery give her a gentle nudge.

'Stop worrying about them, Mother. They're going to make their own choices, like me, John and Dorothy. Have you ever been able to dissuade us from doing things that might put us slightly in harm's way?'

Florence thought about John enlisting and then having been disabled out of the army then signing up the Reserves to work in another capacity. What about when Margery had announced her plans to set up the canteen in Northern France?

She looked at her daughter and shook her head. 'I've never managed to get you to change your mind, if that's what you mean.' She smiled at her to ensure Margery didn't take her words too seriously.

'Well, then.'

It seemed that no sooner had Margery arrived than she was preparing to leave again. Florence hated having to wave her daughter off at Nottingham Station once more. It was a relief to know though that with another Christmas drawing ever closer she had a diary full of appointments that would keep her busy and unable to fret about her daughter too much. Not that the wartime Christmases were as joyous as those her family had enjoyed before, she thought miserably. However much her family might portray a festive spirit, Florence couldn't miss the weariness in their eyes. They were all tired of this dreadful war and having to put on a brave face in each other's company. She hoped that something would soon change to bring to an end the years of dreading what each day would bring.

The first appointment Florence had to honour meant hours of travelling and a night in London. She and Jesse had sponsored a Christmas gift-giving event for wounded soldiers at the Stoll Picture Theatre in Kingsway. However, on the day Jesse wasn't feeling well and was in too much pain to travel hours away from home.

She was met at the station by the man she had been corresponding with, a Major Gilby-Stratton, who seemed very grateful to her for taking the time to travel to London. He dropped her off at the Savoy, where she rested for a couple of hours and had a bite to eat before being collected once again.

His driver took them through the busy London traffic to the cinema. 'Do you come up to London often, Lady Boot?' the Major asked.

'Not as often as maybe I'd like,' she said, aware that each time she visited London she promised herself to return soon but rarely did. 'My husband and I are terribly busy with business and our family, so we don't get away very often.' She didn't add that ordinarily when she did have time for a break away from work she and Jesse liked to return to Jersey and spend time with family there.

'Here we are,' he said, as the car drew up next to the entrance of a vast building that seemed to take up the length of the entire block. Florence gazed at the French Renaissance façade adorned in Portland stone, the Corinthian pilasters on its upper storey and a centre window that she had been told was almost forty feet in height. The entrance hall was flanked by white and gold fluted columns with bas-reliefs that she recognised as being of famous composers.

'It looks like a rather splendid opera house,' she said in awe as she gazed at the boxes high up around the surrounding walls.

'It is rather impressive, isn't it?' the Major agreed. 'The theatre was only bought last year by Mr Stoll and he opened it this April after converting it into a cinema. We thought it the perfect place to hold today's event. I want to thank you and Sir Jesse very much for your generosity in sponsoring the many gifts, and you for coming all this way to meet the men and hand them out.'

'It's the perfect place for it,' Florence said as she was taken through to the stage and welcomed by over six hundred wounded soldiers and officers, who cheered when they saw her. 'And I'm delighted to be here. My husband was sorry to miss this today, but I'll send him your good wishes.'

Florence waited for the cheering to end and for everyone to take their seats in the auditorium. As she smiled at the huge crowd welcoming her Florence could not help thinking how lucky she was to be in a position where her presence and a gift from her could make such a difference to the soldiers' Christmas. She wished Jesse could be here now witnessing how happy these men were to be invited to the cinema for the handing out of the gifts. He would be delighted to see the joy on the men's faces.

Florence stepped forward to address them, happy to know that this small gesture of hers would go someway to making these several hundred brave soldiers happy and letting them know that, whether they had families or were alone in the world, they were respected and remembered by her and Jesse.

Chapter Twenty-Eight

January 1918

The year began with yet more bad news when a boat taking Red Cross nurses, including Catherine Ball and Maud Brown from Nottingham, was sunk in the Mediterranean on its way to Egypt. Florence and Jesse attended the memorial service for the women at St Peter's together with most of their servants, as well as Dorothy and John. Florence was beginning to feel like the war would never end and that this was how their future might be. There was so much heartache everywhere and she found that her only way of coping was to focus her attention on work and her family.

She rubbed her temples as she walked through the hall to the baize door. She wished her headache would go and wasn't sure why it was troubling her. Because she was worried about Jesse's health, maybe? she wondered.

Though that was always on her mind and was something she was used to fretting about. No, this was something else, she decided as she pushed open the green door and walked along the corridor towards the kitchen, where the smell of baking emanated, filling her nostrils with the familiar delicious scent of vanilla.

She needed to speak to Mrs Rudge about the new rationing system, whereby each person was restricted to a weekly ration. It was far less than they were used to, but it was something they would have to ensure they stuck to. She wasn't surprised after witnessing the horrendous queues outside butchers and grocers the previous year.

'Good morning, Cook,' she said, entering the warm kitchen. This must be the warmest room in the house, Florence thought, noticing the two layers of what would no doubt be a very tasty Victoria sponge served to them at tea later that day sitting cooling on two wire racks.

'Good morning, Lady Boot,' Mrs Rudge said, wiping her hands on her pristine apron.

'That sponge smells delicious.'

'Thank you, I hope it tastes good. Sir Jesse requested that I bake one for your tea this afternoon. I'm told that Miss Buttons and your daughter-in-law will be coming.'

Florence had forgotten, which wasn't like her. She decided to blame her lack of memory on having such a dull headache. 'I'm sure we'll all enjoy it very much.'

Mrs Rudge moved a pan off the stove and then looked at Florence. 'Was there something you wished to discuss with me, Lady Boot?'

'There was. The rationing we're now obliged to follow,' she said, relieved that the sponge had been baked before she had to discuss the matter. 'I gather each member of the household must hold a ration book and be registered at whichever shops we purchase our food.'

'So Meadows tells me,' Mrs Rudge said, looking concerned at the thought. 'I suppose I'll need to keep each of your ration books down here with me then?'

'Yes, I imagine you will.' Florence glanced at the larder in the corner of the large room. Each time she had looked in there it had always been filled with tasty things for Mrs Rudge to feed the family and servants. She wondered how the new rules were going to affect the household meals but hoped that with the new rationing in place food would be more evenly distributed to everyone in the country. It made good sense.

'Please don't hesitate to ask me if you need any help deciding on daily menus. I suspect Sir Jesse might find it a little difficult to go without some of the things he's used to eating, but we are all in this together.'

Mrs Rudge pulled a folded small poster from her pocket. 'They haven't given us very much to live off,' she moaned, flattening the sheet of paper down on the scrubbed table and resting her finger on the list of ingredients that each person in Britain now had to be restricted to weekly.

'Look at this, Lady Boot. We are only to have fifteen ounces of meat per person each week, and then there's breakfasts. How am I supposed to make five ounces of bacon last? Thankfully, I'll be able to supplement the breakfast with eggs that we have brought in every few days from one of the farms nearby, but that's not very much at all. I don't think it is anyway.'

Florence walked over and ran her eyes down the list. Jesse didn't have too big an appetite and over the years it had lessened, but she knew there would be many people, especially families with growing sons and larger husbands, who would find this lack of meat very difficult to cope with. She heard Mrs Rudge say something and realised she was still talking.

'How am I supposed to keep everyone to eight ounces of sugar each week? I think those who eat porridge will have to forego their spoonful of sugar.'

Florence had thought about this on her way down to the kitchen. 'We can obtain honey from one of the beekeepers,' she suggested. 'Honey on porridge is very tasty, I think. In fact, I prefer it.' She couldn't recall the last time she had eaten a bowl of porridge, but it seemed to be something that was troubling Mrs Rudge. 'Sir Jesse and I can forgo our sugar in tea. It will do us both good. Then I think that if you collate half of the household sugar and margarine and can make a couple of cakes a week for everyone to enjoy in the afternoons, I'm sure we'll all enjoy eating a slice. What do you think?'

Mrs Rudge pursed her thin lips thoughtfully. 'Hmm, I heard too that milk and flour is to be rationed, which will put an end to most of the puddings and cakes everyone is used to eating here at St Heliers. I suppose this is another way of us doing our bit, isn't it?'

'You're right, Cook.' Florence clasped her hands together, determined to look more enthusiastic about the changes than she felt at that moment. 'Thankfully, we have enough vegetables to bulk up our meals. Who knows, we might find that we enjoy eating less meat?'

Mrs Rudge gave her a look that told Florence she wasn't at all convinced by her suggestion. 'Maybe.'

The woman looked so down that Florence knew she had to cheer her up. She rested a hand on Mrs Rudge's left shoulder. 'I know it's wearisome, Mrs Rudge, but we have to do our best to keep going. Sir Jesse and I have the utmost faith in your capabilities,' she said. 'Neither of us have ever eaten of a meal of yours that we didn't think tasty and thoroughly enjoyable.' Mrs Rudge's face brightened as Florence spoke, encouraging her to continue. 'I'm sure I speak for us both, and the rest of the household, when I say how much we trust you to work with these reduced supplies and continue to offer us delicious meals.'

'Thank you, Lady Boot,' she said. 'I've been speaking to a couple of the cooks at neighbouring houses here in The Park and we've swapped a couple of recipes which we thought might help now food is so scarce.'

'Really?' Florence asked, sensing that Mrs Rudge needed to talk a little longer. 'Can you tell me the sort of dishes you were discussing?'

Mrs Rudge smiled. 'Yes, well, let me have a think. There's one called Saturday Pie. It was my idea. I saw it advertised in a magazine a couple of years ago. It's made up of leftovers, you know, cold meat, that sort of thing.' She thought for a moment and then, raising a finger triumphantly in the air, added, 'You can add mashed potatoes, maybe some onions to give it a bit more taste and if you have some, then a few herbs.'

'It sounds interesting,' Florence said. 'I know you'd make it taste delicious. What else was there?'

'A pudding. Apricot Charlotte, I think it was called. That's made with leftover stale bread and dried apricots. I think I'll give that one a try next week sometime.'

'Whatever you make for us, I know we'll enjoy it, Cook.'

'Thank you, Lady Boot. I'll certainly endeavour to do my best to cater for the household's requirements.'

'I know you will,' Florence reassured her. 'But remember, should you need me to offer you any help with menus, or in finding alternative ingredients, then please do come to my study and ask me. Together, I know we can get through this difficult, dark time. After all, we're all in this together.'

Florence noticed Mrs Rudge's shoulders straighten and her chin rise in defiance at the new laws they all had to live by.

'Yes, Lady Boot. As always, you are right. We will all do our best to work with what we have at hand. Thank you for coming to see me this morning. I'm feeling much better about it all having spoken to you.'

Florence was relieved to have been of help to the loyal woman who had been feeding them for many years. 'Thank you, Cook. I don't know what we would do without you keeping us all fed so well.'

She left the kitchen feeling much better and it wasn't until she reached the hallway that she realised that her headache had almost gone. There was so much to consider nowadays, she thought as she walked through to the living room. She felt certain that the difficulties they were all now facing and the new ways in which everyone in Britain had to alter their eating habits would surely change everyone of them somehow.

To think that only four years ago, they had never considered being short of food. Then the biggest issues she had faced, apart from Jesse's declining health, were his relationship with John, her daughters getting married and bearing grandchildren for them, and how well their business was going. Now, they and everyone else had to think about every mouthful they ate, and each day were confronted with the suffering of others, because of this seemingly never-ending war.

Chapter Twenty-Nine

8 March 1918

Florence was enjoying her poached egg on toast when Jesse gasped and the colour drained from his face. Florence almost dropped her fork when she looked across the table at him, terrified that something was wrong with him, or that something might have happened to someone they knew.

'What is it, my love?'

He swallowed and indicated the broadsheet in his hand. 'They dropped a massive bomb near Paddington Station last night in one of their wretched bombing raids.' He shook his head slowly. 'They're saying here that it was probably around two thousand pounds in weight.'

Florence had no idea what damage something of that magnitude might cause, but knew it must have been devastating to properties and families living in the vicinity. 'But that's horrendous,' she cried.

'It is, my dear.' He shook his head slowly. 'It says that one of the casualties was Lena Ford.'

Florence recognised the name but was unable to place it. 'Remind me who she is?'

'She wrote the lyrics to that song with Ivor Novello. You know, the patriotic one people sing a lot. What is it now?' He hummed to himself briefly before raising his hand triumphantly. '"Keep the Home Fires Burning", that's it.'

Florence sighed. 'Poor woman. How tragic. And to think how much comfort her words have brought to people.'

They sat quietly, each lost in their own thoughts as they continued their breakfasts. Florence struggled to swallow every mouthful, but refused to waste food when others were going without. When she had finished, she drank a mouthful of tea, sadness threatening to overwhelm her. 'Where is all this going to end?' She thought of her children and the impact this seemingly endless war must be having on them. 'I'm glad I'm no longer young and about to start a family with all this terror and uncertainty in the world. I feel for our children and the other younger people just starting out.'

He sighed heavily. 'As do I. When I think how much they all have going against them now, it troubles me greatly. What will be left when this finally ends? How are we all expected to cope? I can't help worrying what state this country will be in when this war is finally over. It's frightening.'

Florence agreed. She was relieved when he turned his attention back to his broadsheet. She hated to cry in front of him but felt worn out from years of fear and struggling to be strong. Florence dabbed at her eyes with the corner of her napkin, and took a deep breath to rein in her emotions. She wasn't sure how much longer she could stand this interminable situation.

Florence focused as much as she could on work. It helped her not to worry too much about all the bad news Jesse mentioned to her each day. Slowly, the weather grew warmer and, finally, it was April 1918. Florence reread a letter she had received from Margery telling her the exciting news that she would be coming home on leave for two weeks to celebrate her twenty-sixth birthday. She couldn't wait to see her youngest child again. It had been far too long since the last time Margery had been back home.

Florence understood her daughter's dedication to her canteen and the other women she worked with as well as all the hard work they were doing and the vast number of men they had helped. However, the break at home would surely do Margery good and Florence planned to spend as much time with her daughter as possible.

'Darling,' Florence called, rushing with her arms wide to welcome Margery as she walked into the hallway. She had been irritated not to have finished her daily meetings and accompanied Meadows to the station to collect Margery, but she was here now. 'I thought you'd never get here. Was the train delayed?'

Meadows carried in Margery's bag, a worried look on his face as if Florence thought he might be the cause of their delay arriving home. 'Miss Margery caught a later train than the one you had expected,' he said. 'I'll take her bag up to her room.'

'Thank you, Meadows,' Margery said, stepping into Florence's arms and hugging her tightly. 'Meadows is right. The channel was very choppy, and the boat was delayed a couple of hours. It meant that I had to catch a much later train and poor Meadows had to wait for me.'

'I could have come to collect you if I'd known,' Florence grumbled, aware that there was no way Margery could have got a message to her so that she could get there to greet her.

'Never mind. I'm here now, thankfully.' Margery breathed in deeply.

'What on earth are you doing?' Florence asked, intrigued.

'You smell heavenly, as always, Mother,' Margery said, stepping back and gazing around the hall.

Florence watched her daughter as she studied an arrangement of pretty pink flowers Florence had selected from the garden especially for her return, and smiled.

'It's so comforting being back here at home where everything smells of floral scents, beeswax polish and wood fires.' She sighed and gave Florence a smile, closing her eyes briefly. 'And I know that if I go down to the kitchen right now there will be even more familiar smells to tempt me.'

Florence loved hearing her daughter speak so fondly about what it meant to her being back at St Heliers House with them. Florence hoped that her daughter wasn't intending to hide her true feelings from her. She didn't want Margery to pretend to be fine when they both knew that her experiences in France had made a lasting impression on her. She was going to have to take things slowly with Margery and allow her to settle back home in her own time. She would watch her and make sure that her daughter knew she could come to her with any concerns at all.

Florence had made a special effort with the flowers and knew that the servants had done the same with the cleaning and the food. Margery was always so bright and popular with the servants and Florence noticed how the house seemed to shine more brightly whenever she was at home. There was certainly more laughter and joy in the place.

'It's wonderful to have you back again, and for your birthday, too.' Florence put her arm around her daughter's small waist. 'I know I'll never be able to fully understand what you've been through or witnessed while you've been away,' she said quietly. 'But I hope you'll come to me if you ever need to talk about anything. I don't want you to keep things to yourself that would be better shared. Will you do that for me?' Florence watched her daughter as she took a deep breath and then looked at her, unshed tears in her large eyes.

Margery nodded, slowly. 'Yes, I will. Thank you,

Mother.' She leant into Florence and kissed her lightly on her cheek. 'I think it's going to take a bit of time for me to get used to being back here in the peace and quiet where everything is clean and calm.'

'It's bound to be that way,' Florence said, hoping Margery would do as she had said. 'Would you rather have something to drink first, or go and freshen up?'

'I'd like to go and wash and change into clean clothes first, I think.'

Florence gave her shoulder a gentle pat. She would have wanted to do exactly the same. 'Then I'll come with you up to your room to settle you in and make sure there's nothing you need.'

Margery laughed as they began walking up the stairs. 'I'm sure you've thought of everything already, Mother. Oh, it is good to be back home.'

Florence's heart lifted to hear her daughter's joy. 'We've missed you so very much. I want you to enjoy your time at home before you leave again. I don't mind what you want to do, whether it's going to visit friends or family, but you must promise me you'll take some time to relax. I've heard reports about how hard you and your assistants work at the canteen and you need to take some time just for you, don't you think?'

Margery nodded. 'Yes, Mother. You're right, as always.'

They reached her bedroom and Florence welcomed her in. Margery stood in the doorway and took in the room. 'Ah, more fresh flowers,' she said, walking over to the dainty vase Florence had made up and placed on Margery's dressing table.

She watched her daughter lift the crystal vase and breathe the smell of the tea rose she had picked especially because she knew it was her daughter's favourite scent. Margery looked at her and smiled before putting the vase back down.

'I love this room. I always forget how sunny and pretty it is until I come back here.'

Meadows placed Margery's bag down and left the room.

Florence wondered if this was always how Margery felt or if there was a reason she was feeling compelled to share her thoughts more. 'Is everything all right, darling?'

Margery sat on the edge of her bed. 'It is. I suppose I'm more wistful than usual being back here at St Heliers because it's been an exceptionally long and miserable winter and for some reason there seemed to be far more desperately wounded men passing through the station than there have been for a long while.'

'It must be draining to live with that day in and day out,' Florence said, sorry for all those who faced such miseries each day.

'It has been. More so recently than before. I feel a little guilty coming home, but I know from the way you worry about Father over-exerting himself that if I didn't come home now I would risk burning myself out. I know I'll be more use to my colleagues with a little time away from the canteen than if I persevered and didn't take this short break.'

Florence waited for Margery to take off her hat and rested a hand lightly on the top of her head. 'You're a very wise girl and I'm grateful for it.' Margery stood and unbuttoned her coat. 'Is there anything else you need?' Florence asked straightening the smaller towel on the wooden towel rail underneath the window.

'No, Mother. I'll just take a few moments to freshen up and come and join you downstairs. Thank you.'

'You take whatever time you need,' Florence said, happy that one of her children was safely back in her care at least for the next two weeks. 'I'll go downstairs to your father. Come to the conservatory when you're ready and we'll take tea.'

She left the room and closed the door quietly behind her. As she walked slowly down the stairs, she had a moment wishing she could go back in time to when her children were younger and all lived at home. She was going to make the most of having one of her babies back with her.

A short while later, Margery walked in, passing the large aspidistra that was shaded by an even larger palm where the conservatory joined the rest of the house.

'There you are,' Jesse said, grinning widely and holding out his hands for Margery to take. 'It's good to have you back with us again, my darling. Can you see the smile on your mother's face? I haven't seen her this happy since the last time you were home.'

Florence rang for tea while Jesse and Margery caught up with their news. A few minutes later, Meadows brought in a tray for them.

'Cake?' Margery said, looking astonished to see it on the tray. 'But I thought you were being careful with supplies?'

'We are,' Florence said. 'But Cook wanted to treat you to her speciality. She knows how much you love her Victoria sponge. Although,' she added, 'it will taste a little different to what you're used to. Cook has to make do with whatever rations are available.'

'I'm sure it will be delicious,' Margery said, widening her eyes.

Florence served them each a cup of tea and a slice of Mrs Rudge's sponge.

'Thank you,' Margery said, as Florence handed a plate to her. 'I'll go and thank Cook as soon as we've finished eating. It was kind of her to bake this for me.'

They fell silent as they ate, and Florence kept stealing glances at her daughter, relishing having her back at home with them. 'We have an ex-soldier working for us now in one of the factories. He said he visited your canteen.'

'You have?' Margery asked, finishing her mouthful and placing her cake fork on the plate before putting it down on the small table in front of them. 'What did he think of it?'

'He was highly complimentary,' Florence said, thinking back to her surprise when Joey Blythe had mentioned meeting Margery. 'He said it was wonderful to be given a taste of Blighty in Northern France, or something like that. I think that his visit to your canteen certainly gave him a boost to help him continue with the rest of his journey home.'

'That's really good to know. Was he one of the wounded soldiers?'

'Unfortunately, he was. His mother worked for us for a long time until she remarried. She wrote to me and asked me for help. His injury was on his face and he was finding it difficult to leave the house.'

'But he's coping much better now?' Margery asked. 'He must be if he's working.'

Florence thought of the strong young man who worked so hard for them and never missed a day's work for any reason. 'Yes. He's doing very well. In fact, I heard that he's now courting a lovely young girl who also works at the factory.'

Margery frowned. 'Doesn't he mind you knowing? Especially as, if they marry, she'll be leaving Boots.'

Florence shook her head. 'He doesn't know that I know about it, but his mother wrote and told me secretly. I think she was so happy to share how much confidence he has, now that his work has given him reason to leave the house each morning, that she didn't think.'

'I hope she doesn't mention to him that she wrote and told you,' Jesse said, a mischievous smile reaching his eyes. 'He won't be too happy to discover that his mother has been sharing his secrets with his and his lady friend's employer.'

'Oh dear,' Margery laughed. 'Poor lady. And you haven't told her, I suppose.'

'No, I was just happy to know that he's making a life for himself again.' She thought back to the sad, disillusioned man sitting across her desk from her who believed he had little to live for. 'I enjoy knowing that he's happy again. He deserves to be.'

'Good for him,' Margery said.

Florence gazed lovingly at her daughter. 'You've grown so much these past few years and I'm so impressed with all that you've achieved, my darling girl. I hope you know that?'

'As am I,' Jesse added. 'You've made a huge difference to thousands of men at what is probably the most troubling time of their lives, returning home injured and unsure what greeting is awaiting them when they get there.'

Margery took one of Florence's hands and one of her father's in hers and smiled. 'Thank you both. Coming from you two that's an enormous endorsement.' She let go of their hands. 'Anyone for more tea?'

As Margery poured, Florence decided she would take a few days off work for once to be available should her daughter need her for company or for any outings. 'Have you given any thought about what you'd like to do this week?'

'I have to see my little nieces but apart from that, I'm happy to do whatever you wish, Mother.'

How lucky was she? Florence thought as her daughter helped Jesse to another small slice of cake. She had so much to be grateful for, especially at a time when there was such uncertainty in the world and millions of others were grieving or struggling to feed their families, or simply alone. She intended making the most of every minute she had Margery back at home, and wouldn't allow herself to think about how upsetting it was going to be to wave her off when she had to return to France.

She realised Margery was talking to her. 'Sorry, what was that?'

'I was saying about them passing that act giving women over thirty with property, or wives of men with property, the right to vote. It's not perfect, but it is a start, don't you think?'

'Yes, I gather it also applies to women over thirty who are graduates. It is hopefully the start to further change for women. I don't see why we can't be treated as equals, especially when so many millions of women have shown how they can do the same job as a man during this war. I shall certainly use my vote when the time comes, of that you can be sure. And in a few more years both you and Dorothy will be able to do the same.'

Margery sighed. 'I know this war has taken a terrible toll on people's lives, but it has given us women much more opportunity than we could ever have imagined being given four years ago. After all that the women's suffrage movement had to go through, working for changes for women, this war has given many of us freedoms we never dared to hope for.'

She was right, Florence mused. 'It's a shame that so many have to suffer though to enable others to have these freedoms. I wonder how long they'll last after the war finally ends.'

'Whenever that might be,' Margery said, quietly. 'Yes, I was thinking the same thing. But then I look at you, now a director of Boots, and all that you've achieved in your lifetime when restrictions were so much harsher for women, and your determination and resilience inspire me every day.'

Florence felt a lump forming in her throat. To hear her beloved daughter say such words was the best gift she could ever receive. She had never set out to be an inspiration to others, only to live the life she wanted and help as many other girls to achieve all that they could in their own lives.

'Thank you, my darling. That's exceedingly kind of you.'

'I mean it, Mother. You and Father have done so much for others. Every day you show Dorothy, John and me what hard work and tenacity can do. But for you, as a woman, it must have been terribly difficult to put all that you have into place.'

'I couldn't have done it without your father,' Florence said, barely able to speak, so much emotion was threatening to spill over from her heart. She beamed at her love sitting quietly and, she noticed, proudly gazing back at her.

'Nonsense.' Jesse said. 'I don't know of another woman who could have thought of all the innovative ideas you've put into place over the years, let alone found ways to make them happen. Margery's right, my dear, you are an inspiration and not just to your children but to me as well. And,' he added, 'I'm sure to many hundreds of others.'

'Father's right,' Margery said, kissing her mother on her cheek.

She pulled her daughter into a hug, delighted to hear

her saying how much she had inspired her. It made the years of hard work and long hours worth all the effort. 'Thank you, Margery. It means a lot to hear you say such things.'

'I'm sure my sister will agree with me when we visit her and the babies tomorrow for lunch,' Margery said.

Florence hoped she would but didn't say so.

Chapter Thirty

June 1918

Nothing seemed to be getting any better, Florence thought miserably as spring slipped into warm May and then a cool, dry June.

Everyone had been coping with the rations imposed since the beginning of the year and Cook agreed with Jesse when he said there was talk of more coming soon. 'But people still appear to be going hungry,' Florence said, frustrated to see so many desperate people on her way to and from work each day. 'If this war doesn't end soon then who knows how people are going to cope?'

It was something that worried her continuously – and now John had been sent away to France as part of his role at General Headquarters. He had insisted it was a managerial role, but as far as Florence was concerned he was once again in France and therefore much closer to danger than he had been when he was in England. This war couldn't end soon enough, she thought, praying that something would happen to turn the tide of the fighting and bring hostilities to an abrupt end.

She made the most of a warmer Saturday morning, taking a copy of *The Secret House*, a thriller she had bought the previous year but had not yet had a moment to read. She enjoyed Edgar Wallace's books and needed something to take her mind off her day-to-day worries. Florence had been sitting reading by her rose garden for only about an hour when she heard the tinkling of a bicycle bell, followed two minutes later by footsteps coming through the conservatory.

Florence heard the urgency in the hurried footsteps and turned to see who was on her way to speak to her.

'Harriet, whatever is the matter?' she asked, seeing her lady's maid's pale face.

'This has arrived for you, Lady Boot. The telegram boy is waiting to see if you have a response.'

Florence's heart seemed to stop for a few seconds as she prayed silently for the message not to be bad news about Margery or John. She wished she didn't have to read the telegram and could put off whatever horrors it might contain. She could hear Harriet's breath as she tried to remain calm, knowing she must read whatever news the telegram was bringing to her.

She placed a bookmark in her book as calmly as she could, closed it and set it down on the table next to her.

Then, taking the proffered envelope in her trembling hands, she opened it with her little finger and read the words. She gasped, relieved to see no mention of Margery or John. Her children were fine. It was her brother who was not. A whimper escaped her lips as she reread the words swimming in front of her eyes, sent by her sister-in-law Florence in Jersey.

Dearest Florence and Jesse,

At pains to tell you that my husband, your brother, Willie Rowe died last evening STOP The cause is uncertain at present, but he did not suffer STOP Ernest and Colin coping well and I do not wish for you to worry about me STOP Fondest regards, Florence Rowe, Mrs

She took a moment to collect herself, unsure what answer to give to the boy.

'Thank you, Harriet.' She tried to think what to say in return to her sister-in-law and wished more than anything that she could immediately board the ferry taking her to St Helier Harbour to comfort her brother's widow and sons in person. Yet another thing this war was taking from her.

She stood, wanting to write down the words to be relayed back to her family at home. 'One moment. Follow me to my study and I'll note down my reply.'

Florence had to force her shaky legs to move and rushed to her study, trying to put her feelings into words with each step. She pulled out a chair, sat at her small writing desk and, picking up a pen, wrote:

Dearest Florence, Ernest and Colin,

Jesse and I are heartbroken to hear your terrible news. We wish that we could come to you at this sad time. If there is anything that we can do, please let us know. As soon as this war ends we will come to you and help you in any way possible. Our love is with you all, Florence and Jesse

She tore the note from her notepad and handed it to Harriet to pass to the telegram boy still waiting at the front door. Florence was sad to think that her only brother had died and, thanks to this dreadful war, she would not be able to attend his funeral and comfort poor, dear Florence and her sons. Ernest, she realised, must now be nineteen and Colin barely nine. They were too young to lose their father, especially at such a dark time. She would have to find some way to make it up to them after the war ended.

Florence had been missing her island home more and more over the past four years. She might have only visited some years for her birthday during the summer, but it was nearly that time again and she was certain that once again there would be no trip back to visit her family.

Florence sighed. This enforced separation was too cruel, for all of them. She thought of all the other mothers, sisters and families held apart from each other for months or years at a time due to this ongoing nightmare. Thank heavens, she still had Dorothy living nearby and her daughter-in-law Margaret with their little girls to visit and pull into a hug.

Florence prayed that one day soon she would be able to bring her entire family together, to look at them face-to-face and listen to their voices. There were a lot of things about this war that inspired her to fight back and she almost always managed to succeed in finding ways to deal with the difficulties that the war flung at them. But this distance between her and her loved ones was not something she could alter in any way, and she hated to feel as powerless as she did now.

She had been imagining returning home to her family for four years now but never thought it would be in such sad circumstances. She tried to recall the last time she had seen her brother. It must have been at Dorothy's wedding. If only they had realised then that there would be such an all-encompassing war, and that the last time they had bid each other farewell had been the last time ever that they would do so.

Florence tried her best not to cry, but it was impossible. Sitting out by her roses, the scent filling the warm summer air, it was hard to connect this perfect afternoon with news that broke her heart and caused such longing to return home to Jersey. She was barely aware of Harriet bringing her tea. How thoughtful, Florence reflected, for her lady's maid to bring the tray herself, knowing Florence wouldn't want the other servants to witness her distress.

'Thank you,' she murmured as Harriet poured her a cup

of tea before leaving her in solitude to come to terms with the sad news she had just received.

Jesse arrived home earlier than usual. Florence imagined it was because Harriet had sent him a message telling him the upsetting news.

George wheeled Jesse's chair outside and stopped it next to her. He covered Jesse's legs with a light blanket and left them alone to talk.

Jesse reached out his left hand and Florence took it in hers, lifting it to her lips before lowering it again.

'Harriet told me about Willie,' he said quietly. 'I'm so sorry, Florence. I know you two were close.'

Florence's throat was tight from emotion and it took her a moment to speak. 'I can't bear the fact that we have no way of going to be with Florence and my nephews, especially now when they probably need us most.'

'I know.'

Florence looked into Jesse's eyes and saw her sadness reflected at her. 'If only we could do something to help them.'

'I can't see that there is anything that we can do, my dear. Unfortunately, we're simply going to have to wait until this war is over.' He gave her a tight smile. 'Then, though, we will return to Jersey and you can do whatever it is you want to help them move on from this.'

Florence dared to ask something that had been bothering her since receiving the telegram. 'Do you think it can go on for much longer, Jesse?'

'I have no idea, my dear. The news doesn't seem to be getting any more positive.'

Florence looked over at her roses. How could they still look so beautiful and serene when everything around them was disintegrating? 'I'm not sure how much more of this I can stand, Jesse.'

He patted her hand. 'You've had a nasty shock and you're bound to miss your home, especially after what's happened, and with your birthday nearing. But we will get through this as we have done every other sadness in our lives. You mark my words, my dear.'

He was right, she knew it. 'I'll be fine once I come to terms with what's happened,' she reassured him, not wishing Jesse to fret unnecessarily about her when he had so many other things to concern him at work. 'Let's just sit here quietly and savour being together, shall we?'

Jesse smiled at her. 'I'd like that. If we clear our minds and breathe in the scents of the flowers and the freshly cut lawn and listen to the birdsong then we might even be able to fool ourselves that all is well with the world.'

Florence doubted she would be able to do as he suggested, but liked the idea and closed her eyes. Whatever happened, she knew that as long as she had Jesse by her side, she would find a way to cope. He was her soulmate and the one person who could reassure her when all else seemed to be falling apart.

'I'm glad I went against my mother's wishes and married you, Jesse Boot,' she whispered.

'I'm relieved you did,' he said. 'I can't imagine having shared my life with anyone other than you.'

Florence stared at him, tears welling up inside her. Here she was upset about her brother when next to her was the man who had given her so much. She hated to see him so frail, the constant pain of his rheumatism draining his energy each day. He would be seventy next birthday and she dared not think how she would cope without him by her side each day.

Chapter Thirty-One

1 July 1918

Florence and Jesse decided to take their supper in the garden and make the most of the warm, sultry evening. 'It's my birthday in four weeks and after last month's sadness at losing Willie, I thought I'd have a small dinner party here with whatever family are near enough to come. What do you think, Jesse?'

'I think it makes sense. It's not as if we could put on anything lavish anyway, even if we didn't have food rationing to contend with.'

'That's what I was thinking,' she said, taking a sip of the delicious cordial Mrs Rudge had sent up with their supper. 'I don't really feel like celebrating, if I'm honest. And, as with the past three years, it wouldn't really be seemly to put on too much of a celebration even if I did.'

Jesse dropped the bread he was lifting to his mouth and

Florence watched as he struggled to take hold of it once more. She wished he would accept help with his eating, but he refused most of the time, insisting that while he had the strength to feed himself then he was determined to do so. She supposed she would be just as determined as him, so didn't bother to argue. Jesse had his pride and, despite the mess he always made at mealtimes, she respected him for it.

'We will have a lot of celebrating to catch up on after this is over,' Jesse said, finally taking hold of the lump of bread and smiling triumphantly at her.

Florence agreed with him but the last thing she felt like thinking about at that moment was celebrating, especially after so much had been lost. No, she was going to enjoy this peaceful moment away from the office at home with her darling Jesse.

Florence opened her mouth to speak when a distant thud echoed around them. Had she imagined the earth shuddering at her feet? Or was it just the sound that had shocked her? She stared at Jesse, frightened to imagine the cause of the sound. 'What was that?'

All amusement had vanished from his face and he lowered his hands to rest on the table. 'It sounded like an explosion to me.' He fell silent, his eyes moving as he listened with her for any further noise.

Florence shivered despite the warmth of the evening air. 'Where do you think it came from?'

Jesse shook his head slowly. 'I've no idea, but I have a horrible feeling that something terrible has happened.'

Florence stared up at the sky, searching the deep blue,

scattered with a few white fluffy clouds. 'Could it be another bombing raid? Should we go inside, do you think?'

Jesse followed her gaze. 'I can't see any Zeppelins.'

Neither could she. 'What could have made that sound, if not a bomb exploding?' Florence asked, a sense of foreboding working its way through her body. She thought of her girls and those that had left Boots to go and work in munitions. 'You don't think it was an explosion at one of the arms factories, do you?'

'I hope not. I suppose we'll soon find out when they report it in the papers.'

Florence shivered. The thought of something igniting in a place where many people worked in close quarters horrified her. She hated having to wait to find out, but knew she had little choice.

The following morning, Florence arrived in the dining room to eat breakfast with Jesse and found him already seated at the table reading his broadsheet. She could tell by the look on his face that he was reading tragic news.

'Is it about the explosion we heard yesterday evening?'

Jesse looked over the top of his newspaper. 'It is, I'm afraid.'

'Where?'

'Oh, Florence, it says here it was at the National Shell Filling Factory at Chilwell.'

Florence knew her mouth had dropped open, but it took

a few seconds for her to make her brain work enough to close it. All those women and men. 'Oh, no. How many?'

'It says here that they suspect sixty people were killed.' He shook his head, frowning. 'If we could hear that explosion from here then I imagine they're being very conservative with their reporting. Surely, more of the employees must have been caught up in that blast.'

Florence thought of the young women who had left Boots to move to Chilwell and earn the thirty shillings a week offered for the dangerous work. She hated that they were sometimes referred to as the Canary Girls, owing to the yellow colour of their skin from the TNT poisoning that all the glasses of milk in the world, let alone the single glass they were offered after their shift ended, wouldn't be able to rid them of. Her heart ached for those lost and for their families who would now be grieving for them.

'It's not only about those who were lost,' Jesse said quietly. 'What about those maimed by the explosion? This is a dark day indeed, Florence.'

Florence felt as if there was a weight on her shoulders. Why hadn't she been more forceful with those of her girls who had given notice to go and work in munitions factories? She had known the risks well enough.

'These women and men should be awarded medals for the work they've done,' Florence. 'Surely, without the munitions they produced the British Army would have no way of defending our country?'

'I agree, my dear. They are truly brave young people who work in these factories.' He lowered his paper and sighed. 'I've heard tales of young women losing legs when one shell explodes, others dying through poisoning from handling the toxic chemicals used in the shells, but this is too horrifying.'

Florence was too sickened by the news to be able to say anything further.

'I'll try to find out more when I go to work. No doubt, there will be talk among the staff.'

Florence nodded her agreement, trying to suppress the nausea rising in the pit of her stomach. All she could think of was Milly, so bright and full of life, and the girls like her who had come to them from school before leaving the safety of their stores and factories to go and earn a larger wage at Chilwell. She prayed that Milly had not been on the night shift the previous evening and had been spared.

Later that day Jesse called Florence to his office to catch up over tea and a few biscuits. After kissing him on his forehead, she sat down next to him. He was looking tired and she could see he was suffering a lot of pain.

'How's your morning been?'

'It's been busy, as usual.' He rubbed his face with his right hand. 'I've been told by one of the directors here who knows someone on the board at Chilwell that they now believe more than a hundred and thirty employees were killed in the explosion. He says that they also estimate now that around two hundred and fifty were badly injured.' He stared at his desk silently for a moment. 'Those poor people.'

'It's too horrible, isn't it?' Florence agreed.

Jesse nodded slowly. 'Apparently, much of the site was obliterated. I gather too that the explosion was so vast that windows were shattered a couple of miles away from the factory, as far as Long Eaton.'

They sat in silence, lost in their own thoughts for a few minutes. Florence couldn't bear to think of so much heartache in the factory only a few miles away.

'I'll leave it a few days and then make enquiries about the girls who left Boots to go and work there,' Florence said. 'If any of them were killed or injured then I'll see if there's anything we can do to help them or their families. They might have left Boots, but to me they will always be my dear girls.'

'Yes, that's a good idea.'

A couple of weeks later, Florence was working in her office when Enid knocked on the door. 'Lady Boot, sorry to interrupt you, but there's a Miss Milly Jones asking to speak to you. I told her that you were busy this morning, but she asked me to please check if you have a minute or two to spare to speak to her.'

Florence waved for Enid to show her in. 'I have a few minutes, Enid. Please, show Miss Jones in to see me.'

Florence waited for the girl to be shown into her office. If she had expected to see someone acting a little nervously, which most younger people did when coming to her office, she was surprised to see that Miss Milly Jones seemed far more confident than she had the last time Florence had met her.

The young girl, whom Florence now recalled as being one of the more popular girls in their factories, strode into the room. Her skin, Florence noticed, did have a slight yellow tinge to it, but if she had been working filling shells for the past year then that was probably to be expected.

'Welcome, Miss Jones,' Florence said. 'Please, take a seat and tell me what I can do for you.'

Milly Jones took off her hat and sat, holding it and her small leather bag on her lap. 'Thank you for seeing me at such short notice, Lady Boot. It's very kind of you.'

'I believe the last time I saw you was when you left us to go and work at the arms factory at Chilwell.'

Milly cast her gaze down to her hat. 'Yes, I thought I was being clever leaving here to go to a job there, Lady Boot.' She looked back at Florence, her expression sad, and Florence noticed she seemed a little lost.

'My husband and I heard the explosion from our home.' She still couldn't believe that they had been eating a light supper when so many young people were killed or horribly injured. Florence shuddered and pulled her mind back to the matter in hand. 'I made enquiries about our girls who had left to work there and was greatly relieved that none of you were working that evening.'

'That's very kind of you to check up on us, Lady Boot. I appreciate you doing something like that, especially after we left you to go there.' Milly's expression appeared somewhat haunted, which Florence thought wasn't surprising after what her colleagues had gone through. 'I was supposed to be working that night,' she said quietly. 'My ma insisted I swap shifts with a friend and accompany her to visit my dad. He's in hospital, you see. Broke his leg falling off a low roof at work a month ago. I tried to argue with her, but she wouldn't listen.' She gazed out of the window briefly before returning to look at Florence. 'I'm glad now that I had to do as she insisted.'

Florence was relieved, too. She wondered what had happened to Milly's friend but hesitated, unsure whether she should ask.

'You're probably wondering what happened to my friend who covered my shift that evening?' Milly said, as if she had read Florence's mind.

'Only if you want to talk about her,' Florence said.

Milly clasped her hands together and Florence noticed they were trembling slightly. 'We were best friends, me and Lucy.'

'And is Lucy all right?' Florence asked tentatively, not wishing to pry but sensing that the girl needed to share her thoughts with someone.

Milly shrugged. 'She survived the blast, if that's what you mean. She's in hospital with burns to her arms and one leg,' she added, sadly. 'I think she'll be there for a few months yet.'

Florence listened as the girl spoke. She could tell Milly was carrying a lot of guilt, aware that her friend was suffering in her place. Florence's thoughts turned to Milly's mother. How terrifying it must be for her to think what could have happened if she hadn't insisted Milly swap shifts that day. Then she thought of Lucy's mother now coping with a badly hurt daughter because her child had been generous enough to agree to take Milly's place. The back of Florence's eyes prickled with unshed tears.

The next thing Florence knew, Milly let go of her hat as she opened her bag and rummaged around inside. Tears were streaming down her face. She sniffed a few times and Florence realised the girl was frantically looking for a handkerchief. Florence pulled open the small right-hand top drawer in her desk and retrieved an ironed handkerchief. She shook it so that it unfolded and leant over the desk so that Milly could take it from her.

Milly grabbed the material and quickly dabbed at her eyes and blew her nose. 'Thank you, Lady Boot,' she said with a sniff. 'I've no idea what came over me just then. I'm so s-s-sorry.'

'Hush, now,' Florence said, trying to calm the distressed girl, 'you have had a terrible shock and it is not surprising that you're upset about your friend. Would you like a cup of tea and then we can start again?'

Milly gave Florence a watery smile. 'Th-thank you.'

Florence walked around her desk and rested a hand briefly on the girl's left shoulder. 'There, now, you take your time. I'll just pop next door to speak to my secretary about that tea. I won't be a moment.'

She opened Gladys and Enid's office door. 'Please, bring in two cups of tea as soon as you can. And some of those lovely bourbon biscuits, I think.'

Without waiting for them to reply, she hurried back to her office and sat at her desk. Milly seemed a little calmer now. Florence watched as she dabbed at her eyes once more and then at the end of her nose.

'I'm so sorry, Lady Boot. My mother would go mad if she thought I'd come here and behaved this way in front of you.'

'There's nothing to be sorry for, Milly. Anyone in your situation would be upset. It's going to take time for you to come to terms with the sort of fright you've had.' She smoothed down her skirts. 'Now, do you want to let me know how I can help you?'

Milly narrowed her eyes as if nervous of Florence's reaction. 'I was hoping you might have a place for me back in the factory where I worked before. I enjoyed my work there.'

'You were working on the gas masks, isn't that right?'

'That's right, Lady Boot. I have some friends in the department and they were saying it's still as busy as ever. I thought— that is, I hoped you might still be looking for girls.'

Florence was unsure if they were without checking first. 'I'll have to find out for you, Milly. But I can assure you that even if there isn't a vacancy for you there, I'll be able to find one for you, probably in one of the departments at Island Street. Would you be happy with that?'

Milly beamed at her. 'Yes, I'd like that very much, Lady Boot. Thank you ever so much.'

'Not at all, Milly. We'll be glad to have you back here

working for us. And I'm sure your friends will be delighted to see you back on the factory floor once again.'

'They will, Lady Boot. It was one of them who suggested I come here and speak to you. I thought you wouldn't want to give me a job, not after I left to go elsewhere.'

'I'm glad you did come to see me though. I'm sure I asked you to do so should you ever change your mind about working there.'

'You did,' Milly whispered.

Florence watched as Enid brought in the tea and biscuits, placing them on the desk in front of her and Milly before leaving again. She felt better knowing that this sweet young girl would be coming back to work for Boots rather than returning to the arms factory. 'Your friend was right to encourage you to come and speak to me and I'm glad she did. Now, how soon will you be able to start work?' she asked, sensing that the sooner Milly got to work and had less time to ponder on the explosion and her friend's injuries, the better it would be for the young girl.

'Whenever you like, Lady Boot.' Milly lifted the cup and saucer, and after blowing on the hot drink, took a sip of her tea.

'Then shall we say tomorrow morning?'

'Yes, please.' She placed the drink back down onto the desk, and stood up. Then, picking up her hat, placed it on her head. 'My ma is going to be very grateful to you.'

'Please, tell her there's no need. I'm happy to help and we can always do with hard-working girls like you at Boots, Milly.' She accompanied Milly to the door and opened it. 'If any of your friends who previously worked at the factory are looking to return to work at Boots, tell them to come and speak to me and I'll do what I can to accommodate them.'

Milly grinned at her. 'Thank you, Lady Boot, I'll do that.'

Enid walked out of her office and motioned for Milly to accompany her. 'Let me show you out, Miss Jones.'

Florence returned to her office and sat at her desk. She felt much better than she had in weeks. It was a relief to know that one of her girls was coming back to work for them. It wasn't much but she felt as if she had done something to help after the dreadful explosion.

Now, she thought, as she stood and walked over to her folder containing the lists of vacancies she needed to fill, was there a position available for Milly in the department where she used to work? She hoped so because not only would the girl be happier among old friends, she also wouldn't need any training, since she had done the work before.

Florence set the folder down on her desk and found the sheet of paper she was looking for. Running her finger down the list she spotted that they had not one but two vacancies.

'Perfect,' she said, relieved that she would be able to send Milly to exactly where she had hoped to be the following day.

Chapter Thirty-Two

September 1918

Florence and Jesse were missing John now that he was working at General Headquarters in France. Florence wished he could share a little about what he was doing on the Western Front, but all John was able to do was reassure her that his was a managerial role rather than a fighting one. It was still at the Front though, Florence thought anxiously, hoping that he was safe from danger.

She sat in her armchair next to the fire, listening to Jesse tell her about how he was hoping to help their customers fight this dreadful Spanish flu that had now spread right across the country. She noticed the blanket on his knees slipping slightly and stood, walked over to him, pulled it up over his lap and tucked it into the sides of his wheelchair.

He waved her hands away, irritated. 'Stop fussing,

Florence. You know how I hate it. I'm more than capable of sorting out my own leg covering should I need to.'

'Never mind all this talk about how we're to help the country fight this flu pandemic,' she said, going to sit back down in her chair. 'You're not going to be any help to others if you don't look after your own health, Jesse.'

He shook his head. 'That's just the trouble, my dear. I know that ordinarily it is us older, less healthy people who are the ones to suffer with flu, but this is something new entirely. It seems to be most aggressive with healthy adults in their twenties for some reason.'

Florence had heard two of the servants saying something similar, and Gladys at work had mentioned it, but she had thought they must be wrong. 'Surely this generation have suffered enough with four years of war? They can't cope with being targeted by this pandemic as well.'

'It seems that is exactly what's happening though, I'm afraid.'

Florence stared at the flames dancing in the fireplace, saddened almost to the point of tears. 'How will this young generation ever recover from what they've had to face?'

Jesse groaned. 'I've no idea, but I'm going to see to it that Boots does all we can to help them.'

Florence wasn't surprised to hear him say as much. How typical of her beloved Jesse to see a gargantuan, invisible enemy and want to find a way to fight it. She looked over at him. 'How do you intend doing that?' she asked, intrigued.

His face brightened and she could tell by the glint in his

eyes that he was already doing something about it. 'I've been in contact with the Ministry of Health. I've offered them any help I can come up with.'

'That's wonderful. Like what?'

'I'm not sure yet, but they're going to consider a few options. Boots is a much-loved brand known to everyone in Britain and they believe that if I put some advice together people may be inclined to take note of it. I've given a few suggestions of how I can do this and they're going to come back to me at some point.'

'That's wonderful news, Jesse.'

'Thank you. I have to admit I'm rather pleased. In the meantime, we need to supply our stores with as much aspirin as possible to help sufferers with pain caused by the flu.'

Florence had heard that the worst thing about the dreadful illness was that some victims, who seemed well when they rose in the morning, then experienced initial symptoms of tiredness, fever and a headache and went on to develop pneumonia, getting a blue hue to their skin.

She shared what she knew with Jesse. 'Why do they turn blue though?' Florence shivered.

'It's what happens when they're suffering a lack of oxygen.' He shook his head. 'There are other symptoms which I don't want to share with you. A lot of these poor souls wake seemingly healthy and then die by the early evening. Entire families are dying in some cases, Florence. It's heart-breaking and I fear it's going to get far worse before it gets better.'

Florence had heard similar stories. 'How can doctors treat something that takes hold and kills within hours though?'

Jesse shook his head. 'I've no idea,' he said miserably. 'If only we could find a way to fight this thing.'

'Or alternatively, we will have to work out the best way to protect ourselves and those around us, if there is no way to fight it medically.' She had seen people wearing cotton masks and decided that it would be a good idea to either buy some or make them. 'I also heard that things are bad in France and am going to write to Margery pleading with her to return home. She's done her bit for the war effort now, surely.'

Jesse frowned. 'You think she'll agree to shut up her canteen and come back?'

Florence shrugged. She had no idea, but she was going to at least broach the subject with her daughter. She couldn't bear to have her across the Channel when this horrible illness was decimating people in towns across the country and Europe. 'I don't know but I'm going to write to her and see what she says.'

As always when things got particularly dark, Florence wanted nothing more than to gather her children around her. She thought back to when they were small and how much easier it had been to keep them close. Now though they were all adults and independent people with their own lives to run. When did life become so complicated? she wondered miserably.

She studied Jesse, noticing how exhausted he seemed,

his shoulders stooped and a sadness to his mouth. Working hard to find ways to help the British soldiers and their customers had given him an extra determination to find solutions to problems, or create medicines and items that people needed, but she couldn't miss the toll it had taken on his health. He was suffering colds more often and the days were becoming more frequent when he didn't fight her suggestion that he spend the day resting at home or even in bed. It troubled her greatly.

Jesse noticed her staring at him. 'What's the matter?' He shook his head. 'And don't bother denying that you're more concerned about something than usual because I can see by the look in your eyes that you are.' He narrowed his eyes slightly. 'Are you thinking about Margery, or maybe you're worried about me?' He sat back in his chair, a satisfied look on his face. 'That's what it is, isn't it? You've decided what you're going to say to Margery and now you're turning your worries to dealing with me.'

She didn't bother trying to argue with him. 'You obviously know me well enough, so I shan't try to pretend otherwise. Yes, I am worried about you, Jesse. The company and you have achieved a huge amount during this war, but your health has suffered.'

She saw the downturn in his mouth and knew he was irritated with her for pointing out how delicate his health was. 'I don't mean to upset you, Jesse. Truly I don't, but you do need to take things much easier from now on.' When he didn't reply, she asked, 'Or at least try to do it for me, if not for yourself.'

Jesse shrugged. 'Yes, you're right. It's just so frustrating being trapped in a body that doesn't do all I want it to, that's all.'

She stood, walked towards him and crouched in front of his chair, taking his hands in hers. 'I know, my love. But it's not just your body now that you have to consider. You're going to be seventy next year and you should also take your age into account.'

His face reddened and she knew she had to act fast if he wasn't going to lose his temper. She rested one of her palms against his cheek and, rising, bent forward to kiss him on his lips. 'Don't bother arguing with me, Jesse Boot. It's a fact, whether we like it or not. You're getting older, and I hate to say it, but you're also suffering from overwork and things have to change. Surely you can't argue with that?'

Jesse stared at her, his expression slowly softening. Florence felt her heart-rate slow slightly. Relieved.

'You are right in what you're saying, my dear. I know that well enough. To be honest with you I do feel somewhat exhausted today. I think I'll spend the next few days at home taking it a bit easier.'

Florence sighed. 'I'm relieved to hear you say that and I think that's a very sensible thing to do. I'll stay at home with you. We can spend some time here quietly. What do you think?'

'I'd like that very much.'

Florence kissed him lightly on his lips once more. She didn't add that it would make her feel much safer knowing he was spending time safely away from others, at least for a time while this Spanish flu ran rampant through the town.

By November, Florence allowed herself to hope that the end of the war might finally be in sight. She knew by the hint of excitement in people's voices that she wasn't alone in feeling this way. It seemed clear that an Armistice was almost certain. She thought back to the start of the war and how they had all prayed it would be over by Christmas. How naïve they had been to even consider such a thing. While Florence's relief grew at the thought of an end to four years of war, the increase in deaths due to the Spanish flu dampened any excitement she might have felt. So far they had been lucky in that none of their family or their servants had fallen ill. Florence prayed daily that they all remained safe and healthy.

She received a letter from Margery to confirm that she was returning home with the other women who had been working at her canteen. *The end seems to be in sight,* she had written the previous week.

> *We are all very concerned about this Spanish flu especially as we've heard that it's running rampant through the soldiers fighting over here. We worry that because we come in contact with so many, one or all of us are more than likely to contract the dreadful disease.*

Florence reread Margery's letter to Jesse. 'I'm so relieved she's finally agreed to come home rather than wait until the very end of the war. I honestly expected her to refuse when I suggested she do this.'

'She's an intelligent girl,' he said. 'As are the others with her. I doubt we will have been the only parents writing to plead with their daughter to do the same as we hoped Margery might do.'

He was right. Whatever Margery's reason for coming home, all Florence wanted was for her daughter to arrive at St Heliers House so she could look after her and spend some time with her again.

She was due to come in on the mid-afternoon train. Florence had sent Alfred Parry to the station to wait for her and bring her home. Now, though, she needed to speak to Mrs Rudge about their evening meal and maybe a snack for Margery for when she arrived.

'You do very well, Cook,' she began. 'I know that we still have to abide by the rationing but the food you prepare for us all certainly keeps us as healthy as possible and we're all benefitting from it.'

'I do my best, Lady Boot,' Mrs Rudge said, her expression serious. 'It helps that we have a good-sized vegetable garden and a few fruit trees.'

There was a twinkle in the woman's eyes betraying how happy she was to hear Florence's comments about all her hard work for the household.

'My husband and I are aware how much harder it must be for you and the other servants at this difficult time,'

Florence continued. 'We are extremely grateful to you all and would be grateful if you could pass on our thanks to the others this evening when you have your evening meal. Hopefully soon we can all begin to experience much happier times. I barely dare say it, but it looks as if this war will end soon, and hopefully soon after that this dreadful flu will die out.'

'Let's hope so, Lady Boot.' Mrs Rudge narrowed her eyes. 'You must be very relieved that Miss Margery is coming home this afternoon?'

'Yes, very much so. I've been very concerned about her working at that canteen, especially with the number of people she comes into contact with each day. Any one of them could be contagious and pass on the Spanish flu to her or her colleagues. The huge number of soldiers being moved everywhere must be the main reason why this vicious disease is being spread so thoroughly through every country. I'm sure there must be many more who have contracted it but don't yet know.' She shuddered at the thought of the invisible enemy among them. How many more trials must everyone have to face before things took a turn for the better? she wondered.

Mrs Rudge gave a solemn nod. 'I've heard that it's come in waves. Like the tide. Just when the hospitals think it's over, then another load of people seem to fall ill from the thing.' She folded her arms in front of her chest. 'It's a terrifying illness, Lady Boot. It really is that.'

Florence agreed. 'I know. And there seems to be little we can do about it apart from try to stay away from infected people with coughs and colds and wash our hands thoroughly before eating. Did you find those masks useful that I sent down for you all?'

'Yes, we did.' Her face reddened slightly. 'I wear it whenever I step out to the shops, but not indoors.' She reached out and moved a wooden spoon to place it next to a pair of metal tongs. 'It's rather frightening, isn't it?'

Florence hated to see her usually confident cook looking so concerned, especially as there was little any of them could do. 'Yes, Cook, I think we're all a little worn down by the past four years and then, just when we all begin to have a tiny hope that maybe things might be drawing to an end for us all, this pandemic arrives. We're luckier than most people though, living here with good sanitation and where the houses are spaced out. At least we can walk in the fresh air. I can't help worrying about those living in tenement blocks, crammed together near so many other families.' She didn't want to worry Mrs Rudge, so she didn't add that she mixed with lots of people when she went to the store. 'Hopefully we'll all come out of this unscathed, as long as we use our masks and wash our hands.'

Mrs Rudge's shoulders relaxed slightly. 'Yes, you're right, all the servants have been reminded often about the need for personal hygiene. Although, to be honest, they were all very good about that sort of thing already.'

'I know they were,' Florence said, aware that Cook was pedantic about personal cleanliness. 'Thank you.'

'Now, as to supper this evening,' Mrs Rudge said.'We don't have much meat, but I do have a tasty stew that I've made. Was there anything else you wanted to ask me, Lady Boot?'

Florence clasped her hands together and tried to think what it might have been. 'Oh, yes, I was hoping you might have a few biscuits or maybe something light for my daughter to eat with a cup of tea when she gets here. She will have had a long journey and I am sure she will be hungry. I know she won't ask for anything but I'd hate for her to have to wait until supper time.'

Mrs Rudge tapped the side of her nose a couple of times. 'I have just the thing, Lady Boot. Miss Margery is a little partial to apricots and I kept back a serving of my Apricot Charlotte from last night's supper for her, thinking she might like it as a treat. It's nice and sweet and I'm sure it will help revive her spirits after her journey.'

Florence laid her hand on her chest. She was touched by Mrs Rudge's forward planning and recalled the delicious taste of the pudding the previous evening. 'You are incredibly organised and thoughtful as ever, Cook. Thank you very much. I'm sure Margery will be delighted to be greeted by something that delicious.'

Mrs Rudge beamed at her, her cheeks reddening. 'It's the least I can do for a young woman who has been working so hard for others. It'll be good to have her back again.'

'It will, Cook.' Florence shrugged. 'Well, I'd better get back to Sir Jesse and wait for Miss Margery to arrive.'

Chapter Thirty-Three

11 November 1918

Florence hurried downstairs to where Margery and Jesse were waiting for her. She could barely believe this day had come and was looking forward to attending the Thanksgiving service that had been hurriedly arranged at their church. She had listened to Jesse's delight that Lloyd George had announced an Armistice and enjoyed seeing a sparkle of happiness in his gentle eyes.

What she couldn't understand was why she didn't seem to be experiencing the same happiness now that the war had been brought to a close. What was wrong with her? she thought, irritated with herself.

She reached the bottom step and stopped, taking a moment to watch Margery and Jesse, both ready and waiting for her to make an appearance. Her heart swelled to see her youngest child standing next to Jesse's chair, smiling down at him as they chatted. So much had changed since they last enjoyed peacetime in this house.

She listened to them talking as she tried to gauge her own feelings and why she wasn't seemingly as delighted as everyone else appeared to be.

Jesse looked up. 'Ah, there you are. Come along, my dear. We're going to be late at this rate and we can't have that happening.'

As they drove the short distance to the chapel, Florence admitted her conflicting feelings to her husband and daughter.

'I don't understand why I'm not deliriously happy right now. It doesn't make sense. This is what we've all been praying for these past four years. I should be overjoyed.'

Margery frowned and leant forward. 'Mother, your feelings are completely understandable.'

Jesse raised his hand. 'Margery's right, dear. We might be celebrating the end of the war, but, like you, I'm sure we're all haunted by the fallen, and by the injured who won't be able to continue the lives they left behind when they enlisted.'

'Father's right,' Margery said, giving Florence's hand a gentle squeeze. 'There's also the flu that we're all at risk from now, and the shortages of food and jobs, and of course your losing Uncle Willie earlier this year.' She shook her head. 'It's hardly surprising you're not in the mood to be cheerful.'

Florence listened to their reassurances and immediately

felt slightly soothed. 'Thank you. You both make good sense.'

Florence enjoyed the service and seeing friends and acquaintances they hadn't had contact with for the past few months. Afterwards, as they drove from church, they passed the marketplace. Florence was deep in thought about how strange the day seemed.

'Look at all those people,' Margery said, her voice barely above a whisper.

Florence gazed over the crowds to see a motorcade of what she assumed were wounded soldiers drawing close. 'Oh, my word,' she said, startled to see a mob surge towards them. She couldn't speak for a moment for the lump in her throat. 'Look, Jesse, the people are wanting to shake their hands.'

She listened as church bells rang all around. All she could think of was the many young men who hadn't made it home and how their families must be grieving for them. The emotion of the day was becoming a little too much. She longed for a few quiet moments in her room to gather her thoughts.

Jesse reached out to her. 'I think we're all a little war-weary.'

She forced a smile, touched by his words and that he had sensed how she was feeling.

'The mayor has given everyone permission to turn the lights back on. We can take down our blinds tonight,' Margery said, her cheerful voice sounding a little forced. 'Won't that be something?'

It would, Florence thought. If Margery could put on a brave face, then so must she. 'It will be,' she said as cheerfully as she could manage. She longed to see street lamps lit and walk past neighbouring houses in The Park and see lights shining onto the street from their living rooms. It brought the area so much more alive to see golden light shining onto the pavements outside.

Despite her sadness at the loss of so many young souls, Florence couldn't help being cheered by Margery's enthusiasm for life. She decided she needed to find that in herself once again. It really would not do to bring everyone's mood down with her own morose thoughts.

'Mother, did you know that food restrictions have been lifted, too? Cook was telling me all about it when I went to speak to her earlier this morning.'

This was good news, Florence thought, her mood lifting slightly. 'They have? I'm so pleased.' She pictured the delight on Cook's face and then realised that even if restrictions were lifted the scarcity of supplies would probably mean that households would not eat much more than they had become used to doing since rations began.

'Yes, apparently butchers are to be allowed to sell turkeys and other poultry, like geese, ducks and chickens. Game too. And no need for food vouchers.' She laughed. 'Cook is beside herself with excitement. She said she's going to make sure we all have a Christmas worth remembering this year.'

Florence sighed. It was good news. 'Good. This will be our first proper Christmas since 1913.' She thought back to that joyous day when each of them had believed that their small worries were all that would trouble them. How different they all must feel now and how much each of them had grown and learned about life.

The previous day, she had returned home and stared out of the car window at the Victory banners in red, white and blue declaring that war was over and that victory was theirs. It was a huge relief to her. As happy as Florence was to see the end of the fighting, she could not forget those whose lives had been changed forever and were now having to learn to live with loss. What about those others, she thought, here in Nottingham and everywhere else in the United Kingdom, who were alone having lost loved ones to the dreaded flu? Her heart ached for all the troubled souls.

She knew she was lucky to have only lost one family member with Willie's death earlier that year, and prayed each day that none of her family, servants or staff would succumb to the flu. It was a worrying time, but Florence wanted to put on a brave face. It would be selfish of her to let her low spirits bring down those who needed so desperately to make the most of the celebrations.

She needed to pull herself together and buck up. Florence knew that the moods of those in the rest of the house were influenced by how she was feeling. It was down to her to boost them and help them feel positive, especially now they finally had something to be joyful about.

'We're going to make the most of being at peace, with the entire family here at St Heliers House,' she declared with as much enthusiasm as she could muster.

'I can't wait,' Margery said. 'Why don't we sit down now and make lists of all the food we're going to have to ask Cook to order? Then we can plan what presents we will need to buy for everyone, especially the little ones.' She beamed at Florence. 'Isn't it exciting to have little ones to celebrate with this Christmas, Mother?'

Florence felt a warm glow course through her chest. 'It is.'

'I wonder when I'll be married and able to bring my own children here for Christmas,' Margery said thoughtfully. 'I'm in no rush to give up my independence but I don't want to wait too long to have a family of my own.'

Her daughter's words reminded Florence of her own wish to be independent when she was young and working for her father in his stationery store in Jersey. How differently her life had turned out, she thought, smiling to herself, and how much better it had been than she could have ever dared dream.

That afternoon, Florence took up a cup of tea to Jesse's room where he was supposed to be having a nap. She opened the door quietly, not wishing to disturb him, and was surprised to see him sitting up in bed reading paperwork. He looked over the top of the file in his hand, a guilty look on his face. She frowned at him as she placed the cup and saucer down onto his bedside table.

'You're supposed to be resting.'

'I know, but I wasn't sleepy and knew I had these figures to go through.'

Florence sat down on the edge of his bed. 'And what figures are those?'

He sighed heavily. 'They're the list of all the members of Boots staff whom we lost during the war.'

Florence's sadness for the people of Nottingham returned. 'Oh, Jesse.'

He shook his head slowly. 'I can't quite believe how many there are, Florence.' His gaze dropped to the names and figures on the page in his hands.

Florence didn't ask any questions. She knew Jesse would speak when he was ready, but she could see he was trying to bring himself to read out what was typed in front of him. He cleared his throat. 'Three hundred and thirty employees were lost over the past four years, my dear. Far too many. It says here that one hundred and twenty-five of the men were from our offices and works, and the other two hundred and five from Boots stores.' He looked at her, his eyes filled with unshed tears. 'So many young lives lost, Florence. It really is too heart-breaking.'

It was. She leant forward and took one of his hands in both of hers. She was sad that they couldn't hold hands properly any longer now his were very misshapen, but Florence could see that Jesse needed the comfort of her hands around his. They sat silently for a few minutes, both trying to come to terms with the loss of so many men. There would not be any celebratory Christmases for those men or their families, this or any other year.

She closed her eyes, unable to push away the emotion that seemed to fill her every nerve.

'I don't think the people of this country will ever recover from what this past four years has put them through,' she said, aware that although they had lost many staff it was those men's families who suffered the most. 'How will we all come back from this?'

He didn't answer but shook his head sadly. 'I have no idea.'

Neither did she. Florence thought of those who had lost loved ones. 'We are so much luckier than most,' she said, thinking of her three children back at home in Nottingham with them once more. 'Our children have all survived and come back to us, and I'm incredibly grateful.'

'I am, too.'

Florence thought of something she kept hearing in the shop. 'They're saying this is the war to end all wars. I hope they're right.'

'As do I, my dear.'

Then it occurred to her exactly what she needed to do. 'Jesse?'

'Yes, dearest.'

'We have to do what we've always done.'

Jesse frowned. 'And what's that?'

'We have to lead by example. From tomorrow, after we've celebrated the Armistice with our family, we are going to sit down and plan how best to take our business forward.'

'We are?'

'Yes. What this country needs now is hope for the future and we're going to do our best to give it to them,' she said.

She had spent four years doing her bit for the war effort; it was now time for her to make the most of the country being at peace.

He smiled and shook his head. 'And how exactly do you propose we do that?'

Florence sighed. 'I'm not certain right now, but I know we'll think of something.'

The End

Author's Note

Dear Reader,

Firstly, I want to thank you for choosing to read one of my books. I've loved writing this series about Florence's life and hope you enjoy reading the next instalment in *Mrs Boots Goes to War*.

In this book Florence's children are now adults and John and Dorothy are married and having families of their own. Florence always wanted to be as supportive to those around her as she possibly could, and so when the war came to Britain, Florence realised that the people of Nottingham needed her, and she wasn't going to let them down.

The Boots family certainly was remarkable and researching Florence's life, or at least her life until the end of the First World War, was fascinating. There was so much more to her than I could have ever envisaged when I first stepped into her world and there was much more to her life in the years after the war. For now, though, I hope you've enjoyed joining her and discovering how she dealt with those traumatic war years that destroyed so many lives and ended with the onset of the Spanish Flu.

We know that Florence was a fighter and did not give up easily, and to me she was truly inspirational. Her strength and determination helped me focus on writing this book when I was separated by my two grown up children and my mother living across the world when our countries were in lockdown. It was – and unfortunately, as I write this – still is a strange and stressful time, but we all find our own ways of dealing with the situation. I'm grateful to have had Florence's life to lose myself in and hope that reading this book might help you to escape for a few hours.

I send out monthly newsletters, and if you want to subscribe please do so here: deborahcarr.org/newsletter.

Happy reading. Stay safe.

Best wishes,

Deborah x

Acknowledgments

Firstly, I must thank my amazing husband, Robert Carr. Not only is he one of my biggest supporters, but he's always on hand to help with research and cook supper. Also, my children, James and Saskia, and my enormous family who encourage me to follow my writing dreams and never mind when my thoughts are with my characters.

I couldn't have done this without the amazing team at HarperCollins' One More Chapter. I've learnt an enormous amount from each of you. Thank you, and thanks to Lucy Bennett for yet another beautiful cover.

My *Mrs Boots* series would not be what it is without my incredible editor, Emily Ruston. Thank you for your dedication and brilliant suggestions, I continue to learn so much from you.

My grateful thanks to Tony Russell for his brilliant copyedits.

I still recall how nervous I was to meet Florence's great-granddaughter, Allison Barrington, her daughter, Heidi Lewis, and granddaughter, Lara Lewis, whose delight that Florence's story had inspired this series, gave me the confidence to sit down and write these three books.

Once again, I was able to make use of information I had gleaned from my visit with Claire Fenby to the Boots Archive in Nottingham, and for that I must again thank Sophie Clapp and Judith Wright, Boots Archivists for all their help.

Not forgetting Michele Leerson, Linda Romeril, and Stuart Nicolle from the Jersey Archive, especially Toni Wolstenholme, whose wonderful last name I borrowed for one of the characters in *Mrs Boots*, thinking I had made up the name myself when, in fact, I had borrowed it from her. Thank you.

To Glynis Peters, Christie Barlow, and Terri Nixon, three amazingly talented authors who make me laugh, give me advice, and generally make sure that each writing day is filled with fun. Also, to Christina Jones, Karen Clarke, Bella Osborne, Noelle Holten, Phillipa Ashley, Maddy Please, John Jackson, Laura Carter, and my fellow Blonde Plotters, Kelly Clayton, and Gwyn GB, two great friends who, thanks to the strange times we're living through, I haven't been able to see this past year nearly as much as I'd like.

Thanks, too, to all the generous bloggers who support writers with blog tours, reviews and sharing writing news, especially Rachel Gilbey, Sarah Hardy, Adele (Kraftireader), and Anne Williams, and a special shout out to Trisha Hayward and Fee Roberts.

Finally, to you, dear reader. Thank you for reading *Mrs Boots Goes to War*. I hope you enjoy discovering how Florence dealt with the First World War and spending time with her as much as I did.

YOUR NUMBER ONE STOP
ONE MORE CHAPTER
FOR PAGETURNING BOOKS